Chris Bunch is the author of the Sten Series, the Dragonmaster Series, the Seer King Series and many other acclaimed SF and fantasy novels. A notable journalist and bestselling writer for many years, he died in 2005.

Find out more about Chris Bunch and other Orbit authors by registering for the free monthly newsletter at www.orbitbooks.co.uk

CHRIS BUNCH

STAR RISK

BOOK TWO: THE SCOUNDREL WORLDS

orbit

www.orbitbooks.co.uk

ORBIT

First published in the United States in 2003 by Roc,
Penguin Group (USA) Inc.
First published in Great Britain in 2006 by Orbit

A CIP catalogue record for this book
is available from the British Library.

ISBN-10: 1-84149-454-2
ISBN-13: 978-1-84149-454-8

Typeset in Garamond by M Rules
Printed and bound in Great Britain by
Clays Ltd, St Ives plc

Orbit
An imprint of
Little, Brown Book Group
Brettenham House
Lancaster Place
London WC2E 7EN

A member of the Hachette Livre Group of Companies

www.littlebrown.co.uk

ONE

The fat man crept out of the hotel's service entrance, peered around cautiously. The night was silent except for a few passing lifters and the buzz of wet circuitry, above, on the primitive electric grid.

All he had to do, he thought, was go down three blocks to the luxe hotel where the lifter cab rank should still be manned, grab the first one, and make for the spaceport. Then he'd be safe.

He swore at himself for thinking he could outthink Them by staying in this working-class hotel instead of at the properly luxurious one his per diem entitled him to. Hotels like this one were where They stayed, saving their credits for alk and bail funds.

The fat man, wishing he'd had some kind of military training, crept along the high wall, moving as quietly as he knew how. It was late, very late, and hopefully They had drunk themselves into oblivion and wouldn't still be looking for him.

He'd fooled them for a while with twin connecting rooms, one under his own name, the other under a false one. They'd broken in to the first room, smashed it to bits, and hammered on the connecting door, but since there was no answer, had given up.

For the moment.

The fat man came to the first street crossing, crouched, and went across, waddling faster than he'd moved in years, except when he was on the field.

The silence held. He went down another block, reached a boulevard, and started across.

He was halfway to the other side when the baying came. A block away, half a dozen stumbling men saw and recognized him.

'Kill th' fook,' 'Tear 'im,' 'Deader'n th' Devils,' the cries came.

The man ran faster. Safety was close, very close.

He didn't make it.

Two dozen of Them came out of an alley ahead of him.

The fat man skidded to a stop, darted across the street, hoping for safety, an open door, stairs, anything. There was nothing but high stone walls.

They caught him within a hundred meters.

Bottles arced toward him, struck. He stumbled on, and then a heavy rock took him between the shoulder blades. He fell, clawed his way up. But it was too late. They were on him with boots, iron bars, fists.

It was almost a relief to let the pain take him down and down into nothingness.

TWO

Trimalchio IV was a very lucky planet. It had no history to speak of, save hedonism. Its diplomats had cleverly played one enemy against another, so Trimalchio was able to stay neutral, uninvaded, and a good place to put money when you didn't want any questions asked. Its semitropic climate and blue seas spotted with islands attracted people who thought themselves beautiful . . . or rich enough to convince others they were.

Jasmine King appeared to fit in perfectly.

She was an utterly gorgeous woman, so beautiful and competent that her former employers, the security firm of Cerberus Systems, had decided she was a robot, and hence no longer deserving of a salary.

That outrage – although she never told anyone whether or not she *was* an android, and if that impossibility was true, what unknown super-civilization had brought her to life – had led her into the employ of Star Risk, Ltd.

She was the office manager, and the head and only member of Star Risk's research department. She was also head and only member of the personnel department, and a junior field operative. While she was quite qualified in administration, her experience out where things got bloody was less exhaustive than that of the four other principals. Her most recent accomplishments included a belt in Applied General Martial Arts and a Master Shot in both pistol and blast-rifle classes.

Star Risk occupied a suite in the forty-third floor of a fifty-story high-rise, a building that used a lot of antigravity generators to give the illusion it hung from the sky without, like many of Trimalchio's citizens, any visible means of support.

Their office was decorated in the incongruous, if currently popular, style of ultramodern leather and steel, along with archaic furniture, and prints on the wall.

The other occupant of the huge reception area was a rather mousy man.

Jasmine keyed her whisper mike.

'A possible client,' she said. 'Not rich-looking. Named Weitman. Said he'd discuss his business with an operative. Suspect he's a little confused, has a cheating wife or partner, and thinks Star Risk is some sort of investigative service.'

Jasmine listened. 'No,' she said. 'There's nobody else out here but me, and no jobs on tap, either.'

She smiled as Weitman looked up. 'Someone will be right with you.' The little man nodded jerkily.

The door to the inner offices opened, and a nightmare lumbered in, all silky fur, and almost three meters tall.

'Good morning, Mr. Weitman,' the creature rumbled. 'I am Amanandrala Grokkonomonslf, which no one beyond my race can pronounce, so you should call me Grok. Come into my office, and we can discuss your problem.'

The little man got up and followed Grok. He stopped, turned back to Jasmine. 'For your information, Miss . . . King, I'm not confused about what Star Risk does, nor am I looking for separation evidence.' He smiled, a not altogether pleasant smile. 'My father taught me to read lips at a very young age.'

Weitman followed Grok, closing the door behind him.

Jasmine King proved she blushed as perfectly as she did most other things.

'Have you ever heard of the game of skyball?' Weitman asked Grok earnestly.

The alien suspected Weitman did everything earnestly.

'A game?' Grok said. 'No, I haven't much interest or knowledge of sports, beyond a little Earth feetball history. My race doesn't practice physical displays of competition, but rather finds pleasure in debate on a higher level. When we aren't killing each other,' he added.

Grok wasn't lying. He'd left his native worlds out of boredom and joined the Alliance's military service as a signal specialist, a cryptanalyst, and someone who really didn't mind if things got bloody out.

Weitman hadn't been listening to Grok after the 'No.'

'Skyball is one of the greatest of all sports, maybe *the* greatest,' he said. 'It requires the utmost of physical development and coordination, plus a high degree of intellectual achievement. There is also a large element of chance, which makes all things more interesting.'

'I assume,' Grok said, 'given the name, that it's

played with aircraft, such as the ancient game of polo-ponies I've read about.'

'There are no mechanical devices in skyball,' Weitman said. 'Except, of course, for the ball the anti-gravity generators, and the random computer.'

'Ah,' Grok said. 'Sheer muscle and skill.'

Weitman didn't notice the sarcasm as he went on. 'Skyball's an invention of the early spacefarers,' he said. 'It was originally played in space, under zero-G conditions. But it grew in popularity, and as few fans find zero gravity exactly easy on their digestive tracts – particularly if they're drinking – its rules were changed, and it is now played in stadiums, on planets.

'The field has antigravity generators above it, so normal gravity is negated. There are ten women or men to a side, and their task is to carry the ball any way they choose, to the opponent's goal.

'The other team, naturally, tries to stop them and secure the ball itself, in any way they choose that doesn't constitute a major felony. Play is in four quarters of fifteen minutes each.

'To complicate matters, the ball has an internal, varying gyroscope, so in mid-throw, it might suddenly change its direction of travel. In addition, there are antigravity generators hidden below the playing field, which turn on and off in a random manner to affect the ball and the players.

'Skyball has become enormously popular within the Alliance, particularly on certain worlds who have vaunted rivalries.'

'This is quite fascinating,' Grok said. 'But we here at Star Risk deal in bullets, as the old saying goes. I assume you have professional athletes playing the sport, and would hardly like to recruit mercenaries and men of violence such as us.'

'The sport is one thing,' Weitman said. 'It is violent enough. But there is violence off the field as well. Certain planets have become absolute fanatics about skyball, so extremely so that actual wars have been fought over interplanetary championships.'

Grok made no comment.

'This is bad enough,' Weitman said. 'But there are also thuggish followers who have attacked players and coaches. More recently, some of them have assaulted members of my guild, which is the Professional Referees Association. A week ago one of our members was beaten to death after a match. This is intolerable.

'The current league finals are between the planets of Cheslea and Warick, whose fans are among the worst of the offenders. We advised them that if they cannot guarantee security to our members, we will refuse to judge these finals. Both worlds seemed unconcerned, and said they would provide officials of their own.'

Weitman shivered. 'For reasons I won't go into, that is a terrible idea.

'PRA has authorized me to investigate various firms who provide security services, and Star Risk is the one I have chosen. We want to hire you to keep the seven referees who'll officiate at these final matches on Warick from any harm, and are prepared to pay one million credits, plus all expenses, to ensure no harm comes to them.'

Grok stroked the fur on his chest, considering. 'Interesting,' he said. 'Very interesting. I think Star Risk will be more than delighted to accept your offer.'

*

'You did what?' M'chel Riss moaned.

Riss was tall, blond, green eyed, and looked more like a model than the Alliance Marine major she'd been before she quit the service, after standing off a lecherous commanding officer. She'd ended up as one of the mercenary founders of Star Risk, Ltd.

'It seems like a nice, simple assignment,' Grok said in an injured tone, 'with a more than acceptable pay rate for a few days' work. It's not like I volunteered us for a war or anything.'

'A nice, simple way to get dead, you mean,' Chas Goodnight said.

Goodnight, a few centimeters taller than Riss, was sandy haired, with a friendly twinkle in his eye. M'chel considered him the most amoral person she'd ever met. He was also ex-Alliance, a 'bester' – one of the handful of bio-modified commandos who did the loose confederation's dirty work. He'd been one of the most respected besters, until he decided cat burglary paid better than assassination and skulking through the bushes.

Star Risk had broken him out of a death cell. Now he wasn't quite a full partner, but was more than an employee.

Goodnight's activities included having eyes capable of seeing in the dark, reaction speeds three times that of an athlete, a brain circuited for battle analysis, and ears able to pick up frequencies up to the FM range. In bester mode, he was 'powered' by a tiny battery at the base of his spine. When it ran dry, after about fifteen minutes or so, he was drained until he input a few thousand calories and hopefully slept around the clock.

Friedrich von Baldur, the firm's head, nodded slowly,

but didn't say anything. Von Baldur was another rogue, who claimed to have been a colonel in the Alliance, but actually had been a warrant officer who hastily left the service ahead of various court-martial charges involving government supplies gone missing. Nor was his real name von Baldur.

'You three *obviously* know something more than I do,' Grok said.

'Skyball's a game,' Riss started, 'and –'

'I know that,' Grok interrupted. 'Weitman gave me a basic briefing, and I looked it up in *Encyclopedia Galactica*. Seems a rough enough, rather predictable sport. Not that we'll have anything to do with the game, merely protecting the officials.'

'Merely,' Goodnight snorted. '*Merely!?* Grok, comfort of my youth, bower of my old age, let me tell you a story.

'A few years back, when I was still somewhat honest and working for the Alliance shilling, me and a few of my teammates were chasing a guy named Purvis around the Galactic lens. The Alliance wanted him alive, because he'd . . . never mind what he'd done. They wanted him bad, so they could work him over and find out what they wanted to find out. We were told we'd get our paws slapped if we came back without him – or maybe worse, if he came back in a body bag.

'Purvis heard he was hot, and so he cut and run. We got word that he'd set up shop as a games advisor on Cheslea, which has one of the teams in this skyball championship. Their team, by the way, is the Black Devils . . . Games advisor, right. So we hare off after his young ass.

'We get to Cheslea, and there's no sign of him. The

planet's a madhouse, which it is anyway, since the people seem to think logic starts in the key of C sharp, and run their society accordingly. But when we arrive, Cheslea's an extra-special madhouse because the Black Devils are facing their worst enemy, the Uniteds, which are from the planet of Warick.

'I see you nodding, Grok. It gets worse.

'So we moil here and there, and there's no sign of Purvis, and then it's time for the games to start. It's one-all, then two-all, and game five is gonna settle matters. We get reliable word that our boy is gonna be at the game, and so we show up. We've got prize seats, two ways out, and a big sack to put Purvis in when we find him.

'The stadium, by the way, is – or was, anyway – sort of open air, with the antigravs hung on spidery scaffolding arcing over the top.

'It was a crappy hot day, and the sun was blistering down. I wanted a beer in the worst way, but I knew if I got one and the mucketies found out I was sluicing on the job, I'd get a strip torn off – which would've been a lot better than what happened to all of us when we got back to friendly waters.

'But I'm getting ahead of things. None of us were paying attention to the game, we're busy looking around for our lad. And we spot him, in the last ten minutes. It was kind of hard to see, because all the stands were glittering. The Cheslea fans had programs that were silver foil, and the dazzle was, well, dazzling.

'There's a lot of hollering going on because it's a tight game, and everybody from Cheslea just *knows* the referees have been bought out by Warick. We're working our way up to the top of the stadium, and the score is tied. Then Cheslea makes a goal, and the officials call it illegal or some such.

'I thought the fans were going to go apeshit, especially when Warick scores a few seconds later, and the clock is running out. Instead, this low muttering starts, and gets louder, and I feel a creep going down my spine. Everybody else with me is looking just as nervous.

'The officials are gathered together, down on the field. Then there's this almighty flash, coming from everywhere, and a gout of smoke, like some kind of silent nuke, and there's no more goddamned referees down there.

'Turns out this was Purvis's ultimate plan if things went awry. Print the programs on this silver reflecting paper. Put a little aiming hole in it – which was disguised as a skyball with an emblem on the cover – and then, if things went wrong, as they just had, hold the program up, catch the sun, and aim it down at the officials.

'The whole stadium was a huge mirror. Fried the refs like steaks – well-done steaks. Barely a few coals here and there. And at that point things went completely berserk, with the fans from Warick trying to get out and back to their transports, and the Cheslea rooters trying to stop them.

'It was a hell of a riot. A *hell* of a riot,' Goodnight repeated.

'What happened to your target, this Purvis?' Riss asked.

'We found out he got dead in the hooraw,' Goodnight said blandly. 'Which of course none of us had anything to do with. But we still got in a world of shit when we got back to base.

'There's no justice in this world,' he concluded, then looked at Grok. 'And that's the kind of thing you've dumped us into for a lousy mil and burial expenses.'

'Sometimes I wish,' Riss said forlornly, 'Star Risk didn't have this tradition of never refusing an assignment unless we don't get paid or the client's lied to us more than acceptably. Who made that idiot policy, anyway?'

'I think,' Friedrich said, 'it was you, m'dear.'

THREE

The madhouse started at Warick's main spaceport. Fans from Cheslea were cascading off chartered transports, arriving in every shape from unconscious and on stretchers to hungover and fighting to sober and looking for a drink.

The five Star Risk operatives came in on a standard liner, and were able to grab a lim to their hotel by virtue of looking sober and waving a large bill. They overflew improvised parades, street fairs, and marching bands.

'So who'd'ja favor?' the lim driver asked.

'Peace and quiet,' von Baldur said.

The driver snorted.

'Damn little of that to be got for the next two weeks. P'raps I best run you back to the port and you can try another system.'

'We are where we belong,' Riss said.

The driver looked back and almost sideswiped a cargo lifter dripping banners: WARICK RULES, UNITEDS CONQUER, and such.

'You folks have something to do with the finals?' He was about to be impressed.

'We're psychologists,' Goodnight said. 'Specializing in the madness of crowds.'

The driver's head snapped forward, and he said no more. As they grounded at the Shelburne – which was not only where the officials were staying but also the most luxurious hotel on Warick – he refused both to help unload their surprisingly heavy luggage, and a tip as well, sitting statue-like behind the controls of his lifter.

'I note they take this skyball most seriously,' Grok said. 'I have never heard of a cabbie refusing a tip.'

'That's a sign and a warning,' Riss said. 'Let's make sure we don't do anything else to show what we think.'

'And, most particularly,' von Baldur said, 'make sure we do not wear any emblems suggesting we back either the Black Devils or the Uniteds. Nor should we mistakenly wear their colors, which are, naturally, black and red for the Devils, and solid blue for the Uniteds.'

'Actually,' Weitman said, 'we're quite prepared for all normal eventualities.'

Six other male and female officials in the hotel suite room nodded agreement.

'First,' the referee went on, 'note my outer clothing. These black-and-white striped pants and shirt are proof against most solid projectiles – although, of course, the impact must still be accounted for. This is why, under the shirt and extending down over my groin, is a shock-absorbing vest, which is also intended to deal with hurled bottles, rocks, and such.

'My little cap is padded, and will take an impact of a kilo at up to twenty kph. My boots are steel-toed and -soled, and I'm wearing knee and elbow pads in case I get knocked down.

'I'll have gas plugs in my nostrils, and baffled plugs in my ears, in case they try to use any amplified sound devices against us.

'Plus, I'm carrying a small gas projector on my belt, and – you must not breathe a word of this to anyone else – I'm carrying a small aperture blaster here, in my crotch.

'And of course there's stadium security, supposedly one for every twenty-five people in the audience, although we've got to assume some of these guards will be as likely to be partisan as the crowds. Which is why we're depending on you five to get us out of any real problems.'

He smiled at the Star Risk operatives.

'Wonderful,' Goodnight said. 'Simply frigging wonderful. Ah, for the life of a sports fan.'

Both the Devils and the Uniteds were at the peak of their performance in the first game. The action swayed back and forth for three quarters, neither side able to score.

Then, halfway through the fourth quarter, with Cheslea having the ball, the Warick team leapt high into the air, trying a drive over the Warick line, going up almost to the roof of the covered stadium, floating for an instant in mock weightlessness, then lobbing the ball hard for the small goal.

The pitch was clear of the antigrav generators and was going straight as hurled, when its gyro came to life and sent the ball spinning into the hands of a Warick end.

He moved instantly, threw hard, under the Cheslea players still coming down from their positions near the roof.

One-nothing.

And that was the only score for the game.

There'd also been no penalties called, even though M'chel Riss, from her position in a skybox, saw at least two kneeings and one punch to a woman's breasts.

The fans were well behaved, and most were fairly sober. Grok saw only twenty or so people grabbed by stadium security for offenses like hurling smuggled bottles at the players, or having a private punch-up in their row.

'If it stays like this,' Weitman said, 'we'll all be home free.'

Star Risk decided they'd spread out through the stadium for the second game, keeping only the most noticeable Grok in the skybox, and a com to their earpieces.

This game was far more open than the first. It seemed both sides had been gauging their opponents, and now, having found weaknesses, they drove for the kill.

And this time the officials seemed to have done the same. Eight penalties were called in the first quarter, six in the second.

The score was 7–3, again with Warick in the lead.

A woman official had just called the first penalty of the third – tripping, which seemed to be one of the few things beyond bludgeons skyball didn't permit.

Von Baldur caught movement out of the corner of his eye. He spun, saw an enormously fat woman dig something out of her oversize handbag and scale it at the referee.

Von Baldur shouted 'Down,' into his com mike and

the official went flat. The something turned out to be a handmade ancient boomerang, and smashed into the turf not a meter from the referee's body.

The obese woman was digging in her handbag once more. Friedrich didn't wait around to see what it was, but swarmed over the high fence separating the fans from the field.

There was a stadium security man who shouted: 'You! Hey you! You can't do that!'

Von Baldur paid him no mind, but went up the steps two at a time, then shouldered his way into the row the fat woman was in, just as she pulled out what looked to be a grenade.

A younger man with the same piggy features as the fat woman came up, fists lifting.

Von Baldur snap-kicked him in the chest and let him stumble into his evident relative, then rolled away as the grenade, hissing, dropped to the concrete.

A few seconds later it went off, and a noxious gas sprayed the area. By that time von Baldur was rolling back down the steps, not turning around to see people gagging, on their knees choking and vomiting, until he was halfway back the way he'd come.

He noted with satisfaction that the fat woman and her relative were among the worst hit, then looked down at what had been his rather dapper lounging outfit.

'New suit,' he muttered. 'Three hundred and twenty-seven credits. Expense.'

The end score was 9–4. Two out of two for Warick. The game had been stopped three times when players were taken off on stretchers. One of them didn't appear to be breathing.

The visiting fans from Cheslea were going somewhat berserk, sure that the game was rigged for Warick, that somehow the antigravs or the ball itself had been rigged to favor the home team.

Goodnight was in the Shelburne's bar – the archaically named Heron and Beaver – and he saw one of the Warick players, surrounded by two prosperous businessmen sporting blue and half a dozen bodyguards – women and men whose eyes never stopped sweeping the crowded bar, and whose hands stayed close to their waistbands.

Goodnight wandered over, and when the player made a joke about a rival team, Goodnight laughed, lifted his glass in a mock toast, grinned wryly.

'You know about the Knights, eh?'

Goodnight had never heard of them. 'Of course,' he said. 'And your story isn't the half of it.' He told a story of his own. The original butt of the joke had been an incompetent and unlucky Alliance unit, but now it became the Knights.

One of the businessmen bought him another beer, and Goodnight was suddenly the player's new best friend, although the bodyguards regarded him most suspiciously. Chas wasn't sure what he was looking for, other than more familiarity with the assignment.

The businessmen got drunk, but everyone else stayed sober. Goodnight let it appear that he was becoming wobblier than he was. The evening wasn't producing much, except the probability of a thick head if Goodnight kept drinking. Fortunately, tomorrow was a rest day.

'So tell me, Dov,' Chas said, deep in the evening, 'I could see today how good you are. But what made you get into skyball in the first place? What else did you consider?'

'Aw,' the man said, 'I always liked playing. I come from money, so m' da had a yacht, and we could always make up a game somewhere in the asteroids or in one of the system's boneyards.

'Why'd I turn pro?' Dov looked around, making sure no one else was listening. 'I got in some trouble, and the magistrate said it was either conditioning, prison, or going offworld. Da had disowned me, so I was thinking about the military.

'But that sounded real dangerous, and so when a semipro team said they needed substitutes, I made damned sure I was there at the head of the line and worked my ass off to play harder and better than anyone else.

'I mean, the Alliance military? You can get actually *killed* doing that.'

Goodnight had nothing to say.

'If you're awake and coherent,' Grok said in what he probably thought was a coo, 'or at least awake, since you're on your feet, Chas, my friend, I have something of interest for you and for the others.'

The Star Risk operatives were assembled for a scanty breakfast in one of the suites' dining rooms.

Riss and Jasmine had little but juice and bran cereal since they were watching their weight. Grok had had four raw eggs and tea, and Freddie von Baldur, also aware of his waistline, had just caff.

Goodnight, who normally shoveled down breakfast platters with both hands, was gingerly putting fruit juice and vitamins down.

'I have acquired,' Grok went on, 'probably from too long an association with you humans – a time period that can be measured in nanoseconds – a certain distrust for humanity.'

'A good thing to have,' von Baldur said.

'Over the past four days, I've taken the liberty to plant some devices, listening devices, in our clients' rooms,' Grok said.

'Imagine my surprise when I discovered that four of the seven have been in negotiations with various elements to shade their judgments.'

'Well, bless my soul,' Jasmine said. 'And we're supposed to be keeping them alive?'

'Let's bail,' Chas said, hangover making him snarly.

'Perhaps we should, perhaps we should not,' Grok said. 'It is interesting that two of them appear to have taken bribes to favor Cheslea, and two to back Warick in their calls.'

'Ah,' M'chel said. 'That makes it two against two against three. Assuming those three haven't already made their own arrangements.'

'Most interesting,' von Baldur said. 'And now I understand why you wanted to talk about this, Grok.'

'Exactly,' the alien said. 'The equation seemed to balance to me.'

'We could just keep on,' King said, nodding understandingly, 'and let matters shake out as they will.'

'No,' Goodnight said. 'Not business as usual. What about the money? If they're getting cute, what's to say they won't get cuter when it's payday?'

'My thought as well,' von Baldur said. 'I think I shall approach our principals, and inform them that circumstances have altered, and we require the million credits to be placed in an escrow account – with, say, Alliance Credit.'

Riss smiled, a bit sharkishly. 'I assume, Freddie,' she said, 'you aren't planning on telling our seven clients or the Professional Referees Association that happens to be the bank we use.'

'I am not,' von Baldur said. 'As I have said before, and no doubt shall say again, never smarten up a chump. If they ask about Alliance Credit, of course I shall tell them. Possibly. But not before.'

'I am not content,' Grok said, 'that we are responding properly to events.'

'Nor am I,' King said.

'Perhaps we should think of some contingency plans, in the event the situation worsens.' Grok said.

'Just what I was thinking,' Jasmine said. 'We might need some louder bangs than what we brought.'

FOUR

'You realize,' Riss said, 'since the series is the best of three, and Warick's already won two, if today's game makes it what I think they call a shutout, there will be serious chaos.'

'I'm aware, I'm aware,' Goodnight said. 'That's why I've got a blaster in my boot and another under this stupid jacket. Not to mention a couple of grenades – real bangsticks, not gas-type like Fatty had – in the pockets.'

'There's also some rifles in the skybox,' Riss said. 'I put them there myself, in the first-aid locker.'

It did get rough.

Goodnight saw his player from the bar kick the legs out from under a Black Devil then 'accidentally' fall on his chest, and he heard ribs crack.

A referee was looking right at Dov, then turned away without hitting the penalty flasher across his uniform's back.

Warick led at the end of the half.

As the players trooped off, there was a roar from the crowd. Riss saw ten fans, arms linked to form a phalanx, charge the stadium security at one of the field gates. Behind them came twenty or so goons, mostly drunk, waving clubs they'd somehow smuggled in through security.

'I don't think so,' Riss said to herself, and ran hard to intersect the miniature mob.

Jasmine King was already there, blocking the gate.

One man swung at her, and she kicked him in the kneecap and pushed him into his mate, then smashed a third man in the temple.

'Goddamnit,' Riss shouted, 'not with your hands!'

Jasmine heard her, looked away, and somebody punched her in the jaw. King staggered, went down, and the man started to put the boot in.

'Enough of this shit,' Riss snarled, drew a blaster, and blew the man's head off. Blood sprayed across the mob, and they shrieked, hesitated.

M'chel shot two more of them in painful places, listened in satisfaction to their yowls, then ran forward and dragged Jasmine away.

Cheslea came from behind to take their first game, 8–6.

'How is it?' von Baldur asked.

Jasmine gingerly moved her jaw. The other operatives were standing around her in the hotel suite.

'No breaks,' she said.

'What about teeth?' Riss said.

'I think a couple are loose,' King said. 'But they'll tighten up.'

'You're sure you don't want a doctor?' Riss asked.

'No,' Jasmine said. 'I'll be fine.'

Riss thought, Of course. A woman who might or might not be a robot would hardly chance discovery by a stranger.

'I don't like this,' Goodnight said. 'Not one god-damned stinking bit. Nobody roughs up our Jasmine.'

'Why, Chas,' King said. 'You're getting sentimental.'

Goodnight grunted, poured a drink. 'If they were to blame, I'd say dump our clients and let the bodies bounce where they will,' he said.

'No,' von Baldur said. 'That would hardly be professional.'

'A thought,' M'chel Riss said. 'This is a onetime contract, right? We're never ever coming back to this world, nor to Cheslea, and we're sure as hell never going to get involved with sports, right?'

'No,' Grok said. 'I have learned my lesson well.'

'Fine,' Riss said, and her voice was very hard. 'These bastards want to escalate . . . we should be able to handle that, as well.'

'Jasmine and I are far ahead of you,' Grok said. 'All we need is permission to implement.'

He explained.

When he finished, Goodnight and King had taut smiles on their faces. Von Baldur and Riss were stony-faced.

'Do we need to put it to a vote?' Riss said.

'I do not see why,' von Baldur said. 'The plan appears to give us the best of both worlds.'

'And we do have a long weekend before the next match,' Goodnight said. 'More than time enough for Jasmine to get things moving.'

'Good,' Jasmine said, getting up from the couch she'd been lying on. 'Assuming my jaw doesn't fall off, I'll start making the calls.'

FIVE

The next game had high stakes. If Cheslea won it, it would be a tie series; if Warick, that was the end.

The fans seeped into the stadium slowly, quietly. The stadium security made no attempt to react when gate metal detectors buzzed, nor did they ever see bulging coats or ask what, either alcoholic or dangerous, might be concealed under them. All of them had their bets down and sides chosen, after all.

Weitman met von Baldur inside the entrance tunnel. 'I'm afraid there might be a riot today,' he said.

'Do not worry,' von Baldur said. 'There is only one mob, and there are five of us. We have them outnumbered.'

Weitman attempted a smile. 'We should have practiced a . . . what do you military sorts call it, an emergency withdrawal.'

'There is no need to practice anything,' von Baldur said. 'We're most competent at what we do.'

A few minutes later, the game began. Play was vicious, but the officials called penalties fairly, or at least evenly. Three players on each side were thrown out for roughness and arguing with the referees.

At the first quarter's end, it was 2–2. At the second, it was 5–3, Warick leading. The stands were restive, and every now and again a bottle, generally of unbreakable plas, rained down from somewhere.

Von Baldur was with Goodnight in the skybox, on a com.

'Child Rowland, Child Rowland, this is Star Risk.'

'Star Risk, this is Child Rowland,' a distinctly cultured voice came back.

'Child Rowland, what's your location?'

'Orbiting at, oh, three-zed meters right over that great box of yours.'

'Are you ready?'

'That's affirm. On your signal.'

'Captain Hook, this is Star Risk.'

'Hook here.'

'Ready?'

'Ready, braced, strapped in, and will deploy on your signal.'

'All stations, this is Star Risk. Stand by. Clear.'

Third quarter, 8–5, still Warick's favor.

'Is everybody ready to move?' von Baldur asked into the Star Risk net.

The other three, around the stadium, responded.

'Very well,' von Baldur said. 'Now, assuming that Warick holds its lead, they will assemble the team in the center of the stadium. The officials will present the winners with a trophy. At that time, we shall move.'

'Clear.'

'Understood.'

'Will comply,' came the responses.

Fourth quarter, two minutes left to play, Warick held the lead 10–6.

'I think we can make certain assumptions,' von Baldur said. 'It would appear that Warick has won the series.'

'Looks like, Freddie,' Goodnight agreed, staring out the skybox's window. 'All we have to – holy flipping shit on a centrifuge!'

Goodnight was moving out the door of the skybox, and von Baldur puzzled out after him for an instant.

Then he saw, from another skybox about a quarter around the top of the arena, three men bringing out lengths of steel, fitting them together into a framework with a rail in its center. Then they brought out a tube, let fins extrude, and put the rocket onto the rail. A fourth man brought out a squat tripod, and crouched behind it, turning the sight on.

Goodnight dimly heard a great roar from the crowd as the last seconds ticked down, and he was running hard, pushing past people – but far, too far, from that skybox.

The officials were hurrying toward the field's center, where the Uniteds were nervously waiting.

Von Baldur was on his com. 'Captain Hook, this is Star Risk. Commence operation ... now! Child Rowland, we are in trouble. Come in as soon as you can.'

'This is Hook. On the way in.'

'Child Rowland, beginning dive.'

The stadium was a melee of fighting men and women. Goodnight heard a gunshot, then another – didn't know where they came from.

The man behind the rocket launcher was taking his time, making sure.

Goodnight's hand brushed his jaw, and the world

around him slowed, and the noise rose in pitch. Now the people around him were blurring, and he was darting through them like a hummingbird through flowers.

The rocket man never even saw him as Goodnight cannoned into him, sending the sight crashing away. But the man's finger was pressing the firing stud, and the rocket launched, smashing across the stadium and exploding in the middle of the crowd.

As the screams started, a Type VIII Heavy Lifter starship – a massive oblong carrying a large hook at the end of its drag – hovered over the stadium. The hook reeled out and caught fast on the framework of the antigrav generators on the roof.

On the bridge of the lifter Star Risk had chartered, 'Captain Hook' ordered full power and a thirty-degree up angle. The ship, intended for the heaviest construction and demolition, barely strained as it tore away the stadium's roof in a ragged curl.

'This is Hook, Child Rowland. You got any problem with the sheet metal?'

'That's a largish negatory. Coming in.'

Goodnight came out of bester mode, saw the three rocket-launcher men gaping at him. One was reaching for a gun.

Goodnight's blaster came out firing.

Three men spun and went down.

Goodnight put an additional round into the prostrate rocket-aimer's head just to make sure, and was running, leaping, down the stadium steps.

Riss and King were already on the field as von Baldur was halfway down the steps.

The stadium was filling with smoke and flame, and

then the screams grew louder as an ex-Alliance heavy cruiser crashed through the hole in the roof and came down, in a stately manner, toward the field, smashing everything blocking its way. It filled the huge stadium from end to end.

A lock opened, and a ramp shot out. Two men with blast rifles ran down the ramp and crouched, looking for a threat. There was none. The mob was busy trampling itself, getting away from this new nightmare.

Jasmine and M'chel were pushing the seven referees toward the ramp, shouting at them. Stunned, the striped men and women obeyed, stumbling up the ramp into the ship.

Grok came down the stairs, grabbed Freddie under one arm, backhanded a man waving a nail-studded club and heard his skull smash.

Goodnight was on the field, and the three reached the cruiser at the same time, pelting into it as the two guards came behind them, and the ramp and lock closed.

'Welcome aboard,' the cultured voice said. 'You're welcome to join me on the bridge. I do have a bill for you. A rather large one, I'm afraid.'

'Not for me,' Friedrich managed over his panting. 'For the Professional Referees Association.'

He looked at the shocked, gaping officials.

'They shall be delighted, nay thrilled, to add a fifteen, no, twenty percent performance bonus to your fee.'

'You said they were the generous type, Freddie. Bring 'em on up with you.'

'We are on the way,' von Baldur said. 'I have a credit transfer to make, as well.'

Chas, Jasmine, and Grok were looking out a port as the starship lifted out of the ruined stadium.

'As you said, Chas,' Grok murmured. 'Mess with our Jasmine, will they?'

Goodnight managed an exhausted smile. 'Jasmine, buy me a steak, hey? I need some stimulation, and this tub's gotta have a mess somewhere.'

'Provided you don't get ideas,' King said. They started out of the lock area.

Riss took one more look back down at Warick. 'It isn't winning that's important,' she said, thinking of the million-plus credits and smirking a bit around the edges. 'It's how the game is played.'

SIX

'Now *this*,' Friedrich von Baldur proclaimed, 'is the place for a proper vacation.'

Jasmine and Goodnight looked at the hologram that hung in the air above von Baldur's desk. It was a sandy beach with curling pinelike trees in the background, next to a carefully rusticated hut. The ocean was clear, green to a deep blue, on the right.

'No coms, no mail, no computer links?' Chas asked skeptically.

'No muss, no fuss, no gambling, no parties till dawn?' Riss said.

'Exactly,' von Baldur said. 'No disturbances, no gunplay, no chicanery, nothing to do but laze on the beach or read a good book. Perhaps,' he went on dreamily, 'finally time enough for Proust.'

'Freddie,' Goodnight said, 'you'd go berserko in three days. And who's this Proust character? Somebody who wrote about famous scams?'

Von Baldur looked hurt.

'A man,' Jasmine explained, 'a long, long, long time ago, who wrote about nothing much in particular. You supposedly can learn patience by reading him.'

'I say again my last,' Chas said. 'Berserko.'

'You people have no faith in my inner resources,' von Baldur said.

'This is true,' Jasmine said. 'I'll put my bet with Chas.' The intercom buzzed. 'Yes?' Jasmine said.

'I have a prospective client out here,' Riss's voice came. 'Can I bring him in?'

'Bring him in,' Jasmine said. 'And buzz Grok, if you would?'

'He's already on his way,' M'chel said.

Riss and Grok bowed in a slender, intense, balding man who appeared to be in his forties.

'This,' Grok said, 'is Mr. Jen Reynard.'

Jasmine, knowing a few archaic languages, thought he was well named as the man came forward, eyes flicking left, right, evaluating everyone and everything in the room.

'Welcome to Star Risk,' von Baldur said, introducing the others and indicating a seat.

'I mean no offense,' Reynard said, 'but your reputation far exceeds your size. Unless,' he added with a bit of hope, 'you have vast resources elsewhere.'

'We have access,' King said, 'to anything a client might need, from a lockpick to a naval fleet.'

'Ah?' Reynard said, a bit skeptically. 'I suppose that's financially sound, not having a lot of thugs lying about on the payroll.'

Von Baldur inclined his head in agreement. 'And how might we be of service?' he asked.

'I am the former premier of Dampier,' Reynard said, then went on, dramatically, 'I need you to free a man from where he rots in a death cell, prove his innocence, and find the guilty party.'

'Good,' Grok rumbled. 'I am getting tired of these tasks that require nothing but headbanging.'

'There may well be some of that required,' Reynard said. 'Eventually.'

'Thank heavens,' Riss said sotto voce. 'We wouldn't know how to handle a nice, quiet, predictable job.'

'Who is this innocent?' King asked.

'A former officer in Dampier's army, falsely accused of selling state secrets to our archenemy, Torguth.'

'What sort of secrets?' von Baldur asked. 'Some secrets, such as how many publicity men are on the government's payroll, carry less of a penalty than others.'

'The crime for which the man was tried and convicted of is high treason,' Reynard said, 'which carries an automatic death penalty.'

'That seems serious enough,' M'chel said.

'I'll explain,' Reynard said. 'The system of Dampier is close to Torguth. From the first colonization on, we have been traditional enemies. Between us are the Belfort Worlds, three eminently colonizable planets near Earth normal. By moral and first-landing rights, these worlds belong to Dampier. Torguth, being the morally corrupt, dishonest system it is, also claims Belfort.

'We have fought three wars with Torguth, basically over Belfort, although other issues were brought into play. They won the first war, we won the other two. Not content with defeat, Torguth is staging up for yet another war, or so my intelligence reported when I still held office and had access to these matters.

'Even though the present government of Dampier is putrescent with dishonesty, they recognized this threat, although they do not admit its immediacy. They proposed a new defense system for the Belfort Worlds. Somehow Torguth obtained full details on this system.

'Legate Maen Sufyerd, who has an absolutely unblemished record – first in the field, now in the Supreme Command's Strategic Intelligence Division on our capital world of Montrois – has been accused of stealing these secrets and selling them to Torguth.'

'You said he's in a death cell?' Goodnight asked. 'That means there's been a trial?'

'A kangaroo court,' Reynard said, voice rising. 'A japery of justice. Planted evidence, inept counsel, prejudiced officers on the board.'

'Why prejudiced?' Riss asked.

'Sufyerd, though he doesn't appear wild-eyed or a fanatic, belongs to an ancient cult that is despised by the hierarchy of Dampier, and has struggled against this prejudice his entire career.'

'Mmmh,' Goodnight said.

'It is not merely injustice that I strive against,' Reynard said. 'But the real culprit in Strategic Intelligence must be winkled out. We do not need to have a traitor in high places in this increasingly parlous time!'

Riss thought of telling Reynard he wasn't making a speech to his constituents, but held her tongue.

'Why have you come to us?' Grok said. 'Do you not have investigative agencies on your own world?'

'We do,' Reynard admitted. 'But I trust them not, especially since the opposition party has retained a very large, very efficient agency to make sure Sufyerd meets his date with the lethal chamber. Perhaps you've heard of them, since they're interplanetary. They're an organization called Cerberus Systems.'

The Star Risk operators showed various reactions at the name of their nemesis: Goodnight glowered, von Baldur looked carefully bland, Jasmine's lips tightened, Riss tried to keep a poker face and failed, and Grok's expression, as always, was unreadable.

'Ah,' Reynard said. 'You know – and from your faces, do not like – this Cerberus. They've also impressed me as being less than ethical, since they're willing to do business with those damned Universalists, the party in power.

'So all the cards are stacked against me and my fellow Independents, although there are turncoats even within that party against poor Sufyerd. Our judicial system has reached its decision as to his guilt, the military he loves has abandoned him, our media constantly bays about his guilt, and now even an outside agency moves against him.

'He has no hope at all. And I feel, to the depths of my soul, that the opposition will stop at nothing – not forgery, slander, perjury, conspiracy, not even murder – to make sure the Sufyerd case stays "solved."

'No hope at all,' Reynard said again. 'Except,' he added cunningly, 'if Star Risk, an outside company without any axes to grind, agrees to help him.'

'Mmmh,' von Baldur said. 'Well, we do like to be of service . . .'

'A question,' Riss said. 'How did you hear about us?'

'I consulted certain experts I've had occasion to use during my political career,' Reynard said. 'And they all attested to your honesty in fulfilling your contracts. They also said that you have a most colorful way of doing business,' he added after a pause.

'Thanks,' Goodnight said. 'I think.'

'Very interesting,' von Baldur said. 'If you'll give us the com of where you're staying, we'll have an answer for you within a day or two. We may well need to ask you further questions.'

'Well?' von Baldur said, a few minutes after having escorted Reynard out.

'You know my prejudice about people who're about to get fried,' Goodnight said. 'Justly or not,' he added a bit sheepishly.

'Why not?' Riss said. 'It is, as Grok said, something different than bashing skulls.'

'My vote is obvious,' Grok said.

'We could use a good cushion with Alliance Credit,' King said.

'I was looking forward to my vacation,' von Baldur said. 'But then, all things are better after a degree of anticipation. So it's unanimous. Usual rates?'

'Yes . . . no,' Riss said. 'Reynard said he talked to some people. Which means our names are known around Dampier. Which increases our risk.'

'Which also means,' King said grimly, 'our prospective presence will also be known to Cerberus, since I assume any politician talks about anything and everything to everyone.'

'Strong point,' von Baldur said.

'Not to mention we're going to be dealing with politicians,' Goodnight added. 'Double down, double down.'

'You shall be pleased to hear,' von Baldur said into the com, 'that we are as upset about this blatant injustice as you are, and have unanimously agreed to accept your commission. Our rate shall be twenty thousand credits per day, plus full expenses.'

Von Baldur listened to the sputtering from the other end for a moment.

'I am sorry, Mr. Reynard, if your cause cannot afford proper representation in this matter, and that you were evidently misinformed about our fees. But our price is our price, and it is a pity that you feel it exorbitant. I might add that we never haggle.

'I shall wish you luck in your search for justice for the unfortunate Legate Sufyerd.'

He listened again, and a smile came and went.

'Very good, Mr. Reynard. Very good indeed. I'm delighted you decided to change your mind. We're looking forward to ending this gross miscarriage as much as you are, and will devote the firm's entire executive talents to it. We shall arrive on Montrois within the week.'

SEVEN

The liner was luxurious, with everything from gaming to gymnasiums to around-the-clock gourmet meals.

Star Risk didn't take much advantage of them, other than Grok's watching with great amusement the work-out facilities for the humans, and von Baldur's dropping a thousand credits the first night out on the gambling tables.

'Which,' Jasmine, their bookkeeper, announced briskly, 'shall not be allowed on your expenses.'

'When will I be able to convince you, m'dear, that honesty should extend only so far?' von Baldur whined.

Jasmine didn't bother answering.

The team was quite busy swotting everything the ship's library or its computer links could dig up on Dampier and Torguth.

'Listen to this,' Riss said to King. 'From one of their local rags: "While I do not mean to imply in this mild critical essay that the good representative is a lily-liv-ered scoundrel whose parents were never formally introduced, and who seems to have trouble with the simplest tasks, as witnessed by the constant urine stains on his trousers, I do think his qualifications for public

office might be exceeded by the average ant-bear."
Whoo. And this writer was talking about a fellow
Independent.'

'I guess these Dampierians have trouble with frank-
ness,' King said. 'Not to mention that their libel laws
are a trifle loose.'

'Interesting sort of army the Dampierians have,' von
Baldur told Goodnight, who was mooning at a young
woman flipping through a fashion fiche in the library.

'Um,' Chas said.

'They beat the Torguths badly the last time around,
primarily through a system of constant attacks.'

'Um.'

'So now they have decided there is no value in
defense, but attack, attack, always the attack, as one of
their strategic writers wrote.'

'Um.'

'Which might be valid, but their defense spending is
small, and being cut regularly.'

'Um.'

'You are not listening.'

'Yes I am,' Goodnight said. 'It sounds like one good
hit and they'll fold up like sheets, and their morale'll go
straight into the shitter.'

'Very good.'

'Yes,' Goodnight said. 'Yes, she is. Now, if you'll
excuse me . . .' And he got up and went across the library
to the young woman, who turned to him, smiling.

'At least,' Grok said, 'we shall eat well. Very well. These
Dampiers seem to export chefs to every expensive
restaurant in the galaxy.'

'I just hope,' von Baldur said, 'that some of the local talent remains.'

'Our employer,' King said, 'is a very feisty man. He's fought half a dozen duels. One over his first wife, two over his second, three over his third.'

'Which would suggest,' von Baldur said, 'that each wife has been prettier and younger than the last.'

'Correct.'

'What does the current one look like?'

'He's single once more,' King said. 'His third wife left him for his dueling opponent.'

'Tsk,' von Baldur said. 'You should always finish off your enemies. Or, at any rate, shoot them in the groin.'

'Or else,' King suggested, 'either keep your trousers buttoned or learn to pick less generous women.'

'Men aren't that smart.'

The liner lowered toward a huge dock, a U-shaped open-roofed hangar.

Goodnight, standing with the others in a long line near one of the passenger locks, looked out an uncovered port.

'Looks like it's raining out there,' he said. 'At least at the moment, Montrois is a gray, rather ornate-looking world, as far as I can see.'

'I can use a little real weather,' M'chel said. 'Recycled air gets to me after a while.'

The liner's antigravs whined up the scale, and the ship settled into its mooring slot. A roof slid across the hangar as the ship's locks opened, and a speaker bayed: 'All passengers, have your customs declarations ready. All passengers, have your customs declarations ready.

After collecting your luggage, move to any open booth. After collecting your luggage, move to any open booth.'

There was supposed to be somebody waiting for them to spirit them through problems. But so far, no show. King started to worry about what would happen when any given case of their gear was opened.

But an officious man, who'd evidently been given a picture of the team, came bustling up just as they were getting in the customs line, as Reynard had promised.

'Mr. von Baldur and company?'

'We are.'

'I'm Deacer, from the Department of Foreign Affairs. I'm also a member of ex-Premier Reynard's party. I'll help you clear customs without the necessity of dealing with any minor officials. I assume you're carrying nothing but personal possessions.'

'Thank you, sir. We are.'

Baggage lifters were found, and their gear, which was quite considerable, was piled on them. Pistols were concealable, but blast rifles, rocket launchers, crew-served weaponry, and mortars could get bulky.

Uniformed men bowed them through a gate, and they were out on the streets of Montrois's capital of Tuletia, sheltered from the rain by an overhang.

'Now for a lifter to your hotel,' Deacer said, looking about. 'Ah, there's —'

He broke off as three shots echoed off the stonework overhead. Deacer crouched, and four of the Star Risk operatives went flat, Jasmine going down just after them.

A man waving a gun ran out into the street, ducking past lifters. He jumped in one, and it took off, ignoring

the outraged whistles from the cab rank officer and two
belated shots from policemen.

'My god,' Deacer said in horror. 'Murder, in broad
daylight! What are things coming to! My god!'

'Yeah,' Goodnight said flatly. 'A tragedy. You four
hang tight right here.'

He pushed through the gathering crowd, looked
down at the corpse. A gray-haired man lay flat on his
back, a look of complete surprise on what was left of his
face.

Goodnight looked about the corpse, made a wry face,
and went back to the others as policemen ran toward
the scene.

'Interesting,' he said. 'As we were coming off the
ship I happened to notice that guy who got his head
shot off. He looks . . . looked . . . a lot like you, Freddie,
which is why I noticed him.

'A lot, a lot,' Goodnight went on. 'Close enough to
be your brother.'

Von Baldur had picked himself up, brushing off
muck from his trousers. 'I assume there was no sign the
murderer stole anything so we can relax in the assump-
tion it was a mere robbery?'

'Nope,' Goodnight said. 'His pockets weren't
turned out, and he dropped a wallet with his tickets in
it when he got plugged. I saw an Alliance passport
sticking out of it, so the shooter probably wasn't somebody local with a grudge who heard his target was
coming back into town.'

'We are blown, then,' von Baldur said, helping
Jasmine up.

'Looks like,' Goodnight said. 'We surely should operate on that basis.'

Grok waved to a lifter driver, picked up a huge case, and carried it over.

'We did not ask for *nearly* enough money,' von Baldur concluded bitterly as he motioned for another lifter.

EIGHT

'What an utterly *chah*-ming dump,' Chas Goodnight said. 'I suppose it has a ballroom.'

'It does,' Jasmine King said.

'Wonderful,' Goodnight said. 'So we can get gunned down by assassins at the height of the masked ball.'

'There *is* a ballroom,' King went on. 'It's got two sniper posts in the hanging chandelier, and two auto-cannon mounts covering the grand staircase.'

'Who was the proud owner of this palace?' M'chel Riss asked.

'He was the former head of the secret police,' King said.

'A careful man?'

'Very careful,' Jasmine said as she led them up the stone steps toward the high-double-doored entrance.

The building was a sprawling manse, half hidden from the quiet residential street beyond by high walls topped with alarm circuitry and broken glass. There were spotlights around the house, and the garden had been carefully laid out so there were no blind spots.

It was most rococo, four stories and three wings, with gingerbread frills and scalloping.

'Very careful indeed,' she repeated as the five entered.

Von Baldur nodded. 'These mirrors in the entrance are one-way?'

'They are, with gunposts behind them, and this inner door has a panic lock.'

'What about the rear?' Grok asked.

'Automated security posts,' King said. 'Plus you can seal any part of the house, especially the servants' areas, from the rest. Also there's a tunnel that leads into a rather commonplace garage on the street behind, for an easy, quiet, exit.

'The bedrooms – there's twenty of them – are each miniature suites, and there's hidden passages connecting them, plus the six biggest have slides for life and security chambers.'

'Twenty bedrooms,' Goodnight said. 'Did he have a very big family . . . or a lot of popsies?'

'How many operatives is it going to take to keep us safe?' von Baldur asked, not paying any attention to Goodnight. 'I would rather not spend more of Reynard's money in front than is absolutely necessary.'

'Let him relax before we jackroll him, eh?' Goodnight asked.

Von Baldur sniffed.

'Not many,' King said. 'As I said, it's mostly automated. I'd guess we could get by with twenty or so, uniformed types, which we can use for other tasks as well. I'll bring them in from offworld, naturally, as I shall the household staff.

'That'll be after I tighten things up – put crushable gas crystals around the grounds, change the locks, add a radar sweep, and things like that.'

'It takes a heap of living to make a fortress a home,' Riss said.

'You want to stay a target like we are in that airport hotel?' King asked.

'Not particularly,' M'chel said.

'It's big, ugly, impressive, and I love it,' Goodnight declared. 'I vote we take it.'

'I do as well,' Grok put in. The other two nodded agreement. 'By the way,' he said. 'what ever happened to that secret policeman?'

'They blew him up as he was going out the gate in his lim,' King said. 'I guess he wasn't that careful after all. You can still see the blast bulges in those wrought iron gates out there.'

Riss snickered and was about to say something, when two shots came from outside. Then came a fusillade.

They went back to the door, everyone but King reaching for concealed blasters. King noted, drew her own.

'Sorry,' she told Riss. 'I'm still learning.'

'Aren't we all.'

The mansion-lined street was a swirl of running, fighting men and women. Some carried signs: FREE MAEN; WE DEMAND JUSTICE; FIND THE REAL SPIES.

M'chel saw a young woman about to hurl a rock as a gunshot blasted, and she went down.

There were screams, and shots fired back, then the mob ran on.

They were running from fifteen masked women and men. These were dressed very differently from the demonstrators, wearing shock vests, knee- and arm-pads and were armed with pistols, clubs, knives.

The Star Risk operatives ducked for cover behind the house's stone balustrades.

A masked man glanced through the open gates at the mansion, saw the five guns leveled, and went after easier prey. The mask was unusual: a black domino eye-piece, with a loose cloth hanging from it to below the chin.

Three police lifters cruised after the masked ones. The cops wore riot gear, but lolled at ease in their lifters, casually watching what was going on. They made no attempt to help the wounded or stop the running massacre.

'Very nice,' Grok said. 'This is the kind of world we thrive on.'

'It is that,' Goodnight said. 'Nothing but scoundrels and goons.'

'I suppose,' von Baldur said, 'seeing as how things appear to be a bit stirred up, it may be time for us to go out and earn our keep.'

NINE

M'chel Riss fell in love with the Dampier System's capital city, Tuletia.

A river curled and twisted through the metropolis — a river long tamed and confined, except in extraordinarily wet years, to concrete banks. Studding the river were small islets, on which were built auditoriums, museums, art galleries, even a church here and there to honor various gods the Tuletians ignored.

There were broad boulevards to speed transport, although Goodnight suggested, somewhat cynically, their real function was to allow the deployment of heavy artillery against any revolution.

Away from the boulevards, small streets wound in patterns guaranteed to befuddle. Riss spent happy afternoons when she was off duty getting herself lost, and then found.

The men and women of Tuletia dressed well, almost as if expecting a fashion designer to pop around the corner and ask them to pose. Statuary was scattered lavishly through the numerous parks.

But best of all was the food. Riss didn't remember eating a bad meal, whether it was in the proud and enormous Bofigers, or once having a simple peasant stew in a tiny restaurant hidden in an alcove she could never find again.

The Torguth had a strange saying, 'happy as God on Montrois,' which said something about the Torguth as well.

The only drawback could be the people, sometimes charming, sometimes irascible. One of the planet's greatest philosophers said, 'We Dampierians have the unique ability to reason impeccably to an utterly indefensible point and then go out and die for it.'

Yes, M'chel decided. After arguing with a waiter who said he was entitled to a tip because his job entitled him to one, even though he hadn't bothered to wait her table without being summoned, she wondered why the Dampierians, all too often, had to be so damned Dampierian . . .

Von Baldur had called for a meeting with ex-Premier Jen Reynard, to brief them in detail about the players in the Sufyerd case. The meet was scheduled during noon meal at Tournelle's, which Jasmine looked up in a guidebook and discovered was 'And I quote, "the longest-reigning high cuisine palace on Montrois, traditionally the meeting place for high-government officials, the cultural elite, and the very, very rich."'

'Real underground,' Goodnight observed. 'Secretive-like.'

But the five were there on time. Their lifter was most unobtrusive next to the long banks of lims with liveried pilots.

'Very, very underground,' Goodnight muttered.

The older men and women looked rich and confident;

the younger ones confident that they'd soon be as well off as the oldsters, or else well protected by them.

The main room was a blaze of baroque paintings and wall hangings, with tables set discreetly apart. However, Riss noticed that the richest of the patrons were escorted into private rooms — as were they, when von Baldur announced their names to the rather supercilious maitre d'.

Reynard was waiting.

'Good morrow, my friends,' he said. 'I am very happy to see you.'

'We are, too,' Goodnight said. 'But isn't this place a little public to be briefing your thugs?'

'Pah,' Reynard said. 'First, everyone worthwhile on Montrois already knows who you are, that I've hired you, and for what end.'

'Still,' Riss said. 'I'm not sure if I'm happy assuming that the oppos know exactly what you're thinking about them.'

'They are dolts!' Reynard said. 'They know nothing.'

'Are you sure this room is secure?' von Baldur asked.

'Of course I am! I have been coming to Tournelle's since I was a boy! They know me here, and I like to think of them as my friends.'

'Friends,' Goodnight said, 'can be bought. Or things can happen when their backs are turned.'

'You are mistaken, Mr. Goodnight,' Reynard insisted. 'We can say anything at all inside these rooms. Besides, I've had trusted members of my own party sweep the room within the past week.'

'Still . . .' von Baldur said, and nodded at Grok.

The enormous alien unslung a small pack, took a small gray box with an earpiece out, and turned it on.

Reynard watched Grok, tight-lipped, as he moved around the room.

'There,' he said when Grok had finished. 'Now are you satisfied?'

'I am,' Grok said. 'There are four bugs. One here, in this table leg, another up there, in the chandelier, another here, at the door, inside this fixture, and a fourth, probably meant to be discovered, under this chair.'

Reynard was purpling. Grok paid no attention, taking very small ovoids from his pack, turning them on, and sticking them next to the taps.

'Now all they'll hear is a dull roar,' Grok said. 'If we had more time, I could synthesize your voice, Mr. Reynard, maybe reading children's dragon tales or something to completely charm your listeners.'

'I shall complain to the management!'

'Why bother?' Riss said. 'They won't be able to do anything until we're gone.'

'That is true,' Reynard said. 'But you may rest assured I shall have a word with the owners.'

'Better you should maybe check the bank accounts of the trusted members of your party who supposedly swept this room,' Riss suggested.

A waiter came in, bowed.

'You'll forgive me if I order for everyone,' Reynard said. 'There are some very famous dishes found here that you will curse yourself if you do not try.'

'Proceed,' von Baldur said.

'My first question,' King said, unobtrusively turning on a recorder, 'is –'

'No,' Reynard said. 'First we eat. Dining is important.'

He ordered, and then they ate wild fungi and meat terrine with a roasted pepper sauce; spiced game steaks with a cabbagelike confit and red wine sauce; roasted wild vegetables; a braised endivelike gratin; a fruit and vegetable salad; and finished with a chocolate chestnut torte.

Riss leaned over to King and whispered, 'I'm never going to eat again.'

King said, 'I'm never going to be *able* to eat again. If this is a midday meal, I don't want to even think about what they do for dinner.'

Goodnight, in spite of his ability to slug down thousands of calories to refuel after going bester, foundered before the salad.

But Grok and von Baldur kept apace with Reynard to the last plate.

Finally, the former premier dabbed at his mouth with a napkin and said, with a bit of regret, 'And now to work.

'Your opponents,' he went on. 'Of course, there are the never-to-be-sufficiently-despised Universalists, traitorous bastards that they are. They –'

'A moment,' Grok asked. 'Traitorous? In what way?'

'That is, or should be, obvious to any citizen of Dampier. Rather than follow sensible policies, and stand against the Torguth, they are a party of the rich, and care for nothing but their bankbooks.

'Domestically, they think that if the rich get richer, the poor will inevitably benefit from this, which of course is foolishness.

'As for foreign relations, they would prefer that we remain at loggerheads with Torguth – never quite going to war, which is destructive, but maintaining a constant state of tension, which allows them to keep spending tax money for useless weaponry. They're not aware that they're teasing the tiger, and that Torguth is in deadly earnest in having designs on first the Belfort System, then on Dampier itself.

'Their members come from the hierarchy of the military, as well, and frequently include church authorities. Plus they've retained your enemies, Cerberus Systems.'

'A *heavy* load of guilt,' Grok said. 'Please continue.'

Missing Grok's sarcasm, Reynard went on. 'The army, Sufyerd's own, has turned against him as well, and will be well content to end this matter with his execution.'

'Why?' Riss asked.

'Because they are embarrassed by the sale of these state secrets, and wish the matter ended as quickly and quietly as possible.'

'You told us,' Jasmine King said, 'that Sufyerd is also hated because he is a member of a cult.'

Reynard sighed. 'My solar system is not perfect. Yes, the Jilani have always been discriminated against. They're an ecstatic, pacifistic cult, but mean no harm and keep themselves and their ceremonies to themselves.

'At one time, our church, now fortunately driven from power and in decline, used them as the whipping boys for any problems. There are still those archconservatives and the uneducated who see them as a threat.'

'You say the Jilani are pacifists,' Goodnight said. 'But Sufyerd was in the army . . . a career officer.'

'I know,' Reynard said. 'But don't all of us carry contradictions with us?'

'Perhaps,' von Baldur said. 'Go on. So the army's

Supreme Command is leagued with the Universalists.'

'Certainly. It's said of the Universalist politicians that they never met a weapons system they didn't like. Not,' he added hastily, 'that we Independents are unaware of the building danger with Torguth. We merely wish defense spending to be sensibly and properly allocated.'

Which most likely meant, Riss thought, they wanted their own contractors to be feeding at the trough, rather than the Universalists'.

'What about the secret police?'

Reynard reflexively glanced over his shoulder and lowered his voice. 'The Dampier Information Bureau claims to serve the state and its current rulers. Of course that means it has its private agenda. The DIB is headed by a cunning, dreadful rascal named L'Pellerin, who, it's said, is so crooked that he can walk a straight line down a spiral staircase.

'As far as Sufyerd, they failed to winkle out the real spy within Strategic Intelligence, which is generally called IIa – and so of course, like the army, they wish the matter over and settled. They will be on the side of the winner, which, gentle people, we *must* be, not only for poor Sufyerd's sake, but for the men and women of the Belfort Worlds and my own, dearly loved people of Dampier.'

Riss was slightly impressed – Reynard had managed that last sentence without taking a breath or seeming winded at its end.

'Quite a roster,' von Baldur said. 'So who is on our side?'

'I am, of course. Those Independents who've remained true to their oath and duty to Dampier.' Reynard made a face. 'There is also Fra Diavolo and his band of crazies, which I'm not sure aren't more of a handicap than a benefit.

'Diavolo – of course, that's not his real name – is a sometime novelist, sometime pamphleteer, sometime politician, sometime revolutionary. The people – by that I mean the workers – love him, and have made him very rich. He spends this money not only on a lavish lifestyle, but in supporting a rather large armed band, who will do his every bidding without question.'

'Why is he backing Sufyerd?' von Baldur asked.

'Because he loves setting himself against the powers of the establishment. When I was premier and the Independents were in office, he was our enemy. Now, for the moment, Brother Devil is on my side. As I said, I'm not sure if I'm grateful.'

'We happened on a bit of a riot yesterday,' Riss said. 'Pro-Sufyerd. They were being harassed by a dozen or so armed thugs wearing masks. The police made no attempt to stop them.'

'The Masked Ones,' Reynard hissed. 'They're nothing but Universalist goons, and some suspect in the secret employ of Torguth. They claim to have nothing but Dampier's best interests at heart, and will commit any crime they think can be covered with the banner of patriotism. No one knows their master. Some say many of their members are of the police, which is why the Masked Ones are permitted to wreak their outrages unhindered.

'So there you have the major participants in this building disaster of ours.'

'Quite a list,' von Baldur mused. He looked down at the napkin he'd been scribbling cryptic notes on. 'First, we shall need to talk to Sufyerd, and we shall need as much access to Strategic Intelligence as possible.'

'That shall be hard,' Reynard said. 'But I'll call in some favors and do what I can.'

'I think, sooner or later, we'll need to meet this L'Pellerin, as well.'

'If he doesn't want to talk to you first.' Reynard looked at them a bit plaintively. 'Do you have any ideas at all who might be guilty?'

'At this moment,' von Baldur said, 'we suspect everyone on this planet except you, and I am not entirely sure of your reliability, either.'

Reynard chose to take the remark as humorous.

TEN

'Imposing,' Grok said. 'But I'm not sure it's a good idea to have your spy service with a listed address.'

The building was a block of ornate stone, sitting on a solitary block.

'Strategic Intelligence maybe *needs* to be on the map,' Goodnight said. 'After all, all these movers and shakers sometimes get lost, buried in their Deep Thinking, and we wouldn't want them to get lost and wander over to the river and drown, now would we?'

The three – von Baldur, Grok, and Goodnight – went through the parking lot, toward the steps. Goodnight eyed a parked lifter.

'Somebody around here's got expensive tastes,' he said. 'That's a Sikorski-Bentley.'

'So?' von Baldur asked, a bit irritated.

'No reason,' Goodnight said. 'I just admire men – or women – who appreciate fine machinery. Especially on a civil servant's salary.' His grin had a nasty edge to it.

They went up the steps, past four sentries, who hesitated, then presented arms, goggling at Grok.

'Guess there aren't many foreigners show up around here,' Goodnight said. 'Especially big fuzzy ones.'

Grok growled.

They went inside the huge doors, where a caged pair of guards examined the pass Reynard had been able to arrange.

'Yes, sir,' one of them said, impressed. 'You'll go on up to the top floor, and Division Leader Caranis's offices are all the way to the back. You can't miss them.'

'Thank you,' von Baldur said, and they started for the lifts.

'That's one, and two,' Goodnight murmured.

'One and two what?' von Baldur said.

'I'll tell you later.'

They went up in the lift and got out on the top floor. They started down the corridor, then Grok realized Goodnight wasn't there.

He went back, just as Goodnight came out of an office.

'I was going to ask for the loo,' he said, 'but there wasn't anybody around. And three.'

'No,' Grok said. 'I won't ask.'

'Good. Don't.'

Division Leader Caranis was a well-built man a few centimeters shorter than Goodnight. He clearly kept himself in shape, and his uniform was nattily tailored.

Goodnight wondered, since there hadn't been a war lately, where he got the four rows of ribbons, then decided he was becoming too much of a snotty bastard.

Caranis had a broad face comfortable with smiles, although von Baldur noted the smile didn't go much above his lips.

He looked around at the three.

'I'm happy to meet such crusaders for justice,' he

said, and his voice was completely free of malice. 'However, it seems that the Sufyerd case has been thoroughly tooth-combed, and there don't seem to be any loose ends, let alone any reason to believe the man is innocent.'

'You knew Sufyerd?'

'Not really,' Caranis said. 'If I had, I might be looking embarrassed right now, since I pride myself on my ability to judge men, although no one involved in any area of intelligence should be naive enough to do so.'

'True,' von Baldur said. 'That is something we all should be cautious of. Now, I think I have read or viewed everything unclassified on the Sufyerd case that is available. One thing that I did not run across is just how, and through whom, you believe Sufyerd was able to pass this purloined data to Torguth.'

'I can only give you the vaguest answer, Mr. von Baldur,' Caranis said. 'Suffice it to say there was a junior clerk at Torguth's Interplanetary Relations Bureau here in Tuletia who was hastily recalled.'

Caranis chuckled. 'Someone on the Torguth worlds has a sense of humor. Interplanetary Relations, which is supposedly their commercial rights agency, is an excellent name for an espionage bureau, isn't it?'

He turned serious. 'I'm afraid, gentle . . . uh . . . men, that I have some bad news for you. I certainly wish former Premier Reynard well, and admire his completely quixotic search for what he determines is justice. And I wish I could accede to his request to allow your firm . . . uh, Star Risk, access to this building and cooperation in your investigation.

'Unfortunately, that will not be possible. We have very tight security here at Strategic Intelligence, and couldn't possibly allow anyone to roam around at will, even with an escort. Nor, of course, will our files be open to you.'

'That *is* a disappointment,' von Baldur said. 'It will also be somewhat distressful to Premier Reynard.'

'I certainly don't doubt that,' Caranis said. 'But in his long career in politics, I assume he's encountered setbacks before, and shall again.

'Now, if you'll excuse me, I'm very late for a meeting, and was barely able to squeeze in a few minutes to personally give you the bad news.'

Von Baldur got up, nodded in a bit of a bow, and the three left.

Outside the building, Goodnight wandered over to the luxury lifter.

'Reserved,' he read from the parking bumper, 'for Director, IIa. How nice. How very, very nice. I'd sure like to know how Director Gotrocks Caranis got his rocks.'

'Now can you tell me what those numbers you were muttering meant?' Grok asked.

'As soon as we're away from that building, and make sure nobody's got a parabolic mike on us,' Goodnight said.

Around the corner he stopped.

'One, is nobody checked on our pass to see if it was for real. Two, nobody, but nobody who knows anything about intelligence should let strangers just wander up to the director's office, and possibly make stops along the way. Two-A is that Caranis then gets all concerned about our having access to his little cakebox without escort. Three is the capper.'

He reached in a pocket, took out a sheaf of documents.

'Where did you get those?' von Baldur asked.

'I happened to see an open door, and a desk, with nobody around. I popped in, saw these here papers, which are stamped MOST SECRET, with a gibberish access code on top of that, and snagged 'em.

'Let's see what they are. Ah. 'Current Strength Estimates, Torguth Reconnaissance of Belfort Worlds.' No doubt very interesting to someone.' He flipped the papers into a trash can.

'One, two, three . . . Strategic Intelligence leaks like a frigging sieve, whatever a sieve might be.

'With no security at all, there's no reason to believe almost anyone couldn't have tippytoed in, snookered those plans, and gone away, no one the wiser. I think this is pretty good evidence that Sufyerd was working for, like they say, a crook outfit.'

ELEVEN

'As our resident expert on prisons, Herr Doctor Goodnight,' Friedrich von Baldur asked without looking away from the controls of the small yacht, 'what do you think of yon bastille?'

'Pretty frigging impressive, like they say in the trade,' Goodnight answered. 'As a prison, that is,' he went on. 'As a defense position, not worth sour owl shit.

'Damfino why people think putting this big fat blob up in space is gonna save them from anything like attackers. All you gotta do is drift a missile close, taking your time, and *whambo*. Or find yourself a nice suicide crew and a spitkit with a limited-yield nuke, and *whambo whambo*.

'But I'm veering. As a prison, it seems to do just fine. I don't think I'd like to try to bust out of there . . . or try to bust someone else out, either.'

'Nor I,' M'chel Riss said from her seat behind the control console. 'So the easy, fast way doesn't look like it's going to work to make Legate Sufyerd a free man.'

'I do not think just freeing Sufyerd will be enough for Reynard to give us our bonus,' Grok said. 'I'm afraid we're going to have to find out who the real villain is, as instructed.'

'Assuming, nacherly,' Goodnight said, 'Sufyerd is innercent. Wouldn't be the first time a whole bunch of people have decided somebody's not guilty when he is.'

'True,' Riss sighed. 'All too flipping true.'

'Which brings up the question, Freddie,' Goodnight said, 'on just why you insisted on dragging all of us, especially me of the delicate sensibilities, out here to visit this depressing ball of iron. I would've cheerfully watched any home vids you made of Sufyerd.'

'I merely wished all of us to meet our client, so to speak,' von Baldur said. 'Perhaps one of us will have some kind of blinding flash about things.'

'Like don't get caught selling state secrets,' Goodnight put in.

The old orbital fortress had three layers of patrol ships around it, plus its own defenses. But as the Star Risk yacht closed on it, it was obvious those defenses were disused, and some had even been removed.

At least the external security was sound – in spite of the pass Reynard had gotten them, their ship had been boarded and thoroughly searched once, and given an electronic sweep twice.

'To return to the subject we were discussing before,' Grok said. 'It seems there are three possibilities, assuming this Sufyerd is innocent: first, that the real culprit worked alone and was able to not only steal, or more likely transmit, the secrets alone, and also mount a cover-up without accomplices, which will make his or her discovery most difficult. The second possibility is there was a small group of conspirators, which improves our chances, since the more mouths, the less security.

'The third is a large conspiracy, such as Reynard seems to favor, with entire political parties involved or some such. If this is the case, then we're not only in worse shape than if it's the first option, but most likely in serious personal danger, as well.

'Does anyone have any additions, or thoughts that might eliminate one of the possibilities?'

Silence, except for ship-hum.

'You've further brightened my day,' Goodnight said. 'First I've got to visit this goddamned prison, then you start talking about big fat conspiracies after the Daisy Hill Orphanage's favorite graduate. Wonderful, wonderful.'

'If no one has anything to add to Grok's rather succinct summation, shall we announce ourselves?' von Baldur said, and swung down a mike. 'Fortress Pignole, Fortress Pignole, this is the ship *Marchiale*, requesting landing instructions. I am traveling on authorization Romeo Alpha Niner Two Zulu.'

'This is Fortress Pignole. Stand by.'

After a bit, the voice came back.

'Your authorization is approved. Kill your drive and forward speed, then zero your controls and stand by to be landed.'

Nothing was left to chance. A tug came out to meet the gently drifting *Marchiale*, and brought it in close, but not close enough for a bomb to damage the fortress.

A long passage, controlled by two suited guards, came out from an airlock and connected to the *Marchiale*'s lock.

'You are authorized to enter the station,' the control said. 'You are not authorized to be in possession of any arms.'

Gathering recorders and notepads, the five went out through the lock and down the tube toward the stage.

'Slipping gently down the large intestine of life,' Goodnight murmured.

'Thank you for the colorful image, Chas,' Jasmine said.

'It was nothing,' Goodnight said. 'I merely think we should have the proper orientation on prisons in general, and this one in particular.'

'Especially remembering,' Riss said, a bit of edge to her voice, 'they probably have every inch of this can bugged, so let's be sure and say things that'll make the warders uncooperative.'

'Sorry,' Goodnight muttered.

Six guards waited for them inside the prison's inner lock. They were scanned, then searched. They were relieved, in spite of their protests, of their recorders, and escorted down passageways to a visiting room bare of anything except four chairs.

'Careful sorts, aren't they?' Goodnight said.

Riss realized he was more than a little nervous; decided anyone who'd ever been a prisoner would probably always twitch around a prison, and hoped she'd never have a chance to test her theory.

The door slid open, and two guards ushered Legate Maen Sufyerd in. He was tall, very thin, and his face looked as if he rationed smiles on a very careful basis. He wore gray coveralls with a large black cross, front and rear, obviously an aiming point for a guard in the event of an uprising.

He was introduced around, then sat down, surveying the Star Risk operatives without expression.

'It is very odd to have out-system people supposedly

working for you,' he said, his voice as dry and emotionless as his face, 'when your own people have decided you're a traitor.

'I don't suppose you have any ties to the Alliance, which would offer a certain justification for your actions. I must say, though, I have no reason to suppose the Alliance might have an interest in Dampier, Torguth, or Belfort.'

'No links at all,' Riss said cheerfully. 'We're mercenaries, working for the mighty credit.'

Sufyerd nodded. 'My apologies, I suppose,' he said. 'But living in conditions like mine, with the death chamber looming close, you become most direct.'

'Which is why,' Riss said, 'we've got to work fast.'

'That would be appreciated,' Sufyerd said. 'Although if I'm not exonerated in this life, I shall be in another.'

'Some of us,' Riss said, 'don't have the comfort of believing in reincarnation.'

Sufyerd said nothing.

'First of all,' von Baldur said, 'you should know that your superior, Detachment Leader Caranis, has refused to give us any cooperation whatever, and is completely convinced of your guilt.'

'Of course,' Sufyerd said calmly. 'He was never my supporter, and was one of the first to decide I was guilty.'

'Now, that's interesting,' Goodnight said. 'He claimed he barely knows who you are.'

'Caranis has always been good at covering his tracks,' Sufyerd said.

'Why do you think he was so quick to decide you were a traitor?' Grok asked.

'I'm not sure I want to answer that.'

'Why not?' Jasmine asked.

'The primary reason is one that I have accepted reluctantly, and don't like to mention, since it makes me sound most paranoid.'

'Because of your religion?' Goodnight guessed.

Sufyerd inclined his head in agreement.

'Is that the only reason?'

'That is the only one I can think of, other than that I do not have a high regard for either Caranis's intelligence nor for his probity. And he knows it.'

'In what way is he dishonest?' King asked.

'He fiddles his expense account, to my certain knowledge. Also, he has been known to use his position to gain certain . . . personal favors . . . from some of his more impressionable female staffers.'

'We noticed his speedster,' Goodnight said. 'It looked expensive for someone of his rank.'

'He is evidently of well-to-do birth,' Sufyerd said. 'Or so I've heard. I do not,' he said somewhat primly, 'make a point of being curious about my fellow officers.'

'So he cheats and likes to get laid,' Goodnight said. 'But is he – could he be – a traitor?'

Only Riss noted the slight hesitation in Sufyerd's voice.

'No. No, he couldn't be.'

'Why not?' Riss asked. 'He seems more than willing to accept you as a patsy. Villains love to do things like that.'

'No,' Sufyerd said, sounding more positive. 'He's spent too many years in the service of his system to suddenly turn traitor.'

Riss was still skeptical, but there was no point in continuing the debate.

'Very well,' von Baldur said. 'Would you mind describing your office routine? No, wait. First, did you ever have access to this proposed defense system for Belfort?'

'I did not,' Sufyerd said. 'I was told of its existence less than a week before my arrest. I was supposed to vet it and write an appreciation, but was arrested before it arrived. It was late, by the way.

'Someone above me, the real culprit, must have shortstopped the information and sent it on to Torguth, although how we discovered these plans had been copied is also beyond me.'

'Since we're not getting any cooperation from IIa,' von Baldur said, 'would you mind describing your section?'

'I do this with a deal of reluctance,' Sufyerd said. 'I suppose the information has low classification, but I still hesitate at describing anything about Strategic Intelligence to an outsider. But I suppose there's no harm, and I certainly don't want to be taken as unco-operative.

'IIa works in small sections, to increase security. My own team of four was one of several dealing with Torguth.'

'Specializing in Torguth's interest in the Belfort System?' Grok asked.

'No,' Sufyerd said. 'My section worked the general field, and would be given specific assignments in any given area as our superiors saw the need.'

'No dealings with Belfort normally,' von Baldur said. 'Was this brought out at your court-martial?'

'My defense, such as it was, attempted to introduce that fact, but it was denied admission.'

'Premier Reynard has given us a copy of your transcript,' Jasmine said. 'That isn't mentioned in it.'

'There was a great deal of testimony presented sub rosa,' Sufyerd said.

'I think it would be helpful if you would tell us what information wasn't permitted,' Grok said.

Sufyerd took a breath.' Very well . . . but I assume any recording devices you brought along with you have been confiscated, as with all my other visitors . . . such that were permitted.'

'Don't worry,' Jasmine said. 'I have an excellent memory.'

Sufyerd licked his lips and began.

'So much for the exciting life of an intelligence type,' Jasmine said. 'All that poor guy ever did was read reports, write summaries, and read summaries and write reports. For which they're going to gas him.'

'Like that's new data?' Riss asked. 'Weren't you paying attention to what you were doing when you were shuffling papers for Cerberus Systems . . . or when we stuck you with running the home office while we were off playing?'

'Setting that aside,' Grok said, 'why was Sufyerd picked as the patsy?'

'I do not know,' von Baldw said. 'If we can get a clue as to that, we might have a lead as to the real culprit. Perhaps just for his religion, even though that sounds somewhat thin.'

'Speaking of which,' Goodnight said, 'M'chel, would you care to accompany me to one of Mr. Sufyerd's group's services? Being as how the Jilani are supposedly an ecstatic sort of cult, from what Reynard said, things might get interesting, and I've never been to an orgy and would hate to be unsupervised.'

'I have,' Riss said. 'In the course of business.'

'And?' Goodnight asked.

'And I found out that mostly ugly people like that sort of thing. Normal folk seem to be able to get their ashes hauled without having to go to a meeting.'

'Mmmh,' Goodnight said.

'While these two are being ecstatic,' Grok said, 'Jasmine, would you care to accompany me to dinner? I've found a new sort of eating here, and you might appreciate it.'

'Enchanted,' King said.

'Leaving me odd man out,' von Baldur said. 'I guess I shall just wander over to Tournelle's and pile on the calories in a solitary fashion.' He touched keys on the yacht's secondary console. 'Assuming no charming or powerful person has called me with another invitation . . .'

The screen lit. CHECKING MESSAGES flashed three times, then two items came up.

'Powerful,' von Baldur said. 'I did not want someone this powerful.'

'Who bonged you?' Goodnight asked from the control couch he was sprawled on.

'We – that means Star Risk, not just me – have been contacted by a certain Mr. L'Pellerin, of the DIB, and a certain Fra Diavolo. Both suggesting a meet over dinner.'

'I'd suggest,' Riss said, 'you go call on the secret policeman. Writers can always be put off until tomorrow. Even writers with their own army.'

'Only sensible, my dear,' von Baldur said. 'Only sensible.' He tried to hide his worried expression.

TWELVE

The name of the restaurant was L'Montagnard. It sat down an alley, and looked to be a fairly small place.

Jasmine King looked at its entrance suspiciously. 'What sort of god-awful dining experience am I to expect this time?' she asked Grok.

The alien put his nose in the air and snuffed, a new affectation he was very proud of having learned from humans.

'I'm insulted.'

'Who was it who decided it was time for me to learn to appreciate that old Earth delight steak tartarater, or whatever it was?'

'It was steak tartar, it was raw, and it was wonderful,' Grok said firmly. 'And if you did not appreciate raw animal tissue sufficiently, who was it who brought you to a place that served chocolate cake with chocolate syrup with chocolate icing and chocolate liqueur drizzled over it?'

'True,' Jasmine said. 'Yum. I'm following you.'

They went in. The restaurant was tiny, a long box with an open kitchen at the back. A cheery fat man seated them, and his equally jovial and heavy wife brought them each, unordered, a glass of wine.

'I shall take the liberty of ordering,' Grok said, 'since I ate here three nights ago.'

Jasmine inclined her head in agreement, sipped her wine.

Outside the two men who'd been following them conferred briefly, and one took out a com.

THIRTEEN

It had taken a bit of work, and some credits changing hands, for Goodnight to find a Jilanis service – if that was what it should have been called. It was in a small warehouse, with no signs outside.

Riss thought it was pretty clear the Jilani were at the least frowned on, if not persecuted – she'd never heard of a religion that didn't cherish the spotlight.

The two Star Risk operatives waited in their lifter until, most unobtrusively, men, women, and children began filtering toward the warehouse.

They looked like typical residents of the working district the warehouse sat in.

Goodnight and Riss joined them. They entered and noticed – Goodnight with interest, Riss with a bit of alarm – the floor of the warehouse was covered with padded exercise mats in front of a few rows of folding chairs.

Goodnight was about to whisper something lascivious about the mats being necessary to keep your knees and elbows from getting chafed, when a lank, middle-aged man with gray hair and a tidy chin beard was at his elbow.

'Welcome, strangers.'

'Uh . . . welcome, yourself,' Goodnight said.

'I see you are not one of us, since you appear a bit perplexed.'

'We're not,' Riss said. 'We've heard of your, uh, faith, and were curious.'

The man smiled. 'I'm Elder Bracken. You were expecting more panoply, perhaps?' His smile grew broader. 'Or what? We don't mind, by the way, being referred to as a cult.'

'I didn't know what term to use,' Riss half apologized, damning herself for blushing.

'Use anything you think appropriate,' Bracken said. 'Please, take a seat. I'll be available after the lesson to answer any questions you have.'

There were about sixty people in the congregation. Bracken led the service, beginning with a prayer that could have been used in almost any church service anywhere. After that came announcements.

Riss almost yawned, then started listening, for those were a bit unusual. A child announced she wished to be raised by a couple other than her parents, with all respect. The parents had agreed. A woman said that she would be taking an additional husband by next Spring Festival. There would be a peaceful protest scheduled outside a prison against an execution.

Then a man and a woman, at either side of the room, began tapping softly on small drums. A woman got up and told a little story about seeing a woman walking along in the rain, and noting a gutter was blocked. She knelt and cleared it with her hands, an obvious good deed, since she thought she was unobserved. Goodnight rolled his eyes back in disbelief.

Two or three people got up and started slowly dancing to the drumbeat. One of them shed her clothes.

Goodnight, remembering Riss's comment about those who go to orgies, winced. The woman would have been better advised to wrap herself in a tablecloth. A very large tablecloth.

A man stood up, shouted 'Praise God,' and sat down abruptly. Others started dancing as well. A man, writhing like a dervish, began chanting in a tongue Riss had never heard. Others followed, each in a language of her or his own.

Goodnight noted that the only woman he considered pretty, other than Riss, sat primly in her chair, lips moving soundlessly.

That went on for too long. Then, without a signal, everyone returned to their seats. The naked fat woman didn't bother to dress.

Elder Bracken recited another equally bland prayer, bowed, and the worshipers got up and started out.

Bracken came up to them. 'What do you think?'

'What *should* I be thinking?' Goodnight asked.

'That, perhaps, our ribaldry or devil-worshiping is a bit exaggerated?'

Riss laughed.

'There've been quite a few other outsiders at our services,' Bracken said. 'Unfortunately, few of them come more than once. And many of them leave disappointed.'

'Why?' Goodnight asked.

'They expected something different,' Bracken suggested. 'We have enemies – have had them for generations – who spread the most dreadful calumny. Now, with the unfortunate incident of Brother Sufyerd, the holos are also spreading these lies.

'I fully expect, any day now, they'll claim we sacrifice newborn infants.' He shook his head sadly.

'We're from offworld,' Riss said, 'and have wondered why you Jilani are badgered.'

'Because we live our lives separately, yet within the Dampier System's culture, just as we do on other worlds, other systems. We do not vote, we pay taxes reluctantly, and avoid military service as much as possible, practicing pacifism. We do not espouse treason, nor even passive resistance to the state.'

'But this Sufyerd –' Goodnight said.

'Some feel Brother Sufyerd had backslid into apostasy, but the truth is that he, and some of our more progressive thinkers, feel we should amalgamate ourselves more into society.'

He shook his head sadly. 'I'm afraid his current predicament suggests to me the possible incorrectness of the theory, although there are still those who persist, and who have dedicated their lives to that belief.

'On the other hand, since Brother Sufyerd's conviction, there are those . . . respected members of our group . . . who think pacifism is an outmoded tool in a society that sneers at peacefulness and persecutes us. They think we should be willing to take up cudgels against those who are our enemies.

'I – and most other Jilani – disagree, and think the best way to end persecution is to continue to live blameless lives.'

'Boring from within?' Riss said.

'I could wish,' Bracken said. 'Of course I would that everyone on this planet believe as we do. But we do not proselytize, never have, and most likely never shall. Our ultimate dream is to simply be left alone, as we attempt to leave others alone.'

'Let me ask you another question,' Goodnight said. 'How many of these strangers who came to your services did you suspect were police agents, or counterintelligence operatives?'

'Such as yourselves?' Bracken said, and grinned broadly, seeing their reaction. 'I just said that to see what would happen. As to your question, I'm not one of those who can recognize a plainclothesman, which I've heard members of the criminal class are frequently able to do.

'But there were those who had recorders, or were jotting things down that I noted. No doubt looking for material, either pro or con, for poor Brother Sufyerd's trial.'

'Why did they choose your . . . congregation, if that's the right word?' Riss asked.

'Brother Sufyerd and his family have worshiped here once or twice,' Bracken said. 'The interesting thing about these police spies is that I didn't see the last of them after Brother Sufyerd was convicted.'

'Oh?' Riss said, letting her interest show, since it was obvious Bracken was on to them.

'Yes,' Bracken said. 'There have been at least half a dozen visitors since the trial, which I can only ascribe to the fact we're the most open of the various chapters here on Montrois. I just wonder what they're looking for.'

'I do, too,' Goodnight said thoughtfully.

'Well,' Bracken said. 'I have business elsewhere. Be advised, no matter who you're working for, that you're welcome back to any of our services. Even a spy might benefit from a little peaceful meditation.'

FOURTEEN

Von Baldur didn't know what to expect from his invitation to meet L'Pellerin at his offices for dinner.

The secret police, the Dampier Information Bureau, were housed in an ominous old-fashioned steel building just off a fashionable boulevard in Tuletia. There was no security visible outside, although von Baldur knew it had to be there. Secret policemen are always more paranoid than intelligence agencies.

He'd been asked to be there around normal quitting time, and workers were streaming out to the heavily guarded parking areas down the street. He didn't see anyone wearing a cloak, nor a dagger or a set of thumbscrews in her or his back pocket.

He entered through double doors into a blast-resistant room, quite large. There was a receptionist, male, who looked as if he'd been hired from a police emergency response team, but who was civil enough.

He asked if von Baldur had any arms, smiled politely at the negative response, and touched a sensor. Two silent men searched him, one using a handheld solid-object detector, but found nothing.

Von Baldur was given a photo badge, and the two

men escorted him down an empty corridor to a lift that shot him up to the second from the top story of the building, then down another empty corridor to an unmarked door.

They bowed him into L'Pellerin's office, a large, comfortable-looking suite. There were no papers or holos visible.

L'Pellerin came out from behind his desk, greeted von Baldur in a tone that was probably meant to be friendly, but actually sounded like a bureaucrat about to deny a last appeal.

L'Pellerin was a slight man, balding, who clearly would never bother with follicle regeneration. He had a nervous, gray face, and, von Baldur noticed, nails bitten close.

'We shall eat in my private dining room,' L'Pellerin announced. His voice was that of a small-town teacher, used to being obeyed.

Von Baldur expressed pleasure at the idea, and was led into a small dining area paneled in wood and incongruously hung with archaic hunting prints.

There was no menu.

The meal was very simple and excellent: crudités, then crusty, warm, fresh-baked bread with home-churned butter, a smoked meat and fowl bean stew, salad, and a cheese course. Von Baldur was offered a red or white wine, L'Pellerin drank mineral water.

L'Pellerin ate hurriedly, in spite of the fact his face suggested he was ulcerous. He behaved as if he'd been given a task at birth, then told he wouldn't have enough time to finish it.

However, like Reynard, L'Pellerin observed the most sensible custom of not talking business with his meal.

Near its end, von Baldur complimented him on the meal.

L'Pellerin looked at von Baldur disbelievingly. 'You mean that?'

'I seldom lie,' Friedrich said. 'Except, of course, when the job dictates.'

L'Pellerin flashed a smile, less humorous than a polite acknowledgment of the jest.

'There are enough elaborate palaces for eating in Tuletia,' he said. 'I prefer the peasant food of my own province.'

There didn't seem to be an answer to that.

L'Pellerin finished before von Baldur, waited patiently. When von Baldur put his plate aside a man came in, cleared the table, left the wine and the mineral water on the table.

'So you . . . and your team . . . are going to prove Sufyerd innocent.'

Von Baldur saw no point in dissembling. 'We are going to attempt that.'

'You will fail,' L'Pellerin announced. 'My investigators are already quite satisfied as to his guilt. I ordered the case closed, and any men assigned to it were assigned new tasks the same day the verdict was handed down.'

'There are others who disagree about Sufyerd's guilt.'

'Reynard? Fra Diavolo? The bleeding hearts of Dampier? I don't worry about their opinions.'

Von Baldur touched the wineglass to his lips.

'I asked you here because I always like to size up an opponent before battle is joined,' L'Pellerin announced.

'I am not necessarily your enemy, am I? I thought

you would be more interested in the truth than in conflict,' von Baldur said.

'The truth has been determined,' L'Pellerin said.
'To challenge that decision is to question the state
itself.'

'The normal police's job is to support society,' von
Baldur said. 'At least publicly. I am a bit surprised that
you take that absolute and simplistic a stance.'

L'Pellerin laughed harshly. 'Absolute? I'm hardly a
fool. But once the state has declared itself, that is the
position we all must take, or society itself is in danger
of crumbling.'

'Obviously I disagree,' von Baldur said.

'Obviously you do. But you're right about one thing.
There's no particular reason I should see you as my . . .
as our . . . enemy. Not yet, at least.

'I have no objection to your taking as much of
Reynard's money as you can. He's entirely too rich, and
a longtime mischief-maker, in or out of office – which
is your first warning. Reynard is growing increasingly
desperate, as are the fringe elements of his party, the
Independents.

'Dampier is quite content being ruled by the
Universalists, and Reynard's scrounging about for a
scandal will accomplish little, I'm afraid – save to stir
up the masses, who're always ripe for trouble.'

'You think that the current situation between
Torguth and Dampier is satisfactory?'

'I do,' L'Pellerin said. 'I speak off the record, but I can
say that we have their dozen or so agents here on
Montrois under constant surveillance, and should the
political situation worsen, can have them all under
arrest within a day.

'As for Torguth itself . . . I think it's quite healthy for two systems to be in competition with each other.

'Some of this competition, of course, is military, which in one regard is a waste of the taxpayers' credits, but on the other does provide work in the various arms industries.'

'I am not really concerned about that, though I certainly do not agree,' von Baldur said.

'You, an ex-soldier, disagree?'

'Perhaps that is one reason I am an ex-soldier.'

'Well spoken,' L'Pellerin said. 'So let me move on to my next warning. You, and your teammates, can be in personal danger if you pursue your quest too diligently.'

'From you and your policemen?'

'Probably not,' L'Pellerin said. 'I would think all of you are too intelligent to chance treason or involving yourselves with the Torguth, which is all the DIB concerns itself with.

'There are wheels within wheels here on Montrois, and I must caution you that little is as it appears, and the situation can change completely from day to day. Be warned that even Reynard may, if it becomes expedient, turn against you.'

'Thank you for the warning, sir,' von Baldur said. 'Now, may I ask you two questions?'

'You may ask,' L'Pellerin said carefully. 'I do not guarantee an answer, though.'

'First,' von Baldur said, 'what is your, and the Universalists', connection with a private security firm called Cerberus Systems?'

L'Pellerin lifted an eyebrow. 'Your intelligence . . . or, more likely, Reynard's . . . is superior to what I thought it to be. The retention of Cerberus Systems, while not classified, was not felt worthy of being brought to the attention of the public.

'Cerberus Systems has operatives here on Montrois, and a small observation team on the Belfort Worlds. They were retained quite against my – which means the DIB's – wishes, by certain nervous Universalists, to act as an outside oversight group on current events.'

'I was told,' von Baldur said bluntly, 'they'd been hired to make sure Sufyerd dies.'

'That might be one of their responsibilities.'

'It's my turn to warn you,' von Baldur said. 'They are less than scrupulous in their methods, and less than honorable in their practices.'

'No doubt,' L'Pellerin said, 'they would say the same about you. And since when, in the shadow world we both work in, is morality, real morality, ever in play?'

'A point,' von Baldur conceded. 'However, Cerberus can be terminally inept in their practices. That, in my view, makes them a risk.'

L'Pellerin inclined his head. 'I stand cautioned. You had a second question?'

'A multiple one. Why are members of what are called the Masked Ones permitted to operate with not only police nonintervention, but with their blessing? I speak from personal observation,' von Baldur said.

'I have heard this.' L'Pellerin nodded. 'An investigation is under way to see if that is, in fact, the case.'

'How many members of the Dampier Information Bureau also belong to the Masked Ones?'

For just an instant, L'Pellerin's face twitched. Then he recovered. 'None that I'm aware of.' He stood. 'But if any are unveiled, they shall be dealt with most harshly. Most harshly indeed.

'Now, I thank you for taking the time to visit with me, and I think – hope, at any rate – we now understand each other better.'

'I am certain that we do,' von Baldur said.

FIFTEEN

'You're forgiven for the raw beef,' Jasmine told Grok, patting her lips with a napkin. 'At least this time it was air-dried. Next month, we'll investigate the joys of cooking.'

Grok daubed cheese on the last of his berry tart, and washed it down with a prune liqueur the restaurant's owner had recommended.

'That is good,' he rumbled. 'I mean, that you forgive me. The meal as well.'

They'd eaten well: the beef, viande de grisons; then raclette, cheese melted in front of the open fire next to them and spread on baked tubers; then salad and dessert.

Jasmine suppressed a genteel burp, saw, on the next table, the printout of a holo someone had left, and noted the headline. Curious, she slid it toward her.

'The *Tuletian Pacifist*, hmm?'

Grok was looking away, at a man who came in and went through the restaurant, into the facilities. That was the second time he'd seen the man do that.

'Condition Yellow,' he said quietly, shifting his weight so the holster behind what looked like a sporran was easier at hand.

Jasmine frowned, then got it, moving her hand closer to her pistol.

But nothing happened. The man went back out. Jasmine returned to the printout, read an ear beside the masthead. 'Coming soon . . . Scandalous Details from Inside the Universalist Party on the Connivers of the Capital, Their Loves, Their Secrets. Read the Secret Letters of Premier Ladier. Mysteries of the Innocent Sufyerd, the Stolen Belfort System Plans, and More, More, More.'

'Perhaps one of us should look up this editor and see if there's anything really there.'

'Perhaps one should put work aside for the moment,' Grok said, 'and concentrate on digestion, and perhaps a nice walk along the river.'

'Do you expect me to shut off my brain?' Jasmine said.

'Of course not,' the large alien said. 'Merely divert it to thoughts of the night and –'

Three men came through the door of L'Montagnard. Two had pistols, one a blast rifle.

Jasmine King was learning about life on the sharp end. She went instantly to Condition Red.

Her pistol, carried in a sleeve holster, was out, and she snapped a bolt into the rifleman's stomach.

He shrieked, stumbled sideways as one of the pistoleers was aiming at Grok.

The shot went wild, punching a sizable hole in a rather grotesque print of two men wearing leather shorts and blowing on ridiculously long horns.

Before he could correct his aim, Jasmine shot him in the head. He dropped like a rock.

Grok's enormous blaster fired, and put a fist-sized

hole in the last man's chest. He collapsed on his knees, died there.

The restaurant owner screamed. Grok was on his feet. 'Call the police,' he ordered. 'Now!'

Her scream cut off, she nodded dumbly, went to the back.

Jasmine King stood, looked down at the rifleman as he gasped his last. She paled a little, found control.

Grok was hastily shaking down one corpse, and King managed to go through the pockets of another.

'Look,' she said.

She was holding a rather unusual mask, one with a black eyepiece, and a cloth hanging below it to hide the rest of the wearer's face.

'The Masked Ones,' she said.

'Just so,' Grok said. 'I suppose it's nice that we are doing something to attract the attention of villains. I just wish,' he said somewhat wistfully, as sirens screamed toward the restaurant, 'I knew what.'

SIXTEEN

The next day was detail time around the mansion.

The first order of importance was debriefing. All of the Star Risk operators carried recorders when they could, and when they couldn't, used their memories, which had been carefully trained to remember everything.

Just to make sure, when they were between assignments on Trimalchio IV, they took mnemonic courses.

Riss was keeping an eye on Jasmine, who was still a little shaken by the previous night's shooting.

King was on a scrambled com to one of the many suppliers Star Risk used, which was one of the ways they were able to keep their mission costs far below other, more lavishly staffed operations.

'Hold on a beat, Asamya.' She muted the mike. 'Friedrich, is there anything we need from outside?'

'I can't think of anything,' von Baldur said. 'Except maybe an expat cook from here, who's been gone long enough to be safe, so we're not dining out and being targets so much.'

King shuddered at the memory, opened her mike. 'No, Asamya, we don't ... wait a second. M'chel's waving at me.'

'I can think of something,' Riss said. 'We don't really have a back door on this one. How's about a nice patrol boat . . . maybe one of those little Pyrrhus-class tubs . . . two crews?'

King asked, listened. 'There are more than a few available,' she told Riss.

'Good,' M'chel said. 'Standard options, standard contracts. Full time. Tell them they're intended to just stand by and play Parcheesi unless the shit hits the fan, and then they'd best be ready to play hero. One ship can be on the ground, the other in orbit, unless things get tense, and then we'll want both of them in the sky.

'Jasmine, write the contract up like that. We get killed, they won't get anything more than expenses. They can start anytime.'

'Untrustful sort, you are, Miss Riss,' Goodnight said, leaning against a doorway of the large mansion library they'd decided to use as an office. 'How could you think a lovely assignment on a charming world like this could be anything other than warm and cuddly?

'Especially after those murderous thugs tried to do some lightweight killing, without even giving us the chance to explain.

'Although I think we ought to develop some sources, and go teach some idiots with masks they should not be messing with our Jasmine.'

'What about me?' Grok said, putting on a hurt voice.

'You're big enough to take care of yourself,' Goodnight said. 'Miss King is our responsibility.'

'Why the paternalism?' Jasmine asked suspiciously. 'Is this another way you're trying to hustle me into bed?'

'Gad,' Goodnight said. 'Now you're getting positively kinky. Can't you suspect me of a little benevolence ever?'

He heard noise outside, went to a window.

'Jasmine, your door-rattlers are here. Must've come down on this A.M.'s liner. You want to brief 'em or for me to do it?'

'If you wouldn't mind,' Jasmine said. 'I really want to get the transcriptions collated.'

'Not to mention someone has got to get ready to have dinner with this Fra Diavolo,' von Baldur said.

'Being of a philosophical bent,' Grok said, 'I would leap at the chance, were I not going to spend the evening considering various electronic security measures.'

'With a name like that,' Jasmine said, 'Diavolo's got to be a lech.'

'Good,' M'chel said with a sharkish smile. 'I'll take the job. Been a while since I've fed a reprobate his own gonads.'

She went upstairs to her quarters. Goodnight looked after her, shook his head. 'What a waste of a lovely, lovely . . . ah well.'

He picked up a pistol belt from where it hung on the back of a chair, slung it over a shoulder.

'Why that?' Grok asked. 'Are you planning to shoot anyone who doesn't suit your eye?'

'Negative,' Goodnight said. 'I just want to have a bit of intimidation handy.'

He buzzed the outside gate open and went outside, as two medium-sized transport lifters came onto the grounds, landed, and some twenty men and women unloaded with an assortment of luggage.

Goodnight noted with approval that none of them were wearing anything vaguely military, although their carriage and haircuts didn't conceal their backgrounds very well.

He sat down on a porch railing and waited until he was noticed, and the chatter died away.

'Good morning,' he said. 'I'm Chas Goodnight, one of your bosses. Some of you know me . . . I saw from your resumes we'd worked in prox sometime in the past. If you do, tell the others.

'All of you have experience with a gun and a suspicious nature, one way or another, one place or another.

'The most important thing you've got to remember is that the only friends you've got are standing around here, and inside. We've never sold any of our people out, or refused to back them up. We expect the same of you.

'I don't make pretty speeches or screw around on a job, and I won't tolerate anybody who thinks this is a game or a chance to do some he-man or -woman posing.

'There are four more of us. You'll meet them inside. You do what they say, no questions, no argument. We don't run an especially taut ship as far as haircuts or uniforms, as long as you're clean and shipshape.

'But don't screw up. A first, minor mistake'll cost you a heavy fine. A second, or a serious one, will get your contract canceled and you'll be using the back half of your ticket before you know it.

'A real bad mistake could get you dead. By me, if not the other side. We don't go to the law, but take care of our own headaches.

'You've all signed contracts. We'll honor them. You don't have to. But if you quit, you better get your ass offworld in a blazing hurry, because I'll be looking for you if you don't. None of this "going to work for the oppos" after you've cased the turf here.

'Your primary job is to provide security for this horrible-looking place we all live in. You'll have the left wing to live in, which has enough room for all of you. Keep it clean. The housekeepers aren't paid to take care of slobs.

'There'll be local work crews in sometime today or tomorrow putting in razor wire, sensors, gas crystals . . . the usual stuff. You'll be watching them to make sure they don't get cute and maybe "forget" to wire something up. Once they're gone, one of us will make some changes in the way they set up things, just in case.

'Like I said, your job is to provide security around the mansion, and occasionally as basic backup if one of us goes out. You'll be assigned shifts and partners. They'll be changed on a regular basis.

'We don't trust anybody.

'We may need some additional heavy work in the event of an emergency. We pay bonuses for anyone volunteering for anything outside the contract specifications.

'You'll be briefed on who our opponents are. There's more than one set of them, and we're not sure we've even got all of them identified.

'One set is Cerberus Systems, which is why the recruiters asked if you'd ever worked for them, or had any problem working against them.

'All of you said no. Don't make yourselves out to be liars.

'You can draw half of your outstanding pay at any time from Jasmine King, who manages our finances.

The rest will go into the offworld escrow accounts you specified, on an E-weekly basis.

'There's a bonus if we accomplish the mission; a nasty taste in the mouth and whatever you've managed to get paid if we screw up or if the contract is canceled.

'It's a very standard deal, and all of you've signed it before we took you on. Don't try to be a barracks lawyer and change things. We will not love you for trying it . . . and you won't succeed. We have better lawyers than you do, nanner, nanner.

'You'll be free, offshift, to go off the grounds into the city or anywhere else – in pairs or more only. Some of that's to keep you safe – some people tried to take out two of us last night. For your hot skinny, all three of them are dead now.

'But the other reason I don't want you wandering around on your own is obvious.'

'You *really* don't trust us,' a bearded man called. 'Do you, Chas?'

Goodnight grinned. 'Glad to have you with us, Erm. It's been a while. And you're right. I *don't* trust any of you, like I said before.

'Now, get to work keeping us alive . . . and we'll do the same for you.'

SEVENTEEN

Fra Diavolo, contrary to M'chel's expectations, wasn't a lecher at all.

Diavolo — no one ever claimed they knew his real name — was gaunt, medium height, austere and ravaged like a Greco Christus. Most solemn, he showed Riss around his vast estate, just outside the city of Tuletia.

He explained that he'd been a writer for more than fifty years, but it wasn't until twenty years ago that he'd discovered the 'way to my people's hearts' — passionate exposés of social evils, mixed with more than enough sex and violence to keep the reader nailed to his screen.

'Then one day,' he said, 'I realized I had no more interest in fiction, at least not as long as my people were burdened with injustice and the evils the rich do with never a thought.'

Now, he wrote shorter pieces that were lapped up by the holos as he railed against injustice.

'Particularly poor Sufyerd, a man doomed to die for his religion who's a judas goat for the real culprits.'

'Culprits?' Riss asked. 'Plural?'

'Of course,' Fra Diavolo said. 'One man . . . or woman . . . couldn't manage to steal a copy of those plans, and convey it to the Torguth without backup. He or she must have accomplices, and I'm determined to winkle them out, and then, once they've confessed, to not only free poor Sufyerd, but assist him in restoring his reputation and winning monetary satisfaction as well.

'I only wish,' he said, losing a bit of his Jovian dignity, 'I had a specific plan to accomplish that.

'That is why I was delighted to hear Reynard was bringing in outside experts, although I expected a much larger team.'

'We bring in support when we need it,' Riss said. 'There's no point in wasting the client's money with a bunch of straphangers.'

Diavolo nodded understanding. 'Do you have any plans?'

Riss smiled. 'We certainly wouldn't be broadcasting them to anyone, even someone who's Sufyerd's ally.'

Diavolo nodded. 'You're right. For obviously you've realized almost everyone involved, including probably myself, has, ultimately, his own agenda in this matter.'

Riss made a noncommittal noise.

'So let me try again. How may I assist you?'

'You, personally?'

'Yes . . . and, as I'm sure you're aware, there are a fair number of people who've decided to devote their time to helping me.'

He took her to a window and pointed out. Riss saw a collection of cottages, in military line. Outside them were a hundred or more people in dark brown uniforms, drilling.

'My organization doesn't have a name. We don't need one, for I doubt if we'll ever have a parade or a medal ceremony. You're looking at some of my people out there, the ones who have been able to join me full-time. Poor people I've been able to help who want to repay me in the only way they can; middle class who see there must be changes in Dampierian society; even a scattering of those rich who have a bit of prescience.'

'Right now,' Riss said, 'I don't think we're in need of marching soldiers.'

'There are many more like them who serve anonymously, when and how they can.'

'Very well,' Riss decided. 'Do you have any sources on Torguth? Specifically, within their intelligence apparat?'

'I have two,' Fra Diavolo said. 'Both of them are purely mercenary, and, I suspect, double or even triple agents. And their services are expensive.'

'Either I or someone else in Star Risk would like to talk to one of them, with a single question. And we can pay very well indeed.'

'Might I ask you a question?'

Riss smiled, but didn't answer, since at the moment she wasn't sure exactly what information would be wanted.

'Very well. Are you prepared to go to Torguth? Their government has become most restrictive on travel permits.'

'I am,' M'chel said. 'Or another of my partners. And we can insert ourselves anonymously, without exposing your person.'

'I'll make the proper approaches, guaranteeing nothing,' Diavolo said. 'What else?'

'Two of my partners had an . . . encounter . . . with the Masked Ones last night,' Riss said. 'It came out badly for them.'

'I have heard of the gunplay at L'Montagnard,' Diavolo said.

'I would like the address or addresses where I might encounter a few of those people.'

'Might I ask . . . no. Even an old man such as I can learn, eventually, when someone has been gifted with a closed mouth. I can provide some names quite easily.

'But first I'll have to give you a warning. You should know that most of the Masked Ones have close ties with L'Pellerin's Dampier Information Bureau, as well as with some of our less savory right-wing groups.'

'I've heard that some of them are, in fact, *members* of the DIB,' Riss said:

'Ah,' Diavolo said. 'And you're not afraid?'

Riss shook her head. 'We don't worry about cops. Especially those who don't have the guts to come into the open.'

Diavolo looked at her with respect. 'From a callow youth, I would expect such brashness. But from a mature woman . . . you clearly are a force to be reckoned with.'

'I would hope so,' M'chel said. 'But I think there are some people on this planet who haven't learned that.'

'I'll give you the names just after dinner,' Diavolo said. 'My intelligence may not be the equal of yours, but it isn't that bad. Unlike that of L'Pellerin, who fancies he has every Torguth spy under close watch, and, should the situation between our systems worsen, will be able to promptly arrest them.'

He laughed humorlessly. 'He is in for a surprise if that occurs. I . . . we . . . know of at least a dozen more. Not to mention whoever stole the Belfort defense plans and then betrayed Sufyerd.

'Now, shall we go into the dining room? I'm anticipating the one daily drink my doctor allows me.'

He smiled wolfishly. 'Yes. Yes, Miss Riss, I'm very glad to have met you, and hopefully will be able to help your cause. For it is time, time past, for this lazy, complacent society of ours to be picked up by the scruff of its neck and shaken until its teeth rattle!'

EIGHTEEN

Grok left the mansion making quiet burbling noises – his race's version of humming. He wore, in spite of the evening's mildness, a large cloak over his long, silky fur, and on his head, a rakish, bright red beret.

Under the cloak he carried a folding-stock carbine and a pouch of grenades, plus the usual dagger and blaster on his combat harness.

He, too, wasn't pleased with what had happened the night before. Three bodies wasn't nearly enough to compensate. Grok had thought he'd go for a stroll, hoping some of the Masked Ones would be following and, even better, try for a rematch.

He was across the street, heading for one of the river-front walks, when a man stood up from a bench. Grok's hand moved inside his cloak.

The man held up both hands palm out, signaling peaceful intents, and limped toward Grok. He was very thin, tall with broad shoulders. One side of his face was a bit shiny, immobile, the result of extensive recon-structive surgery.

Not believing anyone except his partners had peace-ful intentions, Grok had a blaster half-drawn, safety off.

'Amanandrala Grokkonomonslf, I greet you,' the man said in Grok's own language, even if rather vilely accented, his voice not much above a whisper.

'I return your greeting,' Grok said.

'I am Walter Nowotny, Cerberus Systems,' the man said, switching to Basic. 'I thought we might talk.'

'We could,' Grok said. 'But if you think you are leading me into an ambush, it will prove very expensive. For you.'

'I could offer my word, but I know Star Risk doesn't think much of that from me.'

'We think nothing of it, in fact,' Grok said. 'You can walk about a pace in front of me until we reach the river, then I shall pick a spot where we can talk more comfortably.'

'At your command,' Nowotny said, nodding his head.

They walked in silence until they reached the river. Grok stopped by a commercial lifter station, indicated its bench.

Nowotny sat down. 'I came to offer you a warning,' he said without preamble.

Grok grunted. 'You mean a threat.'

'Not at all,' Nowotny said. 'You present no danger to Cerberus, so why should we threaten you?' He sighed. 'I'm afraid the way you, and of course Miss King, were treated by us when you were our employees hardly makes you friendly, nor trusting of us. I'm afraid there's nothing that can be done to change your opinions, nevertheless, in this case, my motives are fairly benevolent.

'The warning I came to give you is to trust no one in this system,' Nowotny said. 'You don't have the resources to adequately cover your backs, let alone help this fool Reynard clear Sufyerd.'

'Everyone not only gives us warnings,' Grok said, 'but knows our business, as well.'

'Come now,' Nowotny said. 'Reynard has been babbling his intent all over Montrois for some months, that he is determined to find someone who'll prove what he knows to be the truth. One and one and one and like that . . .'

Grok grunted.

'First, I don't believe you'll accomplish anything more than spending Reynard's money. Second, I don't think offering you a bribe to cancel your contract would work. I've tried that before, and it failed. Your von Baldur has an absurd system of ethics, considering the trade both our companies practice.'

'He is most romantic,' Grok agreed.

Nowotny almost completely covered his sudden interest except for a brief widening of the eyes. 'You should be aware that the current situation here is quite perilous. Torguth has determined to right historical wrongs in the near future.'

'You mean, invade the Belfort Worlds,' Grok said. 'Are you on their payroll for that, as well?'

'If I said we weren't, you wouldn't believe me. But we're not.'

'So I've been warned,' Grok said, standing. 'Now, may I continue my digestive stroll?'

Nowotny looked at him closely. 'In a moment. Something you said a moment ago struck my interest.'

'Ah?'

'I got the impression you might think Friedrich von Baldur's insistence on holding to a contract until it's completed, failed, or the client fires him is not that, shall we say, realistic?'

'It hardly is that, considering the world we live in,' Grok said. 'Correction – galaxy.'

'Perhaps you yourself might consider accepting a retainer from us.'

'For what?'

'Nothing that would put your partners in jeopardy,' Nowotny said hastily. 'But it might be advantageous to both of us to know what Star Risk's intent is, in any given situation, and also what sort of information you are able to obtain on the Sufyerd matter.'

Grok growled, sat back down. 'Let us talk.'

Grok bounded up the steps of the mansion and through the door. He decanted weaponry on a nearby table, went looking for someone to tell the news.

Goodnight was sprawled in the first lounge off the hallway, flipping through pages on a zine holder. 'You look cheerful,' he said. 'Did you stomp a kitten or something?'

'Not nearly that good,' Grok said. 'I think you should be proud of me.'

'I nearly always am proud of anybody as big and mean as you are.'

'I have sold Star Risk down the river, as I think you say.'

'To anybody I know?' Goodnight said, undisturbed.

'Cerberus Systems!' Grok said excitedly. 'Their man Nowotny approached me, and sounded me out to report on all our findings.'

'And you accepted?'

'I did.'

'For how much?'

'Ten thousand credits per meeting. That should help defray expenses, I would think.'

Goodnight was on his feet, and clapped hands with the alien.

'Good. Very, very good. I was starting to think you were a little too clean-cut for the likes of us.

'Did you get the first payment?'

'Nowotny said he would have it at our next meeting.'

Goodnight sat back down, shaking his head.

'You're still not there, young Grok. A *real* scum bucket, like me – like you want to become – always, always, always gets the money up front.'

NINETEEN

Screamer from the Montrois World (*a supporter of the Independent Party*):

Torguth Fleet Imperils
Belfort System

Maneuvers Threaten
Worlds Peace

From Our Correspondents

Torguth's Grand Council today announced their fleet's annual maneuvers would be held no more than five light years from our Belfort System, a move which was immediately denounced by Dampier's Supreme Command as being a possible threat to our two systems' peace, which has twice been broken by Torguth armed strength.

However, Premier Ladier advised calmness, and said a special envoy will be dispatched to Torguth to present Dampier's thinking on the matter at the appropriate time.

'I have no doubt that calmness and rationality shall prevail,' he said, 'and I advise no member of our citizenry to become concerned or inflamed about the matter.'

However, former Premier Reynard viewed the matter somewhat differently, saying 'the Torguth have very short memories, and once again are planning to test our strength. This matter should be met firmly, and Torguth advised that our own forces will be placed on standby, in the highest degree of alert, and not for peaceful maneuvering.'

Other members of the reigning Universalist Party refused to view the matter with the same gravity as Reynard, and . . .

TWENTY

Riss and Goodnight went over Fra Diavolo's list of the Masked Ones' residences and hangouts, found one that seemed perfect.

It was an elaborate mansion in a once-grand part of Tuletia, now gone badly to seed.

'First, poor people don't go to the cops every time there's a loud noise,' Goodnight told Jasmine. 'Second, what went and run de neighborhood down in de first place is thisyere commercial lifter station two blocks away. More nice noise blocking unpleasant things like screams and gunshots.'

'What . . . exactly . . . are we going to do?' Jasmine asked.

'Why, lass,' Goodnight said, and his voice had never been silkier, 'merely offer some object lessons as to correct moral positioning.'

His . . . and M'chel's . . . smiles were not pleasant.

Riss found an announcement on one of the city's holos.

'Perfect for us, I would think,' she said. 'A nice lecture, not far from our friends' place, debating the need for More Equality and Less Secret Justice. Something staunch patriots like the Masked Ones will be sure to object to. Two nights from now.'

'Heh. Heh,' Goodnight agreed. 'Perfect like a mamoo.'

That night and the next, Goodnight and Riss, wearing black coveralls under their street clothes, took a lifter to the mansion's neighborhood.

They carefully watched comings and goings, and shot several dozen amplified light films.

'What we need,' Goodnight said, 'is to catch these idiots just putting their masks on, before they start terrorizing the widows and orphans or whoever's dumb enough to want to go to this damned talk.'

'So,' Riss said, 'if the suckers' lecture is at nineteen hundred, I'd guess our friends will be assembling at eighteen hundred, maybe a little earlier, getting ready to go out and beat the hamhocks off these poor dissenters for being potentially traitorous and, worse for them, unarmed.'

'Are you sure this is necessary?' von Baldur asked. 'I know he is what he is, and that eventually we shall be on a collision orbit with L'Pellerin, but is it necessary this early in the game?'

'I think so,' M'chel said. 'The only thing a cop understands is greater violence.'

'True,' von Baldur agreed.

'Besides,' Grok rumbled, 'I think an object lesson in how to correctly apply violence and terror is more than needed in these parlous times.'

'You,' von Baldur said, 'just want to go kick holy hell out of something or someone. And where in the hell did you learn the word parlous?'

'This is true,' Grok said. 'But, like humans, I should

be able to put a most pious front to my sadism. As for my vocabulary, all of you should be envious of someone who realizes education is a continuing process.'

The afternoon of the lecture, Goodnight posted a note in the guards' wing. It said that anyone not on night shift who wanted to pick up an extra hundred credits or so, doing nothing all that illegal, should sign at the bottom of the sheet. All of the guards not on duty signed.

'What we'll need you for,' Goodnight instructed, 'is to seal off both sides of a street. Keep the curious away, and if any police lifters show up, which I think they've been carefully instructed not to, give the alarm and haul ass. This isn't an exercise in fair fighting.'

The troops were fed early, then issued black coveralls, blasters, gas and blast grenades, and truncheons.

The Star Risk operatives armed themselves more heavily. Grok picked a semiautomatic, semiportable – except to the enormous alien – grenade launcher.

Riss strapped a small flamethrower on her back.

Jasmine shuddered, checked her own blaster and small backup unit, holstered them, and was ready.

The others had blast rifles, pistols, grenades. All of them wore available-light helmets.

Lifters were waiting in the mansion's yard, and the men and women, not talking, boarded.

The lifters took off and headed west, away from the slum district. It'd been leaked that Star Risk planned a night exercise in the wilderness, to make sure all their people were as qualified as they claimed.

The lifters, beyond Tuletia, circled wide around the city, keeping well below any radar sweeps, then reentered. They landed at a bankrupt loading yard a block and a half from the Masked Ones' lair, put guards on the lifters, and moved in on the mansion just at dusk, making sure their hiding places were off the street.

As night fell, men, mostly young, made their way toward the mansion, pretending elaborate innocence.

By 1800 it was full dark, and the last stragglers were inside.

Goodnight moved the guards out into the street, cordoning the area.

At 1815, M'chel Riss slithered through backyards to the rear of the mansion, and opened the flamethrower's valves.

One blast to one side of the back door, another to the left, and a third straight into the door sent it pinwheeling in flames into the mansion's center.

The fire caught handily, flaring up on the backyard trash. There were screams, shouts from within.

M'chel went down the side of the Masked Ones' center, out into the street in front, finding shelter behind an abandoned lifter.

Goodnight and von Baldur came from their hiding places, a grenade in each hand. They lobbed one each, then the second. The grenades hit on the mansion's porch and exploded. Glass shattered, and now the screams weren't just from fear.

The enormous front door came open, and Grok sent three grenades into the house. They exploded, and bodies spun back, and out. A man came out waving a pistol, shouting for someone, anyone, to call the police, and Jasmine shot him.

M'chel squirted flame at one of the front windows. It melted, and she sprayed flammable mix into the room inside, then fired the flamethrower's igniter, and sent a sheet of flame into the mansion.

The flame set off the unignited mix, and a fireball boiled out toward the street.

M'chel felt her eyebrows crisp, decided to fall back a little, especially as Goodnight roared a burst from his rifle just over her head.

More grenades slammed into the mansion, and Riss saw someone trying to jump out a side window. She fired him up, and in flames, he stumbled away, fell.

Riss heard a noise beside her, saw King's white face. 'Screw him,' she said. 'He would've gunned you down if he had a chance.'

King reluctantly nodded, and, holding her blaster in both hands, shot down two figures inside the left side of the house.

'Good,' Riss approved, sliding out of her empty flamethrower pack.

Von Baldur held his blast rifle's trigger back, and, on full automatic, the rifle sent bolts spitting through the mansion.

Flames were rising into the night, reaching high and higher.

Goodnight saw a curtain behind him move aside, waved at whoever was watching, and the curtain closed. He emptied a magazine into the mansion, saw nothing else worth destroying, ran into the middle of the street. 'That's it,' he shouted. 'Let's go!'

All fire abruptly stopped, and then there was nothing but the thud of running feet, the flames, and dying Masked Ones.

*

'Good *Lord*,' Reynard said. 'I hired you to prove a man innocent, not murder some' – he turned away from the mike and consulted the paper – 'the holos say either twenty or forty . . . men and women.'

'Masked Ones,' von Baldur corrected. 'Neither your friends nor ours.'

'I have not gotten where I've gotten by burning to death everyone who didn't agree with me,' Reynard said.

'I'm sorry you're unhappy with that accident of last night,' von Baldur said. 'Needless to say, all Star Risk operatives and their employees were here at our head-quarters.'

'Where, no doubt, you can provide alibis for each other.'

'Certainly,' von Baldur said smoothly. 'And I know you . . . and we . . . prize innocence.'

Reynard's lips pursed, and von Baldur was fairly sure he was trying to hold back laughter.

'L'Pellerin was in contact with me yesterday evening after the, er, excitement,' Reynard said. 'I tried to contact you immediately, but your coms were all out of order.'

'We were checking them for bugs,' von Baldur said. 'It was unfortunate we did not hear about the, er, unfortunate incident until this morning.'

'I was told,' Reynard said, 'that Star Risk's methods could be, and I quote, "rough as a cob." But I didn't imagine this rough.'

'We do what we have to do,' von Baldur said.

'I guess you do,' Reynard said. 'So what comes next? A nuclear strike on Parliament?'

'If it comes about,' von Baldur said, 'we'll try to give you warning.'

'Out of control,' Reynard murmured. 'Simply out of control.' He blanked the com.

'And are we in trouble?' Grok asked.

'I think not,' von Baldur said. 'I think he was recording that for the record so he has something to say to the media if, or rather when, we do something equally nasty.'

'If,' Riss said. 'Or when?'

'Be that as it may,' Goodnight said, 'what's next? I hope it's something we can get the guards in on. They gave me pure hell for not letting them in on the action last night.'

'I think,' von Baldur said, 'it may be time for me to visit Torguth, and see just how justified the hysteria about their purported designs actually is. I'm suggesting myself, M'chel, because I have some suggestions about what you might be doing here on Montrois.

'I think we can make other deployments. Grok, I'd suggest another call on Mister Sufyerd, to fill out our previous meeting. There are things I've thought of that went unasked that I'll give you.

'M'chel, I'd like you to hold down the fort here. Jasmine –'

'I think,' King said, 'I should be calling on this *Pacifist* holo, to see if I can get access to Premier Ladier's letters and find out if there's anything in them about Sufyerd, as they claim.'

'Good,' von Baldur said.

'And what about me?' Goodnight said.

'I think it is time for you to start thinking about keeping a lower profile, Chas. Something is tickling me, I do not know what yet, and we may well have need for your second-story undercover talents.'

'Wonderful,' Goodnight said. 'Twiddling my twiddles again.

'Actually, I'd like to make a short run of my own, as soon as the patrol ships we ordered arrive. Just to see if we've got any friends out there and see if anybody's listening.

'And I'll only need one ship, and with luck there won't be any killing necessary.'

'Go ahead,' Riss said. 'Be mysterious.'

'Thank you,' Goodnight said. 'I shall.'

'Grok,' Jasmine said, 'would you care to accompany me to L'Montagnard this evening, while von Baldur is jetting off to incredible adventures? I don't think we'll be disturbed as we were the last time.'

'Delighted, my dearest Jasmine. Quite delighted.'

TWENTY-ONE

The patrol ships arrived on schedule. There was a small hassle with the crews when they discovered Star Risk meant what they'd said about no lounging around spaceport bars, and that one ship, at least, must remain on duty, in low orbit, at all times.

Goodnight, after making a few coms, took one ship, and gave the pilot a flight plan for a planet about twenty light years away.

When the ship broke out of N-space he had the pilot orbit the small planet three times before he ordered it to land.

The pilot kept looking at him quizzically when they were on final approach.

'Look, junior birdman,' Chas said. 'You've never contracted with Star Risk before. Relax. We know what we're doing.'

'But why the triple transit?'

'Because,' Goodnight explained, 'this is an Alliance world . . . or, anyway, one that's mostly controlled by the Alliance, right?'

'Right,' the pilot said. 'That, you said, was why you wanted me to bring you here.'

The ON FINAL screen lit.

'Never mind,' Goodnight said. 'I'll explain later, when we're on our way out. Meantime, I want you to keep the ship ready to lift, everybody at their station, without getting clearance nor using the taxiway or runway.'

'But that's illegal from a revetment,' the man said.

'Awright,' Goodnight growled. 'You're not in the Alliance any more, right?'

'Correct.'

'They riffed your young ass out without mercy, right?'

'Uh . . . that's also correct.'

'Reduction In Forces, that's you. Which means all of your little dreams about flashin' through the skies and becoming the youngest Alliance Admiral in history are dust. Right?'

The pilot didn't answer.

'That means they're your enemy. If you don't think so right now, if you keep on mercenarying, you'll figure it out pretty damned soon. Now, you just sit here at the controls and stay alert.

'Oh yeah. I've got this little transceiver in my pocket. Should anybody interesting, like say an Alliance warship, suddenly pop around the corner, let me know, all right?

'That, by the way, is an order.'

Goodnight marveled at the Alliance's capabilities. Even here, on this distant world, with only two buildings, the Alliance bureaucracy kept him waiting for almost half an hour.

He spent the time watching out the window on the

spaceport, having no faith in his pilot, checking his transceiver, and watching for any inordinate signs of panic on the part of the clerks around him.

But nothing happened, and eventually he was ushered into an office, where a surprise waited.

The man sitting behind the desk was of medium height, not distinguishable in a crowd unless you noted his chill eyes.

'Good Christ, Kruger,' Goodnight said, 'who'd you do wrong to get sent out here to the tules?'

Kruger had been one of Goodnight's controls, back when Chas was a Captain in the Alliance Military, before he got caught with his hands in a planetary ambassador's jewel chest up to the armpit.

He and Goodnight had not gotten along, any more than Chas had ever shown respect for any of the intelligence mandarins who loved sticking the besters into near-suicidal situations, especially as their own personal hindquarters would be light years from the resulting massacre.

'Sorry to displease you, Goodnight,' Kruger said. 'But I was just passing through when I heard your name mentioned and thought it might be interesting to see what transpired.'

'Do I have to think in terms of hostages?' Goodnight asked, hand going toward his gun.

'No,' Kruger said. 'I'm after bigger game than you. At least at the moment. Did you, by any chance, happen to show up here to turn yourself in? You're still very much wanted, you know, if not by the Alliance directly, by at least one world we have an extradition agreement with.'

'I don't think so,' Goodnight said. 'My interest in

death cells has been thoroughly satisfied.'

'Did you come in thinking there was some kind of amnesty?'

'No. Is there?'

'No,' Kruger said. 'However, if you were interested in returning to your old trade, there might be some sort of arrangement reached that might even allow you to return to Alliance service at your old rank.

'There's more than enough work these days for someone with your talents . . . and modifications. Although you'd have to be willing to accept some sort of conditioning that would keep your larcenous impulses under control.'

Goodnight shuddered. 'I don't think I want anybody stirring around in my brain, thanks. Least of all the Alliance.'

'Then what brings you to our outpost?'

'I came to find out if the Alliance is monitoring the Dampier-Torguth situation.'

Kruger touched a sensor, and a computer screen rose out of his desk. He slid a keyboard over, touched keys.

'Damn,' he muttered. 'Using someone else's computer is like using their toothbrush.'

'Tasteful comparison,' Goodnight murmured, still waiting for the door to come down and a handful of military policemen to hurtle in.

Kruger watched the screen. 'At present,' he said, 'we have no involvement with either system. Should we?'

'If you're still pushing the story that the Alliance is the Galactic peacekeeper, you should,' Goodnight said. 'Things are building toward war out there.'

'And your involvement is?'

'Something having nothing to do with spacefleets,' Goodnight sort of lied. 'I came back here toward Galactic Center to drop the coin on them, since a nice bloody war wouldn't make life any easier for me and my pursuits.'

'You would expect the Alliance to send out a couple of battle cruiser squadrons just to help a wanted renegade?' Kruger asked.

'Come on, Kruger! I think the Alliance ought to get involved to keep a bunch of its citizens from shooting each other full of holes, no more.'

'Ah,' Kruger said. 'Well, I'll certainly bring your report . . . I assume you have full details . . . to the Resident's attention.'

Goodnight stood. He knew what that meant.

'Right you are. I've got the report aboard my ship, and can have it back here within the hour.'

'I'll arrange to have one of the military attachés give it his full attention,' Kruger said. 'As for you, personally, you might consider my offer. You can't run forever, you know.'

'I'll take your advice seriously,' Goodnight said. 'And I'll be back shortly.'

The two men smiled mutually loathing smiles, and Goodnight hurried out.

A few minutes later, without waiting for clearance, his patrol ship lifted, ignoring the bleating from Planetary Traffic Control.

So the Alliance didn't have a clue as to the building war and, worse, wouldn't get involved in stopping the fighting – at least not until the bodies were piled chin high.

Goodnight's fond hopes that life could be simplified

for Star Risk and its investigation were in vain. It was business as usual ten meters away from what the Alliance called civilization.

TWENTY-TWO

Riss came into the room they'd dubbed the operations center, saw Jasmine critically supervising Grok as he wrote names on index cards and taped them to the wall.

'You know,' Riss said, 'this kind of thing is what they build computers for, or so they tell me.'

'It's easier to move people around from category to category if you can look at the whole mess,' Jasmine said.

'Besides,' Grok said, 'I have everything on computer, if you have a distressingly linear mind and would rather wait for printout after printout.'

M'chel noted names; saw, at the top, Caranis's.

'Is this a suspects roster?'

'No,' Jasmine said. 'At least, not yet. We're cobbling together a roster of Strategic Intelligence.'

'As much of it as Sufyerd could recall, at any rate,' Grok said. 'Here's his section.'

Riss considered the three names: Cabet Balalta, Ayalem Guames, Hopea Ardwell. There was a fourth card, Sufyerd's, completing the four-man team.

Over Sufyerd's name was another card: Balkis Faadi.

'Now we have four specific people to investigate,'

Jasmine said. 'Interestingly enough, Grok confirmed none of them, except Sufyerd's immediate superior, Faadi, testified at the court-martial.'

'Now *that* is interesting,' Riss said.

'Even more so,' King went on, 'is none of them are currently assigned to Strategic Intelligence Headquarters.'

'The matter is being buried,' Grok said. 'Very, very deep.'

'I'll see if I can have Reynard . . . or Diavolo . . . come up with home addresses if they're out of the service, or new assignments if they're just being moved around,' Riss said.

Goodnight was in the doorway, doing his usual job of holding up the doorsill with his shoulder. 'Has anybody bothered to ask when they're going to geek poor Sufyerd?'

'I tried,' King said. 'Dampier has the lovely custom of not telling anyone when they're to be executed. Their counsel is notified at midnight of the day, given a chance to get to the place of execution. The victim . . . sorry, the condemned . . . hears about it when he's awakened.'

'Flipping wonderful,' Goodnight said. 'So you never know whether the footsteps down the hall are a warder bringing you a drink of water, or the headsman.'

'They don't use an ax, Chas,' Jasmine said. 'Lethal injection, like most civilized states.'

'There might be those who think that any state that kills people isn't civilized,' Goodnight said.

Riss turned and stared at him. 'Now that's an odd thing for a formerly licensed assassin to say.'

'Wrong,' Goodnight said. 'I never thought I was

moral. I always hoped that the idiots I worked for were. Fool me. Any word from Freddie yet?'

'Nothing,' Riss said. 'I'm not even sure if he's inserted into the Torguth Worlds yet.'

'Hell,' Goodnight said. 'I need a drink, since nobody's come up with any nasty deeds for me to do yet.'

'Actually,' Jasmine said, 'I can come up with one, but regrettably it isn't that nasty. You noticed Caranis's lifter, some kind of exotic. You might want to do a little digging around, and find out if he really is rich. Or if he's . . .'

'"Bent" is the word used in some circles,' Goodnight said. 'That sounds just vaguely interesting.'

TWENTY-THREE

Tristan, the capital of the Torguth System, was the fourth planet of nine, and quite Earthlike.

Friedrich von Baldur had made two jumps away from Dampier, then another two back to Torguth, carefully checking to make sure he wasn't followed, either electronically or in person. He'd planned his second-to-last jump for a fairly cosmopolitan world for this remote part of the Galaxy, and spent two days having an entirely new wardrobe run up in the unlikely event someone had put a bug or a tracer in his clothing or personal effects. He felt especially delighted because everything would be cleverly buried in the expense sheet sent to Reynard.

He packed his old gear and sent it back to Trimalchio.

While he was waiting for the tailors to finish, he made inquiries in some seedier places, and by the time his clothes were ready and he'd bought new luggage, he was also luxuriating under the name of Lord William of Hastings, a distant planet he'd made up.

His trade, he decided, would be import-export of luxury items. Since everyone knew that people who produced luxuries preferred instant cash, that justified the large amount of credits he was carrying.

He sent a coded notice of his new ID and trade to Trimalchio, where the mail forwarding service would send it on to Jasmine King, and her onetime pads. Just in case he needed a rescue or two . . .

Tristan's main city, Mackall, had been carefully planned, nestling in a mountain valley that opened to the south, where manufacturing facilities and the spaceport were located. Public transit lines were readily available, so no one had to live near the smoke and fumes of his job, and there was a prevailing southerly wind.

Mackall had lakes, canals, parks, and sculptery plazas.

Von Baldur didn't much like it. He hated all well-planned cities, preferring those that grew in strange and unexpected ways. But this wasn't his home, and he'd be gone as soon as he could get the information he sought.

Fra Diavolo had contacted his two agents in the Torguth System, not saying how the messaging was done, and notified von Baldur he could proceed into the lion's den.

Passport control at the spaceport was very careful, very thorough. Von Baldur was starting to get a little paranoid until he realized everyone got the same tooth-combing.

Finally, the inspector — after staring back and forth between von Baldur and his money, waiting for Friedrich to break out in a cold sweat or something — grunted, ran Lord William's passport through a pickup where it was stamped, gave it back, and said, clearly not meaning a word of it, for Lord William to have an enjoyable and profitable stay on Tristan.

Von Baldur wished him a pleasant day, also not meaning it, went looking for transport into the city.

Outside his terminal were crowds and lines, but no for-hire lifters.

It was unseasonably warm, the street was closed off, and there was a parade going on.

The paraders carried banners, proclaiming each group of marchers' occupations and places of work.

Friedrich wondered why, if they were workers, all of them carried blast rifles. Then he noted the weaponry was nonfunctional, solid plas pieces, which made things even more puzzling.

The marchers, men and women, kept going past and past and hypnotically past.

Von Baldur really wanted a good beer and something to eat, and parades had always bored him spitless.

But he stood, trying to look as interested as the bystanders were.

There was a pause in the procession, and a man next to him leaned over, and said, 'You're offworld, correct?'

'I am that.'

'Welcome to Torguth,' the man said, pumping von Baldur's hand. 'You will enjoy yourself here.' It sounded like an order.

'I am sure,' Friedrich said.

'You can go back to your own world, whatever it is, and say that you have been here, and seen how Man can order his universe.'

'By marching in parades?'

The man frowned, let it go by. 'We enjoy showing our solidarity,' he said. 'And our workers love to show off that they are as one, which is one reason we have no unemployment.'

'None?' von Baldur asked, just a bit incredulous.

'None,' the man said firmly. 'We have the proper education, and our leaders make sure that each of us is properly directed into a profession we can be proud of.'

'How nice,' von Baldur said, smiling sincerely, having noted the parade was at an end, and a host of cabs were drifting toward them. 'How very nice indeed.'

The hotel he'd picked from a guide holo was more than satisfactory – his suite was very large, and the emergency escape was one window over, an easy jump if someone unfriendly showed up at the door.

The beer in the dining room was also satisfactory, if a little less hoppy than von Baldur liked.

The meal, however, while well prepared, was more than heavy. He'd considered various options, decided he didn't want to take a nap, and ordered a simple plate of bread, cold meat, and cheeses.

It came on a platter he could've fed everyone from Star Risk, including Goodnight after he came out of bester.

He picked at the food, eventually gave up, and the rather overbearingly maternal waitress cooed over him, worried that he was getting sick.

Von Baldur thought of telling her how long it'd take him on a track and with machines to get rid of all these calories, but didn't bother.

Instead, he found a theatrical supply house, and bought a wig. It was just realistic enough to be believable from a distance. Up close, it was clearly false. Like all good quick disguises it was intended to draw attention to the hairpiece, and a witness would hopefully only see the awful wig, and facial features would become an unidentifiable blur to the memory.

Then he reconned the meeting places.

Diavolo had told him the agents would make contact with him, and had given von Baldur meeting points. Both were in city parks, which von Baldur didn't like, since that was one of the signs of an amateur agent. He liked even less that he was at the mercy of Diavolo's contacts instead of the other way around.

The first park was a statuary exhibit, all piled stone and polished metal, with warlike names on the abstracts.

He guessed it was a monument to one or another of the three wars Torguth had fought with Dampier.

Friedrich didn't like that one much, since there were streetlights and open ground on all four sides, and it would be very easy to surround the statues and turn the park into a trap.

Von Baldur found places around the park where he could stash the tiny pistols he'd brought with him, pistols that would go through a metal detector unnoticed, that were part of a solid sheet of plas that served as his suitcase bottom. Small, explosive rounds for the weapons were hidden inside the metalloid carrying strap of the case.

He went on to the meeting place the second agent had chosen. This was a deal better – a long park beside a small winding lake.

Here there were only occasional streetlights, and more than enough avenues of escape.

Two more pistols could be hidden in conveniently hollow niches in trees.

All he had to do was stroll in these parks, at preset hours, wearing a black mourning band around his left, not right, shoulder. Not professional, he thought. But better than carrying a holo, or a stuffed pigeon or such, more recognition signals for amateurs.

Somewhat satisfied, he went back to his hotel, picking up half a dozen holos on the way.

He went to one of the hotel bars, ordered a white wine spritzer, and started reading.

The holos were trumpeting a host of atrocities and near-atrocities on various of the Belfort Worlds, all, of course, committed against Torguth citizens who were either colonists or visitors.

Von Baldur didn't recollect reading about any of those before he left Montrois, nor about the incredible crime rate on the Belfort Worlds, and the constant rudeness Dampier officialry wreaked on poor Torguth businessmen or tourists.

He even found a mention of Reynard as being one of the chief conspirators 'holding Torguth back from their rightful place in space,' and probably secretly planning an invasion of Torguth.

There was no mention that Reynard was rather firmly out of office.

Saber-rattling, he thought, and went to find someone to consult with who might recommend a restaurant that might serve food, not boat anchors.

The restaurant was better than the hotel, but still heavy. After eating, he strolled through one park at the set hour. No one approached him.

*

The next night, he walked in the other park again, without result.

Then back to the first.

He rather enjoyed these nightly strolls, once he had finished stashing his pistols.

The people of Torguth loved uniforms, and it seemed that everyone had one, from the school children to the priests to the mailmen to various military organizations. He saw one woman dressed in a rather paramilitary set of slacks and loose blouse, wearing a small badge that appeared to show a man soothing some sort of beast.

He asked, was told that she was a veterinarian, and he should learn to recognize uniforms better, even if he was an off-worlder. Friedrich apologized and withdrew, wondering how a people could be so in love with uniforms without considering enlistment.

But if Torguth continued on the path it appeared to be on, he thought, they might end up following the colors whether they wished to or not.

Six days passed, without contact.

Von Baldur kept busy. He contacted various craftsmen and got quotes on interesting material, from hand-worked silver to hunting weapons to an odd melon with three separate tastes that would preserve well, even throwing in a couple of artists.

He hoped none of them would be too disappointed when the promised follow-ups never happened.

He decided he didn't like Torguth any better now than he had when he first landed.

Friedrich also kept up with the tabloid holos, and the steadily worsening situation, for anyone of

Torguth descent, on the Belfort Worlds.

No one was calling for armed intervention.

Yet.

On the seventh night, in the statuary farm, a uniformed man walked toward him. Von Baldur had been practicing uniform recognition, saw the man was of the Custodial Corps.

'A shame to lose someone dear to you,' the man said, nodding at von Baldur's armband.

Von Baldur, feeling a bit of a fool, responded as ordered: 'Not as terrible as if it happened to yourself.'

'Over there,' the man said. 'Behind that blob that looks like a man's butt.'

Von Baldur followed.

'So what is your one question?' the man said.

'Torguth Intelligence has or had a control, or maybe a bureau, handling a high-level double agent on Montrois, who is almost certainly in their Strategic Intelligence,' von Baldur said.

The man blinked. 'If it's a top level operation, there'll almost certainly be no way I can get inside.'

'I do not want you to even try,' von Baldur said. 'I just want to know if that operation is still running.'

'That's not very much for what I want to be paid.'

'I am a very generous sort,' von Baldur said. 'I love giving money away.'

'That's all?'

Von Baldur nodded.

'All right. Same contact place, if I can find anything out,' the man said, smiled, and walked away rapidly.

Not very professional at all, von Baldur decided,

using the same meeting ground. But maybe he could get in and out quickly enough for it not to matter.

Two nights later, with no contact from the janitor, the second agent made contact, in the lakeside park.

She was a middle-aged clerk or secretary, a very no-nonsense look on her face.

She had the same contact phrase, and von Baldur responded as before.

A wintry smile came, went.

'Who makes these things up? Of course losing yourself is a pain.'

She took his arm, and they strolled on.

Von Baldur repeated his question about a mole inside Dampier's Strategic Intelligence, and then another thought came, that he might be able to use in the eventuality Star Risk could get Sufyerd an appeal. It was more a hunch than a coherent idea, but he made a practice of trusting his hunches.

'I would like to know the scenario for the Torguth war games that are planned near Belfort.'

'Scenario?'

'Every war game I've ever heard of has some sort of script,' von Baldur explained. 'The heroes go here, are attacked by whoever plays the villains, they counter-attack or whatever . . . that sort of scenario.'

'The war games are still being drawn up,' the woman said.

'Get what you can . . . I do not need specific deployments or units, just where these mock battles will be fought.'

'Might I ask –'

'I collect toy soldiers,' von Baldur said. 'And I am

running out of role-playing games.'

'I don't believe you,' the woman said.

'Neither do I.'

Again, the chill smile from the woman.

'If – I emphasize if – I can get anything, I'll get it to you at the Café of the Dawn Delights. It's two blocks down, six east. Eighteen hundred. Be inside if it's raining, outside if it's nice. Give it an hour, then try again, two nights later.'

Without waiting for a response, the woman pivoted and was gone.

Now she, von Baldur thought, is almost professional.

It was foggy, with a light drizzle blowing across the statues.

Von Baldur growled at the weather, then realized if matters went sour, it might give him a bit of cover.

The man came toward him quite openly, and didn't bother with the code.

Von Baldur knew something was wrong. 'Well?'

'Do you have the credits?'

'I do.'

'Lemme see.' Greed was heavy in the man's voice.

Von Baldur wished he'd gotten one of the guns out of its hiding place, but thought, if the man was going to try to strong-arm him, he might be in for a surprise.

He nodded, put a smile on his face, and took out a clipped-together band of bills.

'Well?' von Baldur said again.

'They've got some kind of operation going,' the man said. 'On Montrois. Real high level. I found out it was for an agent they've doubled in Strategic Intelligence. They told me . . .'

His voice slipped a little, and his eyes looked over von Baldur's shoulder.

Friedrich spun, saw two men coming out of a parked lifter toward him, two other lifters landing on the other side of the park. They didn't need to get any closer for him to ID them as plainclothes cops.

TWENTY-FOUR

'Jasmine King. I have an appointment with your editor,' Jasmine told the young man. He looked at a screen, nodded.

'Met Fall is running a little late this morning, but he'll be with you shortly.'

Jasmine went to a rather battered chair, sat down, looked about curiously. This was the first time she'd been in a holo's office. The furniture was fairly battered, as if it had been picked up at a fire sale, even though the *Tuletian Pacifist* was one of the most prosperous tab holos on Montrois, and the floor looked as if it could do with a determined sandblasting. The walls were glass, and looked out on a large chamber full of computers, intent journalists, and scurrying messengers.

It must be deadline time, King guessed.

There was one other person in the room besides the receptionist, an extremely pretty woman who Jasmine guessed was in her mid-thirties. She wore expensive clothes, and jewelry just a bit too ostentatiously costly. Her face, heart-shaped under a blond coif, had just begun to harden. King hid a smile, thinking that this woman was a perfect illustration of what Goodnight called a 'high-maintenance bimbo,' and picked up a current edition of the *Pacifist*, and fed it into one of the viewers scattered about.

The banner above the logo read: COMING SOON: UNIVERSALIST SCANDALS BARED IN SHOCKING LETTERS. But there was no accompanying story.

Jasmine had read about half of a poorly written piece claiming – with no hard evidence to back the claim – that Torguth had agents riddling Dampier society, when a buzzer went off.

'Miss King,' the receptionist said, 'you can go straight on through the city room to the end . . . Mr. Fall is free now.'

The other woman looked at Jasmine resentfully.

'How come she gets in straightaway, and I've been sitting here for over two hours?'

'I'm sure Mr. Fall is aware you're here, and wants to be able to give you his fullest attention,' the young man said. He touched a button, and the door into the large chamber opened.

Jasmine went through the room, aware that she was getting interested looks from several reporters of at least three sexes. She was used to that.

Another glass-walled office was at the end, with a tarnished brass plate that read EXECUTIVE EDITOR. The office inside was terminally cluttered with printouts, boxes, several computers, and heaped papers and holos.

Behind a desk that looked as if it'd served for fleet target practice was a man, youngish but balding, who wore his hair thinly combed across his pate. He was thin, and had the face of an ascetic. His suit was expensive, and was worn carelessly.

Jasmine introduced herself to Fall and, since there

was no particular reason she could see to conceal her mission, explained that she'd be interested in any information in these letters that might help Star Risk in freeing Sufyerd.

'No doubt you would,' Fall said. 'I've heard of Star Risk, and have tentatively assigned two reporters to investigate. The only reason I'm holding back on publishing your identities is I'm not at all sure how we want to play you people.'

'Play?' Jasmine asked.

'Yes. How does your presence help or hurt keeping the peace between Torguth, Belfort, and Dampier?'

'I didn't know,' King said, trying to keep sarcasm out of her voice, 'there was any purpose in reporting events except they happened.'

'A very old-fashioned approach,' Fall said. 'Today's journalists must choose a side, choose an issue, or risk being left out of the hue and cry.'

'Oh,' was all Jasmine could manage.

'As for your being able to access these letters,' Fall said, 'I'm afraid that will be impossible, even though I personally believe Sufyerd to be innocent, and would hate to see the execution of an innocent man . . . assuming, of course, that he *is* innocent, since all of us should learn not to trust our instincts.'

'We've satisfied ourselves that he is,' King said.

'A good journalist must stay above such judgments until all the facts are clear,' Fall said primly.

'But you just said . . .' King let her voice trail off.

'No,' Fall said firmly. 'The correspondence between Premier Ladier and Miss Hyla Adrianopole must remain secret, until we begin publishing it within the next several weeks or so, and then all shall be revealed.

'By the way,' Fall continued, 'I heard rumors that there was a gun battle in a restaurant across the river between some off-worlders and some of' – he lowered his voice and looked around, without being aware of it – 'those who call themselves the Masked Ones. Do you happen to know anything about it?'

'Not at all,' Jasmine said. 'But if you'd go back to the Sufyerd matter, is there any reason that I could not look at those letters . . . just the ones that pertain to our client . . . to give us a lead in finding the real culprit, the real traitor?'

Jasmine remembered the way von Baldur had taught her that a journalist never gives anything away, but only trades.

'In exchange for which we would be willing to give your holo an exclusive when we uncover this person.'

Fall hesitated.

'That's tempting,' he said. 'But I must tell you that I do not have possession of these letters . . . and, by the way, the most interesting ones come from Premier Ladier. Miss Adrianopole seems to have been far more careful in what she was willing to commit to writing.

'No. The first thing I realized was how easy it would be for someone to break in here, in the wee small hours, perhaps, and then we would be without a string to our bow.'

'The first thing I would've done, in your position, is to make copies of the correspondence,' Jasmine said, in spite of herself.

'That, of course, was done,' Fall said. 'And those copies distributed to responsible hands. The originals, however, were deposited in yet another –'

The door to his office banged open.

Jasmine turned, saw the woman who'd been in the outer office.

'You bastard!' she near shouted. 'You betrayer! How dare you even think of publishing my letters!'

'I gather,' Fall said, seemingly undisturbed, getting to his feet, 'you are Miss Hyla Adrianopole.'

'I am . . . and you are a traitor to your planet, to your solar system, to everything you ought to hold dear.'

King was thinking Adrianopole was getting a bit histrionic, then noted the woman's hand was scrabbling in her rather large handbag.

'Now, please be calm, Miss –'

Adrianopole, screaming wordlessly, pulled out a rather large handgun.

'Wait!' Fall shouted, and King braced for a dive for the gun. But it was too late.

The blaster slammed three times. All three bolts struck in the center of Fall's chest. An enormous amount of blood spattered on the desk in front of the editor, and more blood sprayed on the glass wall behind him.

Fall gurgled, was dead, and went down.

'You shitheel,' Adrianopole shouted, aiming again at the top of the corpse's head.

But King knocked her hand up, and the fourth round punched a fist-sized hole in the ceiling.

Adrianopole stumbled, almost fell, catching herself with a hand that landed in the pooling blood on the desk.

'Oh,' she said, lifting her hand. 'Oh,' again. She looked at Jasmine.

'Perhaps,' she said, very calmly, 'you'd do me the favor of calling the police.'

'After you give me that gun,' Jasmine said, afraid to draw her own for fear it would set Adrianopole off again.

'Oh. Certainly.' She passed the blaster across. 'Be careful. It has quite a hair trigger.'

'And I continue to quote from thisyere black-ribbed tabloid,' Goodnight said. '"A woman in my position, all alone, without a man able to stand beside her, must be able to fight for her rights, to strike out against monstrous tyranny and injustice." She really said that?'

'She really said that,' Jasmine said. 'I was standing there. She also said that, quote, "in olden times there was the unwritten law, which was used monstrously against women. But I now cite another unwritten law, that gives a woman a chance to defend herself against vile calumny," end quote.'

'I do not believe anyone has ever said "calumny" who wasn't a univee lecturer,' Grok said.

'They do,' Riss said, 'if they've got a speech memorized.'

'Just so,' Jasmine said. 'I wonder who wrote it for her?'

'Good question. But a better one is, What about those damned letters?' Goodnight said.

'They're not in Fall's office,' King said. 'While they were cleaning up the gore, I made a search, as best I could. Fall's little floor safe was shut, but not locked, and they weren't in there.'

'How'd you have time to make sure?' Riss said.

'I just stole everything in the safe,' Jasmine said. 'And went through it outside.'

'While there was blood all over hell's half acre?' Riss said. 'I'm impressed.'

'So am I,' Goodnight said. 'I think our little Jasmine is starting to grow up.'

'We'll have to keep looking for those letters, then,' Riss said. 'We don't need the original. A copy'd do just ducky.

'I just hope Freddie is doing better than we are right now.'

TWENTY-FIVE

Friedrich von Baldur didn't waste his breath snarling about being sold out by the double or triple agent beside him.

He turned, crouching, and drove a knuckle-punch up into the side of the man's neck, who was dead in mid-step.

One of the two cops shouted something. Von Baldur paid no mind, but was running, zigging, around the sculpture, toward another one about twenty meters distant.

He was counting, hoping, on two things.

The first was that these cops would be under orders to take him alive, if possible. A dead spy, at least uninterrogated, is about as worthless as they come.

He reached the second sculpture, jumped up, and yanked the tiny gun out of its hiding place.

Von Baldur came down, and snapped a round into the pistol's chamber, took a two-handed stance, braced against the sculpture.

He fired, hit the first cop in the chest, switched his aim to the second, and fired again. The man grabbed his stomach, went down.

Cops who'd been streaming out of the landed lifters went flat, shouting at each other.

Von Baldur's second hope, now confirmed, was that these cops weren't ordinary street bulls, but members of whatever Torguth called its Counter Intelligence Force.

Espionage is normally a fairly bloodless sport, except at the end and the lethal chamber.

These agents weren't used to being shot at, and seeing their two fellows weltering in their blood froze them for a bit.

Time enough for von Baldur to run, hard, out of the park, past a gaping oldster on his evening walk, and down a side street.

Walking the neighborhood before contact had paid dividends. Friedrich had two open avenues of escape — one into a wealthy district, the other into a somewhat seedy workers' district. He picked the second.

Rich people see a man running, and they call the police. Workers, more realistically, get the hell out of the way and pretend they saw nothing.

Von Baldur took the first turning, went up an alley, down another street, then a broader avenue that led, more or less, back toward his hotel. He forced himself to stop running, pocket the gun, and go whistling on his way, just another man on his evening constitutional.

But the street was fairly empty, and those on it were hurrying off.

They'd scented police, and were heading for shelter.

Von Baldur peered around a brick wall. The neighborhood had improved — he was less than ten blocks from his hotel in a straight dash. He'd cut across this street, down an alley, and zig his way to home and . . .

And three cargo lifters landed in the center of the street. Cops in riot gear debouched, formed up in line, and swept toward him.

Von Baldur took to his heels, cursing under his breath. The whole damned Tristan police force was out now, with nothing better to do than look for Friedrich.

Obviously, he thought morosely, L'Pellerin and his DIB hadn't been very successful at inserting agents here on Torguth, or these flatties wouldn't be spending so much time after him, clearly excited at the thought of actually finding a *real* Damperian spy.

At least it was dusk, getting dark.

Von Baldur rounded a corner, then went back the way he'd come. Yet another line of cops was sweeping toward him.

He went down an alley, through somebody's back yard, into another street that, thankfully, didn't have its complement of police.

Yet.

By then it was full dark, and von Baldur was trapped. He crouched behind a reeking garbage can, and looked down two blocks, at a police line. Behind him, nearing the mouth of the street he'd just left, was another swarm of the bastards.

It looked as if he was well and truly cornered.

There were too many for him to be able to shoot his way through. Besides, he'd rather take his chances on arrest and trial rather than being gunned down as a cop killer, although he was already at risk for that.

There had to be a way out. He found it, although it was about as degenerate an escape as could be imagined.

Von Baldur took out his pistol, buried it deep in the garbage can along with the wig, then crept across the street toward an open, lit window. He slipped into the shabby yard, and to that window.

Inside, a young boy, about eight, was getting undressed and into his pajamas. Von Baldur pressed himself close against the window, steaming it up with his breath.

Behind him, he could hear the soft boot heels of the oncoming police and muttered orders. Perhaps, just perhaps, they'd move right on past him, and he'd be able to –

'Hey!' the shout came. 'Look at that?'

'What . . . I got him . . . that old bastard!'

Running footsteps. Von Baldur turned, pretending surprise.

'Hello, officers, I was just –'

'Friggin' pervert,' one of the two cops rushing him growled, and a gasgun hissed.

Von Baldur held his breath, but still caught enough of it to drop him, swimmy-headed, into near unconsciousness.

'Whacher got?' the desk sergeant said.

'Goddamned peepin' tom,' one of the two cops dragging the limp von Baldur into the station house said.

He was coming groggily back to consciousness.

'We were out on that sweep, looking for that spy, and spotted this creep eyeballin' a little kid getting naked,' the other cop said.

'Bastard,' the desk sergeant spat. 'What'd he have on him?'

'Not much,' the first cop said. 'Just a few credits.'

The big wad of money von Baldur had when the cops jumped him had somehow vanished. Von Baldur felt anger, then tucked the emotion away with the other things he could brood on when he was sleepless. Besides, it wasn't really von Baldur's money, but Reynard's.

'Any ID?'

'Lemme see here.'

Von Baldur felt his pockets being rummaged through.

'Yeh. A passport. He's some kinda offworlder. From . . . Hastings.'

'Never heard of the place,' the desk sergeant said.

'We're charging him with violations of PC 2418, Attempting to corrupt a minor; PC 2287, Child pornography; PC 1243, Resisting arrest; PC 090, Attempting to mislead an officer performing his duty,' the second cop said.

'That's pretty good,' the desk sergeant said. 'I'll think up some others. You two want to pitch him in a holding cell, then get back out with the rest of the shift.

'There'll be big, big points for anybody nailing that spy. A lot bigger'n for this pervert.'

'We're on our way,' the first cop said.

There were four others in the holding cell, which was bare except for a stainless steel toilet, a washbasin, and a dozen mattresses and folded blankets on the floor. Three of the four were conscious.

'Got a baby-raper here for you to play with,' the first cop said, and closed and locked the cell. 'Nice off-worlder.'

'Sleep tight,' the second cop mocked. 'And keep one hand over your butt, although I don't think that'll help any.'

The first cop laughed. 'Hell, maybe you'll meet your new boyfriend here.'

Their footsteps went down the hall, and the door clanged shut. Von Baldur went to one of the unoccupied mattresses and sat down.

The jail smelled about like most of the ones he'd been in over the years.

One of the three conscious prisoners was a truck. The second was medium-sized, but had enough scars to prove he didn't mind a good brawl. The third was wizened, small. Von Baldur immediately knew him to be the instigator.

'A kiddie-shafter,' the little one said. 'Nobody likes those.'

Von Baldur didn't answer.

'Comin' in from some offworld . . . maybe some armpit like Dampier, where they 'lows things like that,' the truck growled. 'Oughta be taught how Torguth treats people like you.'

The medium-sized goon nodded excitedly.

Von Baldur sighed, got to his feet.

'Maybe you wanna take down those pants, nice fancy like they are,' the little prisoner said. 'Don't want to get bloodstains on them.' He giggled.

Von Baldur smiled, and stepped toward the biggest goon. Without buildup, he kicked him hard in the kneecap.

The man yowled, grabbed his leg, started hopping around.

The medium-sized man found a rather wobbly martial arts stance, instepped toward von Baldur.

Von Baldur waited until one foot was in the air, sidestepped, came in on the man's off side, and gave him a gentle push against his axis of movement. The man stumbled, fell against the small man.

Von Baldur came in fast, hit the medium-sized man very hard with the back of his fist in the face, spread his nose from his eyebrows to chin.

Friedrich didn't stop moving, but spin-kicked the big man in the side, heard ribs crack. He hit him hard twice in the gut, and the man went down.

'Now, shortie,' von Baldur said. 'Are we going to continue this nonsense, or am I going to be allowed a night's sleep?'

The little man, shaking his head rapidly, was backing away, holding his hands up.

'Then go sit down and shut up,' von Baldur ordered.

The lawyer eyed von Baldur with distaste. 'I have no idea how your crime is handled on your home planet, Lord William. But it is dealt with most severely here.'

'Is it not alleged crime?' von Baldur asked.

The lawyer shrugged. 'The evidence the police will present is most conclusive. However, I shall do what I can do.

'You should be aware that the maximum penalty for your offense is five years penal servitude, mandatory, plus anti-testosterone injections to ensure you'll no longer be a threat to society.'

Von Baldur covered his wince. Maybe his brilliant plan wasn't as brilliant as he thought.

'But there is a possibility,' the lawyer mused. 'Hmm. Yes.'

The judge glowered at von Baldur.

'Were you not a citizen of a foreign world, I would

be delighted to pronounce sentence on you after you were found guilty.

'But Torguth does not have the time or energy to deal with foreign trash.

'You are hereby ordered deported, and turned over to an appropriate Alliance official when one arrives in this system. You will be held on one of our orbital stations until then, or, if no official presents himself within a reasonable time, to be put on the first transport headed in the direction of your home world, under custody.'

Von Baldur looked at the ruins of his suitcases and new wardrobe that'd been delivered to him in the spaceport holding facility. Someone who clearly didn't like pedophiles had gone through his clothes and what wasn't ripped had been despoiled.

However, he wasn't that disappointed. The lifter taking him to the airport had wire mesh over its windows. Loose wire mesh. Von Baldur now had bits of heavy wire hidden about him that would make an ideal lockpick to open the manacles and leg irons he was held in.

And no one had torn the padded ends off his new suitcases. Von Baldur had replaced the padding with credits. Also, the suitcase bottom that had held the four punch-out pistols hadn't been taken away. There was still one gun to be punched out, and there was still ammunition in the case handles, although he didn't think he'd need it.

There were three other criminals being deported with him, who appeared resigned to their fate. They would provide an excellent smoke screen for von Baldur, and he tried to appear as defeated as they were.

Once they reached the orbital station, and someone started going crazy looking for the nonexistent world of Hastings, von Baldur could busy himself getting free, out of custody, and headed out of the Torguth System.

It was not the first, nor the fifth, time he'd used a space station to transship himself somewhere other than where he was supposed to be going.

TWENTY-SIX

M'chel Riss waited impatiently at the spaceport. Von Baldur hadn't sounded as cocky as usual when he'd commed Star Risk. She wondered if things had gone wrong in the Torguth Worlds.

She also wondered why von Baldur was coming in on a tour ship from some unknown world that was way the hell away from Torguth. But she'd made her way to Montrois's primary port, and was leaning against a column, watching the cruise ship unload.

Riss marveled at the way people dressed when they were on vacation, as if sense and propriety weren't required, and a tourist could dress – or undress – as he or she wanted.

M'chel shuddered, turning away from a woman who must have weighed close to 200 kilos, wearing a diaphanous scarf across her bobbling breasts that sagged to mid-chest, with body hair bleached and then stained in three colors as she waddled past, screeching for her two evident sons, almost as heavy, to follow her.

Just behind her was another poor specimen. A hunch-shouldered man, whose job must be selling the least commercial of items, shambled forward. He oozed defeat, from his crumpled, loud, hand-woven hat to his brightly colored sandals. In addition, the poor bastard had a purplish birthmark splattered across one side of his face that he'd never had removed.

Riss had a moment to thank a god or two that at least she hadn't been born like those two, let alone the poor damned children, when the salesman stopped beside her.

'Let us get out of this place at once,' von Baldur said.

'Good god,' Riss managed.

'No,' von Baldur said. 'No, he is not. But we can discuss theology while we are on our way back to headquarters. Or,' he corrected himself, 'after we stop at a decent clothing store, and then a restaurant so I can wash the taste of that abysmal slop they called gourmet dining among the stars out of my mouth.

'It has not been a wonderful month for me. Not wonderful at all.'

TWENTY-SEVEN

Reynard listened closely as Star Risk gave him what information they'd developed, without mentioning von Baldur's trip to Tristan.

'The most important thing we have learned,' von Baldur finished, 'is that there is an agent within IIa – a mole – who is still operational. And L'Pellerin and the DIB, in spite of his boasts, haven't been able to uncover him or her or maybe they.'

'I've always been skeptical of that man,' Reynard said. 'He postures too much about knowing everything about everyone. When I return to the government, I shall certainly be considering his replacement.'

'We have other things to worry about first,' Riss said. 'Such as getting Sufyerd out of the lethal chamber.'

'A question,' Goodnight said. 'Sufyerd's been tried and convicted. What does it take to appeal a court-martial, or, if he's been turned down on appeal, to reopen the case around these parts?'

'Obviously, it takes being able to produce the real culprit or overwhelming evidence of the convicted person's innocence,' Reynard said. 'Or else proof of malfeasance by the court.'

'It seems to me,' Grok said, 'that we maybe ought to be taking this in small steps. For instance, can we get enough evidence . . . of any sort . . . to confuse the issue, and get Sufyerd transferred off that satellite on the thinnest of pretexts?'

'What good would that do?' Reynard asked. 'He'll still be under sentence of death.'

'Right,' Goodnight said. 'But the farther he is from the gas chamber, the longer it'll take for the bastards to kill him.'

'Oh,' Reynard said. 'But of course. Forgive my thickness.'

'If we could get our hands on those letters between Hyla Adrianopole and Ladier,' Jasmine King said, 'that might give us some evidence.'

'Half of Montrois wants to read those letters, the other half seems to want to burn them,' Reynard said. 'Do you have anything that might help us find them?'

'The *Pacifist* is still running teasers, as I believe they're called, that the letters will run,' Grok said, 'in spite of the murder of Fall, the editor. I would guess they would begin running when the trial starts.'

'Which is in two weeks,' King said.

'I'll work on that end,' von Baldur said, deliberately vague.

'In the meantime,' Riss said, 'we want to find and talk to those other three members of Sufyerd's cell in IIa, and Sufyerd's boss. Caranis has told us to piddle up a rope, so we'll get no cooperation from him. Can you get us any leads on the four?'

'Probably,' Reynard said. 'Almost certainly.'

He sighed, rose. 'We seem to be making small, if definite, progress, in spite of the money I've spent,' he said a bit mournfully. 'But I see no other course but to hammer on.'

'One other thing,' Goodnight asked. 'Maybe you could get a location on Cerberus Systems's headquarters and suboffices, if any, for us?'

'What will you do –' Reynard stopped abruptly. 'No. I do not want to know what you want with them. It makes deniability much easier. Yes, I can get that data for you.'

When he left, Riss nodded to von Baldur. 'Good going, Friedrich.'

'Thank you,' von Baldur said. 'I figured you might catch it.'

'Catch what?' Goodnight asked.

'That,' M'chel explained, 'the agent that Freddie killed . . . or anyway, maimed a lot . . . back on Tristan would've been operating under instructions from Torguth's Intelligence or Counter Intelligence.'

'Of course,' Goodnight said.

'Which meant he reported von Baldur's contact with him, without knowing who Freddie represents, and his control decided to pick up Freddie. And this control also would've notified the real mole that someone is looking for him, and Sufyerd didn't work as much of a judas goat.

'Since it's evidently common knowledge as to what we're doing here, A leads quite naturally to B.'

'Which means,' Goodnight said, getting it, 'we're targets for any Torguth headbangers around here. Not to mention the local talent.'

'Just so,' Riss said. 'But with any luck somebody'll take a shot at us, they'll miss, and we'll have another lead.'

'Which is why I asked about Cerberus,' Goodnight said. 'I think we should go out and rattle their cage.'

'Any particular reason,' Riss asked, 'other than we don't like the assholes and for pure meanness?'

'That'll at least make them, and everyone else around, realize that we are not good to have as enemies,' Goodnight said. 'Do we need anything better?'

King was grinning broadly, and Grok was nodding. There was no need for a vote.

'Plus I'll be looking for Sufyerd's old bunkies.' Goodnight sighed. 'Going door to door, ringing a bell, waving a three-D, asking "Have you seen this man-slash-woman?"

'This job sure is different than just running around with guns and blasting people hither and thither,' Goodnight said.

'Cheer up,' M'chel said, patting his cheek. 'With any luck, it'll get as bloody as you like things to be.'

TWENTY-EIGHT

The sniper opened up at dusk, just when the guards were being changed. One of them went down with a ricocheted bolt in the upper thigh, bloody and painful. The sniper's second and third shots went wild.

Another guard kicked the general alarm switch, and everyone within reach of a gun came out, ready for battle.

The cargo lifter the shooter had been hiding in was already in the air, and only Riss and Goodnight got rounds off in time enough to make interesting but harmless holes in the lifter's rear loading gates.

Then it was gone.

They brought the wounded guard inside. He was conscious and, being a new hire and wanting to make sure everybody knew he was a badass, made cheerful jokes about his wound bonus kicking in, and that he couldn't wait to come back.

Riss and King, both medic-trained, stopped the bleeding, hit the man with pain ampoules, and got him off to a hospital, his shift commander riding shotgun.

'Well?' von Baldur asked.

'Not that good,' Riss said quietly. 'He'll get more

than that wound bonus . . . he'll be awhile healing, and they'll have to transplant a fair amount of tissue into the hole, so we'll pay him off and ship him back to wherever was home.

'I don't think he'll lose the leg, but it'll be close. He'll most likely walk with a limp from here on out.

'*Goddamnit*,' she said fiercely, 'I wish it was like the romances, and people who get shot would have nothing but nice, picturesque little drools of gore, and keep right on keeping on with gritted teeth and patriotic slogans.'

'That's one for them,' Goodnight said. 'I think we should be considering a bit of revenge.'

'I think the first order of business,' Grok said, 'will be to figure out *which* them *is* the them.'

TWENTY-NINE

'I have a confession to make, Jasmine,' Grok growled, somewhat tenderly covering her hands with an enormous paw.

King looked a bit alarmed, knowing little about the alien's romantic habits. She sipped from her glass of wine, and managed a smile.

The proprietor of L'Montagnard raised both her eyebrows at what she thought was a mildly passionate moment, but shrugged with true Montrois sophistication and went back into the kitchen.

'I am feeling a new emotion,' Grok continued. 'I think it might have a human parallel, called homesickness.'

Jasmine relaxed and patted Grok's paw.

'This system . . . these worlds,' the alien went on, 'with every hand turned against everyone else, reminds me of my own cluster, and the way each of us competes with everyone else – at least until bribed or convinced a project will benefit them as well. Truly these are scoundrel worlds.'

'As von Baldur said,' King agreed. 'Perfect for our sort.'

'They are,' Grok said. 'And contemplating that, I think one of our priorities should be either ending enmity, in any way we choose, which is unlikely, or forcing our enemies to combine, which will make them more visible and easier to destroy.

'I wonder, for instance, who that sniper yesterday was working for, or if she or he was just someone who dislikes foreigners.'

'Let's consider our list of baddies, then,' King said. 'We have . . . personal choices first . . . Cerberus Systems. Then the Masked Ones. Then the Universalists . . . at least those who're determined to murder Sufyerd. Then there's the mole in Strategic Intelligence. Plus Caranis. And I doubt if L'Pellerin and his Dampier Information Bureau think well of us. Anyone else?'

'Probably the police would be just as happy if we vanished,' Grok said. 'And Torguth, naturally, but they haven't become an active factor. Yet.

'This kind of situation – gears within wheels, or however the expression goes – makes me very glad I chose to invest in Star Risk.'

'Personally,' King said, 'I'll be happier when at least a few of our assorted foes have been taken out.'

'Precisely what we should be planning,' Grok said. 'A worthy topic to discuss over, say, a raclette. We might have some good ideas we can bring up to the others.'

THIRTY

For once, the team was assembled for a common dinner when M'chel Riss stomped in.

'You look disturbed. Not to mention pissed and discombobulated,' Goodnight said, adding, in a breath, 'Haveadrink.'

'I will,' Riss said. 'Maybe several.'

She went to the sideboard, eyed the selections, poured a decent snifter of an old brandy, shot it back, whuffed, then chased it with some ice water and chased the ice water with another brandy.

'So what happened?' von Baldur said. 'Wasn't this Faadi cooperative? Or didn't you find him?'

They'd gotten addresses of Sufyerd's cell from Reynard, and were beginning to track them down.

'I found him,' Riss said grimly. 'And he wasn't cooperative. Mainly because he was dead.' She drank, watched the reactions.

'Clearly,' Jasmine said, 'not of old age. Or you wouldn't be so tight-faced.'

'You read right,' Riss said. 'It seems that about a week after Sufyerd's court-martial – which Faadi also didn't testify at, like the others – he was run down while crossing the street on a midnight stroll. And the vehicle that nailed him was never found.'

'Interesting,' von Baldur murmured.

'I looked up the autopsy,' Riss said. 'He was pretty thoroughly mangled. Almost like somebody pitched him out of a lifter, instead of running him down.'

'I do not like that a lot,' von Baldur said.

'Nor I,' Grok said. 'We'd best accelerate in searching for the others, to mention the obvious.'

'I think,' Jasmine said, 'we also should be pondering who might have interest in causing such a, quote, "accident," end quote.'

'And what's that going to get us?' Goodnight asked. 'I can give you the answer right now. Almost anybody.'

THIRTY-ONE

It wasn't a very good gambling hell, Chas Goodnight decided.

The old-fashioned roulette wheel next to him had hidden electromagnets, powerful enough to send the white ball skidding across the wheel without rolling. They were worked by the croupier, who kept one hand in his pocket. Either that, or he had an amazing case of crab lice.

One of the card games – he wasn't familiar with the game they were playing – clearly had an eye in the sky, somehow sending signals to the housemen on when to bet, and when to fold out.

The six-dice table had the best croupier in the joint, able to switch a straight die for a shaved one while flirting with a mark on the table, generally without Goodnight being able to spot him.

Spotting the various cheats was about all that was keeping Chas awake. He would've turned a card or two himself, but he only bet in honest casinos . . . or at least ones where the rigging wasn't this obvious – or where he thought he could outcheat the cheaters.

Division Leader Caranis, three tables over, hadn't

spotted anything at all. He was plunging madly at Rhadian twist, a game with impossible odds, made worse because any combination of other players could change the scoring procedure with 'wild cards' – actually electronic switching.

Plus the houseman had foot controls controlling the spinners under the carpet.

Twice Goodnight had seen Caranis bust out, go to the cage, and come back with more credits.

'That man sure likes life to be exciting,' he said, pretending admiration to the bartender.

She smiled mechanically. 'Mister Caranis is one of our favorite guests,' she allowed.

Chas knew what that meant in any gambling joint – he was a consistent loser, without a clue as to how any game should be played.

'He was born rich?' Chas hazarded.

'Guess so,' the bartender said. 'He's government, somebody said, and I never heard of any paper shuffler getting paid well enough to flash the lights the way he's doing.'

'Ah,' Goodnight said, finished his drink, tossed a coin on the bar, and started out, having seen enough.

Watching Caranis had been very interesting, especially since Goodnight had done a little basic research, and acquired a copy of Caranis's canned bio, in which he boasted of having come from a poor farming family on one of Dampier's agricultural worlds, a world famous for being eternally poverty-struck.

Division Leader Caranis would definitely need some more investigation.

THIRTY-TWO

'There's nothing to be afraid of, Miss Guames,' Jasmine King soothed through the crack in the door.

The middle-aged woman looked at her timidly.

'No,' she said. 'I always spent my life, my whole career in IIa, being careful of what I said, what I did. And now I'm retired, but I don't see anything wrong with keeping silent.'

'Except if everyone keeps silent, Maen Sufyerd will die.'

'I'm sorry for him,' Ayalem Guames said. 'But the court-martial decided he was guilty, and who am I to stand against them?'

'Someone who believes in the truth,' King said.

Guames glowered at her, fluffed her apron.

'You one of those Jilanis?'

'No,' Jasmine said. 'My firm's been retained to help prove Legate Sufyerd innocent. We're not religious.'

'Hard telling,' the woman said. 'Huh. All those years I worked in IIa, and I thought I could tell what people are, what they think. Look how wrong I was. About Sufyerd, and . . . and other things.'

'What other things?' Jasmine asked.

'Things like . . . no. I swore I'd not talk about anything, and I haven't told any of the people who've come around anything.'

'Why not?'

'You know about Balkis Faadi?'

'I know that he was killed in an accident.'

'Some accident,' Guames sniffed.

'Do you know anything about it?'

'No,' Guames said. 'But I don't need to know anything to figure out that accidents can happen to some of the best people. Especially if they're not really accidents.'

'These people who've come around that you talked about,' Jasmine said. 'Do you have any idea who they might be?'

'I don't. Didn't ask, didn't even speculate. I've got a daughter who's going to have a baby in three months, and I'd like to be around to see what my grandchild looks like.'

'So it doesn't matter to you if Sufyerd, an innocent man, dies. And whoever the real Torguth agent is will be able to keep on with his treason?'

'That's nothing to me,' Guames said. 'All I was, was a statistician. I don't know about any of that anymore, and I don't care.'

'But —'

The door closed very firmly.

Jasmine thought of knocking again, but didn't have anything that she could use to pry whatever — if anything — Ayalem Guames knew.

She went back down the steps to the street, feeling Guames's eyes on her back until she got in her lifter and took off.

*

'A nice day for fishing,' von Baldur observed to the nattily dressed, middle-aged man beside him on the float.

'It's always a nice day for fishing,' Cabet Balalta said. 'It's just that sometimes the fish don't know it.' He laughed enormously at his own joke, then eyed von Baldur. 'Where's your gear, mister?'

'I am not much at fishing,' von Baldur said. 'At least not for fish.'

'I had you pegged as a cop, right off,' Balalta said.

'Not quite a policeman,' von Baldur said.

'You're another one of those who're involved with poor goddamned Sufyerd,' Balalta said.

'I am,' Friedrich said. 'And you are a good guesser.'

'Got to be good at something,' Balalta said. 'Lord knows I wasn't worth sour palilla leaves at spotting a spy.'

'You think Sufyerd is guilty?'

'Now, what I think doesn't matter, does it, since the thing's over and settled, right?'

'There are those who are trying to reopen the case,' von Baldur said. 'I am working for them.'

'Maybe you are,' Balalta said. 'Or maybe not. I didn't spend as many years doing what I was doing, even though it was just a desk job, without learning that people go and lie to you.'

Von Baldur put on his most charming smile. 'They certainly do that.'

'Well, I'm one of those who leave things alone. I'm not saying I think somebody went and murdered Faadi because he was going to talk. Talk to who? The whole matter's settled.'

'It does not have to be.'

'No,' Balalta said. He considered von Baldur carefully.

'I'll tell you the truth, mister. No, I don't need your name or anything. I don't really know anything. All I've got is an opinion, that they're going to hang poor Sufyerd first because he's a Jilani, and they make people nervous, going on about the truth, which they seem to think they've got exclusive rights to.

'The second reason he's for the high jump is because Sufyerd, to be honest, is a fairly unlovable man. I know he's faithful to his wife, and thinks the world of his kids, and always was ready to stand in if you needed a day off in an emergency. But he was . . . is . . . flat cold. I think he thinks that he's got some kind of handle on the truth . . . and that didn't come from his religion . . . but he's what they call self-righteous.'

This time von Baldur's smile was very real. 'He is that, I agree.'

Balalta laughed. 'I guess people like him are always the sorts who end up being made martyrs. Maybe that's what they wanted in the first place.'

'I can tell you that Sufyerd doesn't want to die,' von Baldur said.

There was a long silence.

'Look, mister,' Balalta said. 'When they came around and told us we were going to retire, with full benefits, I didn't object, figuring what people bigger than me wanted was what I should do.

'That's one reason I never had any trouble in IIa, even though it was a sensitive job, and sometimes our analyses made some of the high-rankers angry.'

'You know they retired you to keep you from testifying at the court-martial.'

'I'm not a moron,' Balalta said.

'If the case is reopened, you . . . and the rest of

Sufyerd's team . . . will be called to testify about that.'

Balalta made a face. 'Assuming that whoever asks that question is prepared to offer all of us protection I'll have to tell the truth – but no more. And anybody who asks questions will have to know the right questions to ask. Like I said, I really don't know anything. I just did my job.'

'You said something earlier, about the people involved with Sufyerd,' von Baldur said. 'People who seem to still be interested after the case has been settled. Do you have any idea who they might be, who they might be working for?'

'I honest to Izaac don't. Because I didn't ask.' Balalta took a deep breath. 'Tell you what. You go find Hopea Ardwell. If you can. The rest of us just got retirement benefits one pay grade above what we were entitled to. She got more. A lot more.'

'We haven't had much luck in finding her,' von Baldur admitted. 'Do you have an address?'

'I do not. I wouldn't want it, either. Ardwell is one of those people who likes to move in fast circles, if you know what I mean.' He shrugged. 'She's young, and sharp enough, to be able to get away with it.

'That's the best I can give you, mister. Find Hopea, get her talking if you can . . . and maybe that'll give you something. Or maybe it won't.'

THIRTY-THREE

The mob came in just at midday two days later, and the watch commander set off the alarms.

'Natch,' Goodnight said, staring out a window in the mansion's foyer, 'there's never ever been a good riot at dawn. Hard to get up that early, and have the stomach for the proper stimulants.'

'You disrespect the will of the majority,' Grok said.

'You're making a joke.'

'I am *attempting* a joke,' Grok corrected.

The off-watch guards were tumbling into the dining room.

Von Baldur looked at the mob, which had filled the street outside from curb to curb.

'Interesting signs they are carrying,' he said.

Some of them read: OFFWORLDERS OUT OF POLITICS; MERCENARIES GO HOME; KILL TRAITORS; KILL SUFYERD; DOWN WITH THE INDEPENDENTS; JUSTICE FOR BELFORT.

'I would guess,' he said calmly, 'that what we have here has been organized by the Universalists. I would not think the Masked Ones are behind it, since all we are getting bombarded with is rocks and bottles. The Masked Ones would use guns.'

He turned to the guards' watch commander. 'Go out with hoses, and crying gas. Clubs, if any of them get over the fence. Put filters in against the gas. Pistols only, and try not to use them unless things become ugly. Go ahead when you feel it is right and push them back out of the street. Our neighbors might be complaining.'

The man half-saluted, led the guards out.

'There,' von Baldur said. 'That should hold them for the moment, until . . . and what is this?'

He ducked involuntarily as three lifters swooped low over the gate, and gas grenades bounced into the yard.

'Filters on,' he announced. 'I am assuming this is riot gas they are dropping, not a lethal compound. This house is not gas proof, I think.'

'But it is,' Jasmine said, went to a panel, opened it, and touched keys.

'That should . . . depending on how many open windows there are . . . put a positive air pressure in the house, so nothing can leak in,' she said.

Riss hadn't been paying attention to the chatter, beyond stuffing a pair of filters in her nostril, but had a pair of high-power, variable-magnification binocs, and was sweeping the back of the crowd.

'Looking for ringleaders?' Goodnight asked.

'Just so,' she said. 'That one . . . I think he's either a police agent or one of L'Pellerin's agents. And that one . . . wup! Jasmine, sneak a peek.'

King took the glasses.

'Son of a . . . that's Nowotny.'

'So it is,' Goodnight said. 'Now, I don't mind Cerberus being behind things . . . way behind . . . but running the demonstration hands-on is a bit much.'

'It is that,' Riss agreed, sounding most nasal. She grabbed her combat harness.

'Come on, Grok. I might need some backup.'

The alien rumbled pleasure, followed her as she ran through the house, back through the kitchen, to the panel that led into the mansion's escape tunnel. He snagged a blast rifle and clipped a couple of concussion grenades to his belt on the way.

The tunnel was cobwebby but dry and clean, and there weren't any rodents rustling about. It opened into a small lifter garage on the street behind the mansion. Riss went out through a side door, Grok ducking after her.

The pair ran down the street and up a side alley to the boulevard the mansion fronted on. Riss held up her hand for a halt, peered around.

She saw gas grenades arcing over the mansion's iron fences, into the crowd, and howls of dismay from the mass. There were a few who'd brought masks or filters, betraying their claim to amateur status, but they thought it better to retreat with the others, pelting away down the boulevard.

'Do you see Nowotny?' Grok asked.

'No, dammit,' Riss said. 'He must've hauled ass when the first bang went off. Or maybe when the lifters dropped gas, if it was his idea.'

'So what are we to do?'

'Go on back and . . . no! We'll take this clown!'

A gas-masked man, wearing gray tunic and pants, was running toward her.

Riss stepped out, gun leveled.

'Don't even breathe,' she snarled.

The man skated to a stop, brought his hands up.

'You can't –' he said dimly through the mask. 'I'm an officer of the –'

'I just did,' Riss said, and yanked him into the alley.

'This is kidnapping!'

'You noticed. Your momma didn't raise fools,' Riss agreed. 'Grok, let's run him back into the garage.'

The alien growled, lifted the man up with one paw. Riss patted him down, took a pistol, a gas sprayer and a set of brass knuckles from his pockets, a wallet ID pack from his breast pocket.

Grok ran back, in great two-meter-long bounds, to the rear street and then into the garage, moving so quickly that anyone who saw the snatch wouldn't have time to react or, hopefully, to believe their eyes.

Riss was just behind him. She yanked the man's mask off, pulled her filters out of her nose. 'Don't let him even wiggle,' she told Grok.

'He will not move,' Grok said, held out an enormous paw, and let his claws slide out, showed them to the cop, then retracted them.

The man became a stalagmite.

'Let's see what we have here,' Riss mused, opening the wallet ID. 'Indeedy, he is a limb of the law. So why weren't you out there bringing peace to the premises?'

'I've got my orders.'

'Which is spreading disruption,' Riss said.

The man clamped his lips shut.

'What I want from you,' Riss said, 'is where that man wearing brown is headquartered. The one you were standing next to, and talking to. I don't know what name he's using, but he's very thin, big hands, has bad scars on one side of his face, and limps. Talks with a whisper.'

'I don't –'

Riss slapped him hard, backhand-forehand, twice, on the ears.

'Where can I find him?'

'I can't tell you that.'

'Oh yes, you can,' Riss said. 'And a great deal more. What your boss does to you is a maybe. I'm for sure.'

The man shook his head.

'This,' Riss said sadly, 'is going to get messy, then.'

Half an hour later, they had the location of one of Cerberus Systems's safe houses, and full details, as far as the low-level policeman knew, of Cerberus's cooperation with the Universalists.

The police agent was sprawled on the floor of the garage.

'Is there anything else we might want?' Grok asked.

'I can't think of anything, just now,' Riss said. 'Besides, is he still breathing?'

Grok bent over, shoved a thumb against the man's carotid artery. 'Barely breathing . . . but his pulse is good.'

'We don't need *that*,' Riss said. 'He might decide to take affront at what we did.'

'I agree,' the alien said, and smashed the side of his heel down against the policeman's neck. The man contorted, lay very still.

'After it's dark,' Riss said, 'we'll come back and dump the delicti in the river.

'Now, let's go tell Freddie what we've got planned for how we're going to express our displeasure with Mr. Nowotny around some of those Cerberus offices Reynard got for us.'

THIRTY-FOUR

'I don't know about this Hopea Ardwell traveling in fast circles, whatever they may be,' Grok said. 'But she certainly moves in invisible ones. I've used all the usual methods, and can't find a trace of her.'

'Which means we probably really want to talk to her, if she's gone to ground that thoroughly,' Goodnight said. 'You got a holo?'

'I do,' Grok said, bringing it up in midair.

Goodnight looked at the image critically. It was of a young woman in formal evening wear, smiling a bit seductively into the pickup. She had long blond, nearly platinum, hair, a heart-shaped face and, assuming the gown wasn't figure-augmenting, a rather voluptuous figure. Goodnight guessed Ardwell would be fairly short, no more than just over a meter and half tall.

'When you find her,' Goodnight said, 'I think I want to be the one to talk to her.'

'You would,' Riss snickered from her terminal. 'Which'll raise the question of who gets more information out of whom.'

'I'm shocked,' Goodnight said. 'I may be seducible, but I'm not prone to pillow talk.'

King had entered the mansion's main room, and studied the image. 'What don't you have, Grok?' she asked.

'Any location at all.'

'What about friends?'

'She doesn't . . . didn't . . . seem to have many. I contacted one of her former roommates . . . a dancer as Ardwell wanted to be once. The woman told me Ardwell tried hard, but just didn't have a feel for it.

'I got the idea she didn't think very much of Hopea, although she didn't give me any specific evidence.'

'Strange,' Goodnight said. 'Going from prancing around into Intelligence.'

'I asked,' Grok said. 'She said it was secure. Almost as secure as finding a rich blind man.'

'Interesting,' Goodnight said. 'Somebody who thinks like that might be eminently corruptible.'

'That, I think, was what Balalta was trying to imply to Freddie,' Riss said. 'Which might mean Torguth figured out the same thing. And it just might be that her roommate doesn't like our Hopea any longer because she had eyes for the roommate's romantic friends.'

'Maybe,' Grok said. 'But I'm still hitting zeroes.'

'What does Sufyerd think of her?' Goodnight asked.

'I think he is a little bit afraid of her,' King said. 'Sort of like a man who has a jealous wife who thinks the worst of any of her husband's workmates who're prettier than she is, and so he runs like the wind any time they're alone together.'

'I don't understand why you humans seem hell-bent to mate with anyone other than the person you contract with,' Grok said. 'Truly a strange race.'

'We are that. And people wonder why I never got

married,' Riss said. 'Chas, here's something to try. Go back to her roommate, and ask if she had any particular preferences in perfume.' She considered the gown. 'And in expensive clothes.'

'What will that give us?' Grok said.

'If we're very, very lucky,' Riss said, 'she favors a nice expensive scent or clothing designer, something a little out of her salary range that she'd talk about. Then, if it's special enough, maybe she's now got friends at some of the stores who sell said perfume or labels.

'Remember, Balalta told Freddie that she managed to get more money than any of the other people in the cell. She might be enjoying spending it. Like I said, if we're lucky,' she finished.

'Perfume and dresses,' Goodnight said. 'And aren't we getting personal?'

'Yeah,' Riss said. 'And something else that's personal . . . has anybody been wondering just why all those flatfeet have been greasing around Elder Bracken and his Jilanis?'

'I have,' King said. 'With no results.'

'Try this,' Riss said. 'Maybe they're trying to find . . . or keep track of . . . Sufyerd's family.'

'To what end?' von Baldur asked.

'Who knows?' Riss said. 'But if I'm right, odds are it isn't for anything pleasant.'

'Clever of you,' Grok said. 'We might wish to prevent any unfortunate eventualities.'

Goodnight nodded thoughtfully. 'It might be a very good idea to keep things personal there, too.'

Von Baldur had been listening to the exchange.

'As the old song said, Chas, 'You ain't seen nothing yet.' While these other projects are more than admirable, I think it has now become time, as both you and M'chel have wanted, to reduce the number of enemies we appear to have, or at least to make them aware that Star Risk has fangs. Sharp fangs.'

THIRTY-FIVE

'The first thing we need to do,' Jasmine King explained, 'if we're going against Cerberus, is hit them hard enough so they'll start whimpering and hopefully go home. Which means not just a first strike, but several strikes, since Cerberus is very proud of its backups, both men and data.

'So we'll start with finding out which of these addresses M'chel got is their home office. That will be our first target. That should be fairly simple, because if we assume Nowotny is in charge of this operation, all we need to do is find him.'

She realized with surprise, and more than a bit of pleasure, that the other four Star Risk operatives were listening closely. It was the first time she'd instituted a plan of violence.

'I am disappointed,' Grok said. 'No one has suggested a way to make use of my turning my coat with Mr. Nowotny. Can't my treason be used somehow?'

Von Baldur thought hard, then shook his head.

'I cannot come up with a way, my friend,' he said. 'Plus, the way the situation has developed, with Nowotny taking a personal interest, no doubt at the instigation of his superiors, he might get suspicious, and decide to take you for a one-way boat ride.'

'He would not be the first to try that,' Grok said, 'nor would it be the first time that I came back by myself on the boat.' But he subsided.

'Find Nowotny,' Goodnight said, 'make a buncha bangs, and then I can go off on my mission of love, as soon as Riss tracks down her perfume.' He snickered.

'Don't laugh,' Riss said. 'It's just liable to work.'

'I'm not laughing,' Goodnight said hastily. 'I'm admiring.'

'You'd better be,' M'chel snarled.

Step One was finding Ceberus's headquarters.

That was simple. They put operatives on all of the security firm's offices, noted which one Nowotny visited the most.

They staked that one out around the clock, taking note of half a dozen Cerberus operatives. These, then, were tailed, but not by the experts.

The Cerberus personnel were far more experienced than the door-rattler guards Star Risk had hired, of course, fully trained at detecting and losing a tail. But it's almost impossible to shake a tail when there's half a dozen of them, each working no more than a block or two, letting another operative take over, dropping off and picking up in another half a dozen blocks.

Similarly, when a Cerberus agent would duck into a department store, intending to leave by another exit, all of the store's exits would be covered by Star Risk people.

It took three days of monitoring traffic, and then Star Risk had several Cerberus central offices located, one at a location not on the ex-premier's list.

Cerberus Systems played its cards very close, not trusting anyone.

One office was in a high-rise, the other two were storefronts, including what King and von Baldur had decided was the main office. The other was three doors away from a police station.

'That one shall be yours,' von Baldur decided.

'No problem,' Goodnight purred. 'Just line up the steaks for afterward.'

Jasmine King crouched in a streetside stairwell, behind Friedrich von Baldur. Both of them wore nondescript gray coveralls with back emblems reading: STREET SURVEY.

Inside the coveralls were pistols and blast grenades. Both of them carried tubes a little less than a meter in length, about twelve centimeters in diameter.

Across the street was the office Star Risk had decided was the center of Cerberus's operations. And sitting outside it was a very expensive lifter, a Sikorski-Bentley.

'I would dearly love to know what Strategic Intelligence Division Leader Caranis is talking to Nowotny about,' von Baldur said in a whisper.

King didn't answer, making sure she had the sequence right for that tube under her arm.

'Ah well, ah well,' von Baldur said. 'Another time. Duck down. Here he comes.'

The door opened, and Nowotny limped out, cheerfully talking to Caranis. The head of IIa got in his lifter and took off. Nowotny went back inside for a few minutes, then left with two employees and an obvious bodyguard.

King and von Baldur saw movement inside.

'The watchman,' von Baldur said. 'I shall try to bounce the beastie so we don't obliterate him. There is no need for bloodshed.'

He gave it another five minutes, then nodded to King.

Uncap the cover . . . slide the two-piece tube to its full length . . . snap open the peep sight on top of the cylinder . . . pull the safety pin out of the rear tube . . . break the seal over the trigger housing and pull it down.

Von Baldur did the same with his tube.

'I shall go first,' he said in a normal voice, making King start a bit. 'That will open the place up some, and give you a chance to do the real damage.'

King grinned, feeling the sweat of excitement on her palms.

Von Baldur made sure Jasmine was out of the back-blast area, aimed carefully, and pressed the trigger bar up with a thumb.

The rocket inside the tube swooshed out across thirty meters and smashed into the office door.

It exploded with a crash, and flame spattered the early evening's dusk.

A moment later, a battered, dust-covered watchman tumbled out the door, and staggered off into the night.

'A lucky man,' von Baldur murmured, turned, bowed to Jasmine.

She aimed into the office, and with a convulsive jerk, fired.

Her rocket spat out of the tube, and into the office where it exploded.

A satisfying gout of flames reached out.

'Shall we continue our stroll?' von Baldur said,

stripping off his gloves and depositing them in a trash can. 'Surveying streets and all.'

The young woman walked down the corridor, past closed offices, to one that had no sign at all on the door. She tried the door, frowned ostentatiously to show her disappointment that the firm inside had dared close before her arrival, and put a bulky envelope down against the door.

Unhurriedly, M'chel Riss walked to the lift, and was gone.

Ten minutes later the envelope exploded. The shaped charge blew the door off its hinges, and a cascade of incendiaries sprayed the interior of another of Cerberus Systems's offices.

Chas Goodnight touched his forehead politely to the pair of policemen coming out of the station, continued past to the closed office that was another Cerberus backup station. He slid a parcel out of his bulky jacket, touched three studs, and held the parcel against the glass door that was reinforced with steel bars.

Fat lot that'll do, he thought, walked on to the corner and turned it just as the bomb blew the office apart.

I do love making big things into little things, he thought. He triggered his bester and went across the street, scaring the hell out of two lifter drivers who didn't know whether to brake or scream at the blur in front of them, then continued down an alley.

By the time the cops came after him, he'd jumped into the lifter Grok was behind the controls of, and was headed for an expensive steak house.

*

'How *dare* you?' Walter Nowotny hissed in a lethal whisper.

'Now, now, Mr. Nowotny,' von Baldur said. 'I truly have no idea what you might be talking about.'

'You know goddamned well!'

'I certainly do not,' von Baldur said.

'We've hardly declared war on you!'

'But I thought I saw you lurking behind some goon-ish-looking demonstrators a few days ago,' von Baldur said. 'I am terribly sorry if it was a case of mistaken identity.'

'You bastard!'

'Try to control yourself, my friend,' von Baldur said. 'After all, I remember *you* blowing *me* up not so very long ago on a world named Glace. And did I curse at you?'

Nowotny glowered out of the screen, then jerked as he heard, just off pickup, a giggle from Jasmine King.

'All right,' he said. 'You want to play like that, we can do the same.'

'Tsk,' von Baldur said. 'I thought more of Cerberus Systems than to suspect they could no better than play copycat, although I swear on my mother's honor I am still at a loss as to why you are distressed.'

Nowotny's face got redder, then the screen blanked.

'You should have kicked him some more,' Jasmine said. 'I've never seen someone have a heart attack.'

'I am afraid, my dear Jasmine, that Walter Nowotny is the sort who gives heart attacks, not suffers from them,' Friedrich von Baldur said sadly.

'Once before,' L'Pellerin said quietly, 'I warned you that you did not wish to become my enemy, von Baldur.'

'I thought we agreed I . . . and Star Risk . . . are not.'

'Circumstances have changed,' the secret policeman said, smiled politely, and broke the com connection.

'I do not like people who do not need to make threats,' von Baldur said to King. 'They worry me.'

THIRTY-SIX

Chas Goodnight sniffed.

It was definitely Passion's Embrace.

Ah, he thought. The true instincts of the hunter.

After Star Risk got lucky on Riss's suggestion, M'chel had bought a bottle of what was supposed to be Hopea Ardwell's favorite perfume, and made sure Goodnight had it 'memorized,' not only waving it under his nose at periodic intervals, but drenching his pillow with the scent.

Ardwell lay motionless on a large beach towel three meters away.

Goodnight decided Passion's Embrace wasn't to his tastes. He preferred scents more subtle.

Behind Goodnight was the very old-fashioned bulk of the resort's main building, which included several restaurants, two nightclubs, and the obligatory casino. Planking it were two very modern wings.

The beach was quite empty.

The tenth call that Grok had made to expensive department stores had paid off. King had paid that store's perfumery a visit, figuring that an alien with an interest in perfume would start rather pointless talk.

Deliberately vague, King had said that one of her

friends, a Hopea Ardwell, had always talked about Passion's Embrace, and now that Jasmine had gotten an unexpected bonus, she'd be interested in buying a little bottle, and maybe the clerk knew her friend Hopea, who she'd fallen out of touch with?

The clerk, more than a bit envious, had said she certainly did. Hopea was one of her best customers, and had bought the entire line of Passion's Embrace. She'd come into an inheritance, she could afford it now, and as a matter of fact had ordered some of the line's new body lotion that week, and had it sent to the resort she was at.

Which was?

The clerk hemmed, and said she didn't remember which one, but it was on the Gulf, and it had, what, something Secret Palazzo for a name.

More com work, and the Gulf Palace of Secrets was found. Goodnight was put in motion, booking into a suite at the Palace the next day.

Hopea was indeed there, as a snapshot and a twenty-credit note shown to a clerk proved. Chas Goodnight, sleek, obviously wealthy, and always formally dressed, watched her for two days.

After the first day, Hopea began watching back.

More money to one of the human staffers got more information. Poor Miss Ardwell. She'd really come here before the Season – Goodnight actually heard the clerk capitalize the word – was really under way, and seemed lonely. A pity, the man said, such a beautiful woman was unescorted.

A pity indeed, Goodnight agreed. And so the next morning, wearing a real Earth-silk half robe over his trunks, Goodnight had ambled out to the beach when he saw Hopea spread her towel.

He waited until she looked up, saw him, and smiled. He smiled back, and walked toward her.

'A beach this crowded,' he said, 'makes it hard to find a spot to spread out on.'

'Crowded?' Hopea said, looking about, puzzled. Then she got it and giggled.

Goodnight spread his towel a sensible distance from her, and settled down.

'And who are you?' Hopea cooed.

'Someone who's spent a lot of time looking for you.'

'Oh, that's ever so romantic.'

'Nope,' Goodnight said. 'Accurate, Miss Ardwell.'

She jerked up to a sitting position. 'Who are you?' she hissed, eyes flickering about.

'The name's Goodnight, but you can call me Chas. I mean no harm. I'm working for a man you used to work with.'

Ardwell's lips went into a thin line. 'I'm *sure* I don't know what you're talking about.'

'Of course not, Hopea,' Goodnight agreed. 'And it's a long ways from Ila, isn't it?'

'You're talking strange, mister. Now go away before I call one of the resort guards.'

'I don't think you'll do that.'

'Why not?'

'First, you don't have anyone booked to buy you dinner tonight, let alone a midday meal on one of the floats out there.'

Ardwell relaxed a bit. 'Are you a cop?'

'I hope not,' Goodnight said. 'I'm just somebody who's interested in hearing people talk. And, if it's interesting enough, willing to pay.'

'Pay?' Ardwell's eyes glittered a little.

'Pay well,' Goodnight said. 'Plus, if you're able to help me, you'll have the warm feeling of saving a man's life.'

Hopea looked at him intently, then shook her head. 'No. Oh no. I took my settlement and told them I'd never talk to anyone about anything, and I don't want to get in trouble with them. Trouble or . . . or worse. Like poor Balkis Faadi got into.'

'Oh well,' Goodnight sighed. 'I can tell my boss that I tried.' He stretched out on his back.

Ardwell looked at him, puzzled, for a while, then she lay back down.

Without turning her head, she asked, 'How much could you pay? It takes more money than I thought it would to live the way I want to.'

'Let's say, oh, ten thousand credits a day for being interviewed.'

Ardwell jerked up. 'Ten thousand is a *lot* of money. Just for talking.'

'It is,' Goodnight agreed.

'Interviewed where? Some prison or something?'

'Not unless you call this place a prison.'

'I don't know,' Hopea said doubtfully.

'Plus, of course, there's meals,' Goodnight said. 'And maybe some credits to go gambling with, and somebody to take you dancing.'

'You're no cop!' Ardwell said firmly. 'Cops don't think like that.'

'I told you that already. And did I mention that we'll pick up your bill here?'

'I've been here almost two months.'

'I know,' Goodnight said.

'What do you want me to talk about?'

'I'd like you to tell me about working in IIa. No details about anything that was classified. I just need to get an idea of what it was like, from the time you came in . . . no, from the time you left your apartment, until you got home at night.'

'Will I have to testify? I mean, like in court.'

'I don't think so,' Goodnight said. 'If someone wants you to be a witness, they'll have to clear it with me, and I'll not let anyone at you.'

Ardwell thought hard, worrying her lower lip between her teeth.

'I always kind of liked Maen,' she said. 'I don't know why, I'm sure. Maybe because I couldn't believe anyone could be that tight-butted.

'I mean, I knew he was a Jilanis, and I've read the tabs about what they do in their services. I even got him to invite me to one of them once, thinking that might be kicksey, and he said his wife would be real happy to go with us.

'That wasn't what I wanted, if you know what I mean.'

'I'm sure I do,' Goodnight said, uncapping a tube of tanning oil. 'Or maybe I don't. Would you like some of this fine ointment?'

Ardwell looked at him kittenishly. 'Would you put it on? I mean, I can't really get my back and the backs of my legs.'

'Delighted,' Goodnight purred, and Ardwell rolled onto her stomach. Chas set to work.

'Isn't it funny,' Ardwell said, 'that I'd sort of like somebody who's a real meterstick, and when somebody else tries to come on, I'd tell him to forget it.'

'Somebody else?'

'Never mind,' Ardwell said. 'Nothing happened.'

'Somebody else,' Goodnight persisted. 'Could his name be Caranis?'

'What made you think of him?'

'Something Sufyerd said about his boss not being exactly the most honorable man,' Goodnight said, adding, tactfully, 'and I got the idea from Maen that Caranis had romantic thoughts about some of his people.'

'Romantic?' Ardwell snorted. 'If you think trying for a knee-wobbler against the back of his damned lifter is romantic – which he figured he was due because he bought me a couple of drinks. What did he think I was? I mean, am?'

'Is he rich?'

'Not a chance,' Ardwell said. 'He'd like you to think he is, with that lifter, and his clothes, and the way he tries to put on.

'But when he slips, he uses slang like any other worker, like I did, until I taught myself better.'

'Interesting,' Goodnight said. 'You'd think that someone living a lie . . . or a pretense, anyway . . . would get looked at by the DIB.'

'*Those* idiots,' Ardwell said. 'They think that because they've got truth machines and a whole flock of people trying to follow you around that they know everything. Show you how stupid they are, they think poor Maen's guilty, and they're going to kill him.'

'You don't think he's guilty?'

'I *know* better.'

Goodnight held back his reaction.

'Might I ask how you know?'

'I just know . . . I have a feeling for people.'

Goodnight's hopes sank. 'So who do you think is the traitor?'

'Nobody in our cell, that's for certain,' Ardwell said firmly.

'Caranis?'

Ardwell hesitated. 'I don't know,' she said, her voice deliberately neutral.

'But you wouldn't mind too much if he was?'

'I'm thirsty,' Hopea said. 'Will you buy me a drink?'

'I'd be delighted.'

Goodnight got up lithely, held out a hand, and pulled Hopea to her feet.

'What's that little tiny bulge at your back, just below your waistline?' she asked. 'A gun?'

It was the small battery powering Goodnight's bester powers, at the base of his spine.

'You've got a good eye,' Chas said.

'Maybe. But I like looking at men's butts,' Ardwell said.

'You shameless creature!' Goodnight said, pretending shock.

Ardwell giggled.

'Now, start by telling me about your day.'

'After I see your credits, Chas.'

'Very well,' Goodnight said. 'Then let's adjourn to the lobby bar, and I'll go up to the suite, and bring down the first payment.'

'Will I have to sign for it?'

'You don't have to do anything . . . other than start talking.'

'This could be the easiest ten thousand I've ever seen,' Ardwell said, and greed underlined her words.

*

Once started, it was impossible for Goodnight to stop Hopea Ardwell from delivering her part of the bargain.

Through the day, through cocktails, through dinner, and through dancing, Goodnight learned everything there was to know about being a junior analyst, barely more than a secretary, with Dampier's Strategic Intelligence.

It was just as dull as he'd always envisioned any intelligence post beyond field duties.

In spite of his excellent memory, Goodnight was grateful that he had a tiny mike in his watch ring, transmitting to a recorder in his suite, and thence on to Star Risk's mansion in Tuletia.

At least Hopea Ardwell didn't talk in bed. Not in coherent sentences, at any rate.

Hopea was delighted not only with being with the best-looking man at the resort, but also with Goodnight's continuing the contract for three days, making her go over and over her routine.

He also asked about the way the cell had been dissolved, learned that it had been at the orders of Caranis, found the supposed reason was to give everyone who was innocent a chance to start over.

'Start over,' she said. 'With the government? Hah! As if nobody would know where you'd worked, and they'd be forever picking at you, wanting to know what it was like to be a spy or to be around a traitor.

'And you'd best not shatter their little ideas by saying you knew Maen Sufyerd was innocent.'

On the third day, she was droning on about the problems her cell always had getting proper supplies when requisitioned, when he stopped her in mid-sentence.

'What?'

They were lying naked on the deck of his suite.

'Go back, love,' Goodnight said. 'About the mail-boy.'

'Oh him. Not worth talking about. He came to us from some government program. If brains was power, he couldn't blow his nose.'

'Who was he?'

'Some little yerk who was always looking at himself in any mirror or anything shiny, like he was as good-looking as . . . as you are. Thought he was just the best-looking little flasher ever ever. But he could never get anything right, and was forever giving me Maen's mail or memos, and forgetting to give poor Balkis Faadi his directives. A useless little tweep if ever there was one.'

'What was his name?'

'Runo Kismayu.'

'When they broke up the cell, what happened to him?'

'I don't know,' Hopea said. 'Nothing, I guess, since he wasn't part of our team, our cell. Knowing how the government works, they probably promoted him to something or other.'

She yawned. 'I think I want to take a nap. But come over here first. My throat's dry, and I need some mouth-wash.'

'Ah, the conquering hero returns,' Riss said. 'Are your lustful impulses satisfied for the moment?'

'As a matter of fact,' Goodnight said, 'they are. Gad, but it's hard being a honey trap.'

'But you volunteered,' Riss said.

'Dumb me. Why do people who love to run at the mouth always have annoying voices?' Goodnight asked.

'She does have that,' King said. 'Thank heaven for automatic voice transcripts. Although I kind of wanted to listen to the dirty parts.'

'I'm going to be celibate forever and ever,' Goodnight said mournfully. 'If she wasn't talking, she wanted to screw.

'I'll take my pain out on the bottle . . . and maybe by becoming a thief again. I've got an idea that needs cogitatin' on.'

THIRTY-SEVEN

Chas Goodnight eased through the door of the dingy shop, smiled at the tiny, bald man behind the dusty counter.

'Help you?' the man asked without returning the smile.

'Looking to pick up some tools,' Goodnight said.

'Like what?'

'A good reader, a jumper, an earpiece, some full-size picks, a lighted glass, a jimmy and brace, and if you happen to have any night eyes, I could use them,' Goodnight said, slipping easily into thieves' cant.

'You a locksmith?' the old man asked, playing it straight.

'You have me spotted,' Goodnight said, going along with the game and wondering if the stories he'd picked up in a couple of seedy bars about this man could be lies.

'Happen to have your license about?'

'Afraid I went and left it in my other pants.'

'Can't sell to you without a license.'

'That's a problem,' Goodnight said. 'My other pants are on Capella Seven.' He dug in his pocket, took out a high-credit bill, creased it, and sat it on the counter.

The old man picked up the bill. 'You realize it's illegal to sell anything resembling burglar tools here on Montrois,' the old man said. 'Illegal anywhere in the Dampier System, in fact.'

'That's hard,' Goodnight said. 'Keeping a man from his chosen trade.' He put another bill next to the first.

The old man moved very fast. A small, deadly, if a bit old-fashioned pistol was in his hand.

'I think you might want to stand very easy,' the old man said. 'Some friends of mine might want to meet you.'

'I do hope they're not policemen,' Goodnight said.

The old man seemed to find this amusing. 'They're not. Oh, they're not,' he chortled.

Goodnight sat down in a rickety chair, keeping his hands in plain view. The old man kept his eyes . . . and gun . . . on Chas while he punched numbers into a com, picked up a whisper mike, and spoke into it briefly.

Goodnight waited. He was pretty sure that if he triggered bester, he could get across the room before the man could pull the trigger.

Pretty sure.

Besides, he was curious to see what his request would produce.

Things weren't working out as smoothly as he'd planned, but he had hopes that the old man might be tied in with some nicely corrupt cops that he could further corrupt to be on his side.

He wondered why he'd been stupid enough to leave his burglar's tools back on Trimalchio. Goodnight had known this would be a city job, and since when could you do anything in a city without some sedate thieving and robbing?

Half an hour later, a rather large bruiser swaggered into the shop. On the other side of the street an equally large sort looked for Goodnight's backup, couldn't find any, came into the shop himself.

Goodnight's hopes sank. He was pretty sure what these two represented, not at all what he wanted.

They shook Goodnight down, found one of the small pistols he had hidden on his person.

'Who're you,' one of them growled, 'to be trying to operate without permission of the Thieves' Guild?'

'Bring on your King of Thieves, who I assume's crouching outside the door, and I'll explain everything,' Goodnight said tiredly.

The thug glowered, but went to the door. 'It's copa, boss.'

A very fat man waddled into the shop.

'M' name's Guayacurus. I run all thievin' in Tuletia,' he announced. 'You must be from offworld, not comin' to me for permission to work yer prowls.'

Goodnight shook his head sadly. 'I'm Chas Goodnight, and yeah, I'm from offworld. But I'm no cherry-boy to listen to your jeffin'.'

'You can't –' one of the goons started, reaching for Goodnight.

But Chas had already triggered into bester. The closest heavy went pinwheeling through the outer window. The old man pulled the trigger of his gun, but Goodnight wasn't occupying that space anymore. Instead, the projectile put a smallish, but fatal, hole in the middle of the second bodyguard's chest.

Goodnight reached across the counter, a gray blur, watching the gun's action slowly cycle. He plucked the pistol from the old man's hand, snapped his wrist, and pushed the old man back into a tray full of sharp tools. The man's mouth was opening into a scream as Goodnight turned away to see the fat 'king's' hand reaching into his gaudy, somewhat unclean, tunic.

Goodnight pulled the man's hand clear – accidentally, more or less, breaking his forearm – took his gun, and came out of bester.

Fatty was gaping, the old man was screaming, and the two thugs lay still. Outside, a couple of people passed, and ostentatiously paid no attention to the body on the sidewalk. It was that kind of district.

'I should have just killed you,' Goodnight said. 'Don't you think I'm cereb enough to know every frigging city on every frigging planet's got at least one, generally ten Kings of Thieves, all hustlin' their asses to convince the marks they're for real?'

The fat man started crying.

'Stop leaking,' Goodnight ordered. 'I was hoping you'd be somebody else, but I'll settle for the name of your best fence, in trade for your sorry fat ass stayin' intactico. I may need to move some swag before I move on.

'And I'll need to know where you plug from, in case you double-deal me, in which case I'll hunt you down like a dog and blip you on to your next life.'

The man muttered names, locations.

Goodnight quickly went through the man's pockets, found a knife, another, very tiny gun, and a large collection of credits, all of which he appropriated.

'Now, I'll just get the tools I came here for, and leave you to clean up the remains. I figure I just paid my entry fee and a year's worth of dues into your Guild.'

THIRTY-EIGHT

'Yes,' Elder Bracken admitted, 'I do know where the Sufyerd family is. They are quite safe with us, however.

'We moved them from their own home after some hooligans threw rocks at their house and threatened the children. It was a place that would have been hard for us to guard them in.'

'I don't mean to insult your capabilities,' Riss said. 'But the people who might wish Maen Sufyerd harm are quite used to gunplay.'

'And we are not,' Bracken agreed. 'Even those of us who served in the military before discovering our way are unwilling to choose violence.

'That, I understand, can slow someone down in the moment of action.'

'It can,' Riss said dryly.

'What do you propose to do with them, assuming Mrs. Sufyerd is willing to accompany you?'

'Take her and the children to a safe place,' Riss said.

'Which brings up another matter,' Bracken said. 'We have both been assuming that you . . . and your people, including this rather frightening gentleman with you . . . don't intend harm to the Sufyerds. Before I will help, I'm afraid I'll have to have some proof as to your good intents.'

Grok huffed. Riss couldn't tell if he was insulted or complimented by Bracken's words. He sat cross-legged on the floor of Bracken's rather spartan living room, trying to maneuver a human-size teacup.

Occasionally one or another of Bracken's children would peer around a corner, goggle-eyeing at the alien.

Riss grinned. 'No offense, but I've never had to prove my innocence before, and I'm not sure how to go about it.'

'I have an idea,' Grok said. 'Would a personal call from ex-Premier Reynard be satisfactory?'

Bracken visibly reacted, then considered. 'Would there be any objection to my recording the conversation?'

'If there is,' Riss said, 'I'll get involved as well.' And threaten, she thought, to rip that bald bastard's skull fringe out if he doesn't cooperate.

'That is a level I'm not used to dealing at,' Bracken said.

'I'll even,' Riss said, 'let you place the call, to make sure we don't have a double standing in the wings.'

'My,' Bracken said. 'The world you live in is full of deceit, isn't it?'

'I'm afraid so,' Riss said.

'And I'm afraid,' Grok said, 'that we rather enjoy a universe of such duplicity.'

Shaking his head, Bracken led Riss to the com.

Riss was very curious about what Mrs. Sufyerd would look like, suspecting she'd be a tall, gaunt ascetic like her husband.

Instead, Cahamla Sufyerd was short, long-haired, and wore a saucy expression, even shadowed as it was with worry. Her daughter, Abihu, about ten, and son Hasli, six, were a bit more solemn than children their age should be as well.

'Elder,' Cahamla said, 'I don't know if I should follow your advice.'

'Of course,' Bracken said courteously, 'you have that option, and we'll continue to shelter you among the membership. But what this woman says does make sense.'

'You and the children, as long as you're above-ground,' Riss said, 'are what they call hostages to fortune.'

'In what sense?' Cahamla asked. 'I have an idea what you mean, but would like things made clear.'

'The, uh, children?' M'chel asked.

'We have never tried to hide anything from them,' Cahamla said firmly. 'And shall not start now.'

'First, in the open, you could be kidnapped.'

'Which would produce what?'

Riss blinked.

'I don't mean to me, or to the children,' Cahamla explained.

'Your being in peril could keep Maen silent,' Riss said.

'No,' Cahamla said. 'Maen is . . . always has been, always shall be . . . his own man, serving the truth as best he knows.'

'Your jeopardy also might keep others silent, who might refuse to help prove Maen innocent,' Grok said.

Her two children were as entranced with the shaggy alien as Bracken's had been.

'He talks,' Hasli told his sister.

'Of course he talks,' Abihu said. 'Now don't be embarrassing.'

'I'm not embarrassed,' the boy said.

'I meant embarrassing *him*,' Abihu said, jabbing her brother in the ribs with an elbow.

'He's not embarrassed, are you?' Hasli asked Grok.

'I do not embarrass easily,' Grok said.

'See?' Hasli said. 'Yadder-dah-yadder-dah-yadder.'

'Hush,' Cahamla said. 'I'm thinking.' She got up, went to the window of the small, modest house the Jilanis had put them in.

'Under normal conditions,' she said, without turning, 'I'd ask for a few days to consider what you propose, and would communicate with my husband.'

'I don't think that would be wise,' Riss said. 'I mean, the part about telling Maen what we want. All of his coms are monitored, and, quite frankly, there are people in the government we in Star Risk don't trust, and knowledge of what we want to do might set them off.'

'Star Risk . . . that's a neat name,' Abihu announced. 'Could I work for you when I grow up?'

Riss raised an eyebrow.

'Uh . . . well, we're always looking for good people . . . but I don't really think your family, and your friends, would approve.'

'Then pooh on them,' Abihu announced. 'I want to do what I want to do when I'm big . . . without hurting people, naturally.'

'We better talk about that,' M'chel said.

Cahamla was smiling at her. 'I can tell you don't have any children.'

'I don't,' M'chel said. 'Nor a husband, either. But how does it show?'

'Children can distract anybody except their parents,' Cahamla said.

Grok growled what signified amusement to him.

'How do you do that?' Hasli asked, attempting a growl of his own.

'Children,' Cahamla announced. 'You are not making this decision process easier.'

The two children looked at each other, grimaced, but kept quiet.

'As for your staying here to think about things,' Riss said, 'if you think that's what you have to do, go ahead. With your permission, we'll put guards around the house, to make sure nothing happens.'

'You think we're in danger here?' Cahamla asked, sounding worried for the first time.

'I don't know,' Riss said. 'All I know is what Elder Bracken told us some time ago, about various people who weren't Jilanis coming around to your services. I would think one reason they did so was to keep tabs on you.'

Bracken nodded. 'I'll accept that theory.'

Cahamla took a breath. 'Very well, then. We'll go with you. Can you give me an hour to pack?'

'We'll wait,' Riss said. 'We're in no particular hurry.'

'It won't take any longer. Ever since that gang ran us out of our own house, we've been living out of our travel cases.'

She smiled wryly. 'I guess we should consider making that a routine until Maen is freed.'

Her voice was quite sure that he would be.

*

The Sufyerds had just loaded into Riss's lifter when she saw movement across the street, outside a clearly empty house with an overgrown garden.

'Are we going to see Daddy?' Hasli asked.

'Eventually,' Riss said absently. 'Grok . . . do you –'

'I got him,' the alien said. 'One man, with a com and binocs.'

'Not good,' Riss said, turning the ignition on and starting the drive.

'Not good at all,' Grok said. 'Look.'

'What is it?' Cahamla asked.

Two men were coming out of a small commercial lifter down the street that had PHILBRICK COMS on its side. Both had guns in their hands.

'What the blazes are they doing?' Riss said, bringing the lifter clear of the ground and spinning it through 180 degrees.

'And why didn't they do it earlier?' Grok wondered.

One of the men was waving something that might have been a badge holder.

'And that proves nothing,' Riss snarled. 'I'm not polite to people with guns.'

She went to full power, and drove at the two men.

They gawked, realized Riss was fully prepared to run them down, and went flat. Riss missed them by about a meter.

One man rolled on his back, and snapped a round up toward the bottom of the lifter, which missed.

Abihu shouted 'Whee!' and Hasli laughed.

'I don't like what you just did,' Cahamla said. 'We're law-abiding.'

'We are,' Bracken agreed. 'Perhaps we should –'

'Anybody can get a badge from somewhere . . . if

that's what the man was waving,' Riss interrupted. 'We'll settle things out back at our headquarters.'

'Well,' Cahamla said doubtfully. 'If you think that's what we should do . . .'

'I don't know if it's what we should do,' M'chel said. 'I know it looks to be the only option. Look.'

She pointed to the left, as half a dozen lifters took off from a small industrial site.

'I don't understand,' M'chel said to Grok.

'I can offer a theory,' the alien said. 'Perhaps these people . . . whoever they are . . . were under orders to keep the Sufyerds under observation, and take action only if we . . . or any others . . . approached them, and it appeared they were going to flee.'

'We set off the trap?'

'Possibly,' Grok said.

'Since you're being so bright, whyn't you turn on the emergency band . . . maybe somebody'll get the talksies and enlighten us,' Riss said. 'And along with it, boy genius, who are these sorts who find us so fascinating?'

'Possibly the normal police force, although I doubt it. Possibly L'Pellerin's DIB,' Grok said. 'That's the most benevolent guess I can make. From there . . . the Masked Ones. Cerberus possibly.'

'Simply wonderful,' Riss said. 'I'm running out of fingers and toes to count the bad guys.'

'This is exciting!' Abihu announced.

'It is?' Hasli asked.

'It is,' she said with certainty.

'Oh,' Hasli said. 'Then I won't be scared.'

'So let's smoke back to the mansion,' Riss said, just as the emergency frequency blurted:

'Unknown lifter, unknown lifter, this is the Tuletian

authorities. Land at once. I say again, land at once.'

Riss made a rude noise and Abihu laughed again.

'Sir,' one of the men on com watch told von Baldur, 'we've got something on the aviation emergency frequency.'

Von Baldur frowned, hurried into the com room as the speaker crackled:

'Unknown lifter, this is Tuletian Control. I say again . . . we have your ID numbers, NY3478 . . . ground at once or fly on at your own peril.'

'That's the lifter Riss took out this morning,' the watch officer said.

'Can you scramble and contact her?'

'We've been trying, sir,' the man said. 'So far without result.'

A pair of speakers blared static.

'And now they're jamming.'

'Get everybody on their feet and ready to react,' von Baldur ordered. 'And keep trying to reach M'chel.'

Interference blared out of the lifter's speaker. Grok shook his head, replaced his mike.

'Nothing,' he told Riss. 'And now we know they're not official.'

'Why so?' Riss asked.

'The police . . . even L'Pellerin's people . . . wouldn't need to jam,' he said. 'They'd just stay on us.'

'Which they're doing a pretty good job of,' Riss said, pointing to her right, where another four lifters had appeared.

Star Risk men and women boiled out of the mansion toward lifters being warmed up as von Baldur,

Goodnight, and King, all wearing combat harnesses, waited on the steps.

'I guess the best bet will be to get airborne,' von Baldur said, 'and maybe we can get a location on this jamming. Our M'chel should be somewhere under that.'

'Not good,' Goodnight said. 'But better than nothing.'

Turbine-whine echoed down the street, and half a dozen commercial lifters grounded outside the mansion's high fencing.

Two of them had closed beds. The sides fell away, revealing heavy crew-served blasters, with men at their controls. Men ran out of the other lifters, and took up firing positions across the street.

Then everyone froze.

'Nobody's giving us orders on what we should be doing,' Goodnight said. 'I don't like that.'

'No,' von Baldur said. He trotted toward the gate.

A blaster *clanged*, and a bolt smashed into the ground two meters away from von Baldur's feet. He skidded to a halt, held up his hands in peace, went forward again.

Another bolt slammed into the paving near him, and gravel and sharded concrete sprayed von Baldur's legs.

Von Baldur went back to the mansion steps.

'They don't want to talk,' Goodnight said.

'What do they . . . oh,' King said. 'They don't want any rescuers.'

'I guess not,' von Baldur said. 'I shall check the back tunnel, although what good that being clear might do us, I haven't an idea.' He ran back into the mansion.

'Plainclothes,' Goodnight mused, then shouted, 'All of you . . . get down and stand by for orders.'

'If they're not wearing uniforms,' King said, 'they're either Cerberus . . . or the Masked Ones. Or maybe the DIB.'

Von Baldur ran back out.

'I can hear lifters on the back street, so they must have us surrounded. I tried to use a com to call the police, and all power has been cut off. It'll take a minute for our backup generator to cut in.'

'Son of a bitch,' Goodnight said. 'If they come in –'

'They're not moving,' King said. 'I think they're just intending to keep us right here.'

'Nice to see a world where the laws work,' von Baldur said calmly. Only his tight-pressed lips showed his rage. 'We cannot even notify the parking patrol about these traffic-blockers.'

'We sit here all corked up while they do whatever they want to Riss and Grok,' Goodnight snarled. 'Son of a bitch twice.'

'They're trying to net us,' Riss said. 'Look up.'

Very high above them were faint contrails, moving with them.

'Spaceships,' Riss said. 'I could zig a zag or two, and prove they're on our ass . . . but I don't think it's necessary.'

'At least,' Grok said, 'we've got speed on the lifters around us.'

'Or at least they'd like us to think we do,' Riss said. 'I *really* want to go home and have a nice, quiet drink. Grok, see if you can't get through to the mansion on our freq.'

'This is Headquarters,' von Baldur said clearly into the microphone. 'I scramble on R-four-three. I say again, I scramble on R-four-three.'

The man on the com nodded to von Baldur that the signal was being scrambled.

'M'chel,' von Baldur said. 'We are surrounded by bad people. Do not, repeat, do not, attempt to return home until we have firm communications and you have been signaled that all is clear. I say again . . .'

The lifter was silent except for drive-whine and the blast of wind as Riss and the others listened to the repeat of von Baldur's cast, badly broken by the interference.

Riss was scribbling numbers from memory on the back of the lifter's handbook. She grimaced, read out her intermittent decryption.

'That does not fill me with joy,' Grok announced. 'At least one thing. They will want us alive.'

'No,' Bracken said. 'They want Cahamla and the children alive, I would think. I don't think anyone cares about the rest of us.'

'I thought religion was supposed to fill you with joy and comfort,' Riss said.

Abihu started crying, and her brother followed suit.

'Wonderful,' Riss muttered.

'So where can we go?' Grok asked.

'If it was just us,' she said, 'I'd suggest we head for some town and go to ground. But with all of us . . . that's not a very good option.'

'You are being most polite,' Grok said. 'I think that I might stand out, even if we didn't have friends with us.'

Riss gnawed at her lower lip. 'I have an idea,' she said. 'We can try to reach Fra Diavolo. He's got enough room . . . not to mention people . . . to hide us out.'

'And he is how far from here?'

'About an hour, I'd guess. Maybe two. Uh-oh.'

The lifters were closing toward them, like a gigantic noose.

'I don't think we're going to be given that option,' Grok said. 'There are three ahead of us.'

M'chel looked down at the ground.

'And of course, there's no nice safe town to put it down in,' she said. 'Just goddamned jungle.'

'We're not afraid of jungle,' Abihu said. 'Hasli and I are Pioneers.'

'That,' Elder Bracken explained, 'is our church outdoor youth group.'

Riss looked at the two children, then at Cahamla, who smiled sheepishly. M'chel's lips were moving, but fortunately, she wasn't vocalizing.

'Awright,' she growled. 'I have been pushed around enough!'

She slid into her combat harness and reflexively checked it. Blaster . . . spare magazines . . . fighting knife . . . six grenades, two flash-bang, two lethal, two gas. It was not quite true that Riss never went anywhere – including out for a hot romance or to the bathroom – without the harness.

She pushed the power through to emergency, and sent the lifter down in a screaming dive.

This time it was Hasli's turn to yip gleefully and shout 'Roller-coastie!'

'When we land,' M'chel ordered, 'I want everyone out, and following me. We're going to run away from the ship as fast as we can, and then hide.'

'Hide and seek?' Abihu asked doubtfully.

'Hide and seek,' Riss said as the lifter smashed

through branches. She flared the lifter, went to full lift, and the ship stabilized a few meters above the ground. Riss sent it darting forward, under the cover of a huge tree, then landed hard.

'I wish to hell we had this turd rigged for a booby trap,' she said as she opened all four doors and jumped out.

The other five followed her, zigging, away from the lifter into thick brush. Riss wanted to run like a track star, but remembered the children, and slowed to a trot. She heard the sound of ships coming in behind her.

Riss looked out through the bottom of a bush at the line of men and women sweeping up the bluff toward her. They weren't wearing the uniform of Dampier's military, but dark gray coveralls. But they moved to shouted orders and carried standard-issue blasters.

Dunno, she thought. No idea who they're working for. She slid back to the others.

'Here's the first thing we'll try,' she said. 'We're all going to crawl into the heart of that thicket over there, and nobody's allowed to make a sound, even if they get prickers in them.

'I hope that these people aren't very good, and they'll sweep right over us. Then we'll run back the way we came, and toward that town that we passed over just before I landed. All right?'

Everyone nodded solemnly, and began worming their way into deep cover.

The search line got closer and closer, and M'chel, pistol ready, ducked her head into the dirt, and thought bushlike thoughts.

It almost worked.

She heard underbrush rustle, almost beside her, then bootheels moved on past. Riss gave it an eight-count, lifted her head. The sweepers were about ten meters past, almost hidden by brush.

Then Hasli got to his feet, stepped on a branch, which cracked loudly.

A man spun, saw the boy, and lifted his blaster.

Elder Bracken was up, yanking Hasli down, as the man fired.

The bolt caught Bracken in the stomach, and sent him flopping down.

M'chel blew the shooter's chest into pulp, shot the two on either side of him, then yanked the others up, and they were running, as the beaters realized they'd almost lost their prey, and turned and came after them.

It was nearly dusk. M'chel had led the others into a shallow cave, not good enough for a hide, but good enough for a moment's shelter, while she thought about what she'd try next.

'Is Elder Bracken dead?' Abihu whispered.

'Yes,' Riss whispered back. She saw Cahamla's lips moving in prayer.

'He'll be rewarded for saving Hasli, won't he?'

'Yes,' Riss said.

'I didn't mean to –' the boy started.

'Hush,' M'chel whispered. 'It was an accident.'

'I've decided,' Abihu whispered, 'that when I grow up I want to be an Elder like Elder Bracken.'

'You could do a lot worse, kid,' Riss said, letting her rage build. 'You could do a lot worse.'

She beckoned to Grok. 'I'm getting tired of being chased.'

'I also,' the alien said. 'And so much for the theory that they want us alive.'

'Unless,' M'chel said, 'he was the clown – there's one in every outfit – who never gets the word.'

'Are you prepared to gamble on that?' Grok asked.

'Hell no. Here's what we'll go for. We'll get into deep cover,' Riss said, 'and wait for full dark. Then we'll see what they do next. Maybe they'll just leave.'

'If they don't?' Grok asked skeptically.

'Then there's gonna be a whole bunch of gray corpses scattered around the frigging landscape,' Riss said, not knowing her teeth were bared like a feral animal.

No one heard any orders, but the gunnies surrounding Star Risk's mansion came to their feet, loaded back into their lifters, and the aircraft took off.

'Now what brought that on?' Goodnight wondered.

King and von Baldur shook their heads.

None of them said what they feared – that whoever was after M'chel and Grok either had caught them, or had them trapped.

Campfires dotted the forest, and whoever was after Riss and the others had brought in heavy gunships. Three starships orbited overhead. There were sentries posted.

Riss left the others with their instructions, then slid out into the night. She went through the sentries like a hot wire through butter. Not bad for an old broad, she thought. Guess all that Marine horseshit sticks with you.

Once through the loose picket line, she made for one of the gunships. Military issue, she noted, not jerry-rigged. Armored, with a chaingun on each side and a heavy blaster in the nose.

There was a sentry posted. He gurgled in complete surprise as Riss's knife went into his stomach, driving upward into his heart, and he was dead.

Riss pushed his body under the skirt of the lifter, eased the lifter hatch open, entered.

There was a bored gunner at one of the chainguns, yawning, hungry, looking out at his teammates outside the ship, around their cookstove.

Riss pulled his head back, knifed him in the throat, yanked him to the deck, and slid behind the chaingun controls.

Not a breed of lifter she was familiar with, but a chaingun was a chaingun was a chaingun. It was on half-load. She turned the power on, full-loaded the gun, making sure the canisters for the six barrels were firmly locked in place.

Then she waited.

Contrary to what the late gunner might have thought, his teammates weren't happy. They kept looking out into the darkness, and unconsciously pushing closer to the fire.

'This is screwed,' one woman said. 'Who are these mad bastards we're working for, anyway?'

'Shuddup,' her team commander ordered.

'Like hell I will, L'ron. You're two days' senior to me, and there's no reason you should have a stripe when I don't.

'I think it's shitty when we're told off to follow some asshole who's wearing nothing but coveralls, and not even a goddamned name tag, and go chasing some kids and some women.'

'Look, you dumb bitch,' the other woman said. 'You ever hear of the Masked Ones?'

'Heard,' the first woman said. 'Some kind of terror-
ists.'

'Don't be calling them that,' the team commander
hissed.

'Don't get stroppy with me,' the first woman said.
'I'll call frigging civilians what I want to. And what I
want to know is who gives them the authority to yank
all of us out of training, and send us out here to fart
around?'

'The reason I'm telling you to shut up,' the second
woman said, 'is because these bassids are stone killers.
They'll cut your throat for a laugh. I know. I'm from
Tuletia, not some pisshead place in the outback like you
are.

'I've seen them at work, and don't ever want to see it
again.' She shivered. 'Two whole families in my block
got butchered, shot down, men, women, kids, because
they went and got political and tried to get the plant
where three of 'em worked unionized.

'And they've got pull. Pull enough to get us sent out
here chasing up and down the hills. I'd guess if they've
got that kind of weight, they could probably leave your
sorry ass out here under a bush without even thinking
about it, and there damned well wouldn't be any search
parties looking for your body. Now shut up, and see if
the stew's cooking.'

A wind whispered across them, and the team leader
shivered and looked out into the blackness.

It was too dark.

There had to be something out there.

There was.

Something darker than the night loomed at the soldiers. One person had time for a scream, another was

running, and the team leader was grabbing for her rifle.

Grok shot her in the head, gunned down the man next to her, flipped the switch to full automatic, and sprayed the rest of the group.

He roared mightily, like he imagined a horrid creature of the night should, and vaguely wished he had more of an anthropophagous bent than he had.

Now the screams were louder, and soldiers were pelting away, shouting the alarm.

Grok lobbed a pair of grenades after them, thrown very high, very far, landing in front of the fleeing soldiers.

Other troops heard the screaming, and were up, fear spraying adrenaline through their system.

M'chel Riss opened fire from the lifter, the chaingun spraying lines of fire through the night. Other gunners opened up, firing at they knew not what.

Panic washed over the half-trained soldiers, and they trampled their officers and the Masked Ones who'd brought them into this forest. They ran, not sure which way led toward safety, but anywhere that might be away from this nightmare.

'Come on,' Grok shouted, and the Sufyerds ran toward him.

Riss had the hatch of the lifter open. 'Let's go visiting,' she said, and the Sufyerds piled aboard. Other ships were taking off blindly into the night.

'You know how to fly this pig?' Riss called.

'I think so,' Grok said.

'Good. I'm not through killing assholes yet.'

'M'chel,' Cahamla said. 'It is ill to kill more, and will not bring back Elder Bracken.'

'No offense, Sister Sufyerd,' Riss snarled. 'You mourn Bracken your way, I'll mourn him mine.'

She slid back behind the controls of the chaingun, found a target, and sent cannon fire chattering into a crowd of frenzied soldiers trying to cram themselves aboard a troop lifter.

'Of course we'll take care of the good Sufyerd's family,' Fra Diavolo said. 'They'll be content here, or wherever we choose to conceal them . . . well, as content as they can be, knowing Maen Sufyerd's troubles.

'Perhaps they can even teach me something of the Jilanis faith,' he went on. 'I've always been intensely curious about their practices, and now might be an opportune time to learn.'

'Good,' Riss said. 'Also, Grok and I would like to hide out with your people. I think there's a good chance we're very, very hot, and might need to call in a certain ship we've got standing by in orbit and make our get-away.'

'It would be a pity to lose you and your friend,' Diavolo said. 'Particularly when things appear to be warming up.'

'I agree,' Grok said. 'I am thoroughly enjoying all the scoundrels that we have been meeting of late.'

But there was no hue and cry. M'chel never knew how the casualties were buried on the army's rolls. There was no mention of the firefight in the forest, nor was there any arrest warrant for Riss or Grok.

Riss and Grok said goodbye to the Sufyerds, M'chel reminding Abihu of her promise to grow up like Elder Bracken.

'Quite an admirable pair of offspring,' Grok said as they flew back toward the capital.

'They are, aren't they,' M'chel said, secretly very glad of her solitary state. 'But being around kids . . . anybody's kids . . . for more than an hour makes me nervous.'

'That's interesting,' Grok said. 'I have never mated for progeny, so have no idea what my opinion might be.'

They returned to the mansion and a riotous welcome from von Baldur and the others.

'With you safe, and still operational, we are moving on to the next stage,' von Baldur told them. 'Which shall begin with our Chas attending a masked ball.'

THIRTY-NINE

Chas Goodnight stopped at the top of the steps, catching a reflection of his dapper self in a window glass. He took a moment to admire the way he looked — immaculate in formal whites, clawhammer jacket, pants, and black cummerbund with a matching neck scarf.

His pack of burglar tools showed not at all. Nor a smallish, fairly harmless bomb stuffed down the back of his pants, or the small gun holstered inside the cummerbund.

He also admired his plan.

Goodnight desperately wanted to see that pack of love letters between the Universalists' Premier Ladier and Hyla Adrianopole, his mistress, whose murder trial had begun the day before, since there was supposedly information about Sufyerd in them.

The problem was, where were they?

The *Tuletian Pacifist* kept promising to run them, so unless it was a total fraud, that meant *somebody* involved with the paper had those letters. Or rather, Goodnight corrected himself, several somebodies, since King had been told there had been copies made.

The question was, who had the goodies?

Goodnight figured the *Pacifist*'s boss must have a copy. The holo's publisher was named Bernt Shiprite. From all reports, he was a rather arrogant shitheel, third-generation rich, who'd managed to convince himself that the rich and powerful of the Dampier System really liked him around.

Even Goodnight, hardly a communications expert, knew said rich and powerful of any system thought all members of the press about as attractive as a good case of scabies, and only tolerated publishers and editors as long as they could play them like fish on the line.

So it had been with Shiprite, who'd been a staunch Universalist until he had complained in print about a particularly juicy piece of trough-feeding. Driven into the outer darkness for his sin, he swore revenge. Although, strangely enough, he never got in bed with Reynard's Independents, nor Fra Diavolo's wreckers.

He sulked in the political wilderness, using his publications to sling darts in all directions. Probably he hoped the Universalists would someday let him back into their midst, although going after the current premier wasn't exactly the first step toward redemption.

Shiprite owned a dozen holos. Most were free advertisers scattered throughout the Dampier System, which were ignored but hugely profitable. One was Tuletia's favored entertainment holo. Two more were puzzle holos. Then there was the *Analyst*, a sober, vaguely reactionary holo, and finally, the *Pacifist*, which until two years ago had been the *Tuletian Conservative*. After Shiprite was declared anathema by the Universalists he'd purged the existing staff and brought in a crew of fairly radical hotheads, with the late Met Fall in charge.

Goodnight had puzzled at a way to get into Shiprite's vast estate to look for those letters.

He found out as much as he could about the publisher, found that his hobbies included restoring old racing lifters, lifting weights, collecting spectacular and significantly younger wives, and formal parties.

Goodnight commed Reynard, asked him to arrange an invite to Shiprite's next affair, not under his own name, nor in any way involved with the Independents.

'You plan on wreaking havoc, I assume,' Reynard said. 'Which is fine with me. That man is as dependable as . . . as a Torguth. Don't give me details. I'll arrange everything.'

And so, invitation in hand, Chas Goodnight nee Charanga Guessendo had formal evening wear tailored, rented a lim, and went to Shiprite's mansion.

The parking area outside was a dazzle of the rich. Bodyguards and armed chauffeurs surrounded the area, lifters swooped in and out. Just on the edges of the floodlights, armed guards and automated sniffers patrolled the grounds.

Just inside the door a woman in her thirties, wearing an extraordinarily low cut gown in spangled silver and a matching feather headdress she should have had sense enough to leave on the birds, beamed at him.

'A new face! You're . . . ?' she said.

'Charanga Guessendo,' Goodnight said. He liked picking false names no one could pronounce, in the theory that no one would be suspicious of a clanger.

'Yes,' the woman said vaguely. 'Glad to meet you, Mr. . . . ummm . . . yes. I'm Dorothy Shiprite. You can call me Buffy.'

'My pleasure, Buffy.'

Her eyes ran up and down Goodnight's body. He felt suddenly naked, vowed he'd never leer at a woman again.

'Yes,' she said thoughtfully. '*Very* pleased. I hope that you'll become a close friend of mine. And,' she added quickly, 'of my husband, of course.'

Goodnight had been warned by one of Reynard's people not to let Buffy get him into a corner. He looked around hastily, saw a rather vapid-looking young woman, barely more than a girl.

'Yes, yes indeed,' Goodnight said. 'Excuse me. There's the woman I've been looking for.'

He stepped away, grabbed the woman by the arm. 'There you are!'

'Oh . . . yes . . . here I am,' the woman said in a rather perplexed monotone.

'We were just going to dance,' Goodnight said.

'Oh . . . yes . . . yes, I guess we were.'

Goodnight led her toward the dance floor.

The woman grabbed two glasses of some sparkling wine from a tray, handed one to Goodnight. He pretended to drink, set the drink on a table, and took her in his arms. Chas Goodnight didn't believe in drinking on the job.

This season's musical arrangements for the hoi polloi were evidently strolling musicians, all playing the same melody, coordinated through tiny transceivers clipped to their instruments. They weren't very good, being more intent on not stumbling into their masters than playing.

But dancing to their sounds was better than being chased by Buffy.

*

After a time, after deciding the food was pretty fine, and that the daughters and wives of the very rich could be more boring than he could tolerate, and having had the man pointed out to him, he drifted over and 'happened' to catch Bernt Shiprite as he circulated.

Shiprite was in his early sixties, tall, athletically built, with longish, clearly transplanted hair in a style twenty years too young for him.

Goodnight introduced himself, said that he was new to Montrois, and was a speculative writer, specializing in travel pieces.

Shiprite said, without meaning it, that Guessendo might be interested in doing a piece for the *Pacifist* on what he thought of Tuletia, then eyed Goodnight in a rather interested manner. Chas was reminded of Buffy's recent evaluation.

'I see by your build that you work out.'

'When I get ambitious,' Goodnight said. 'I'm afraid I'm a bit too lazy to have regular habits.'

'So am I,' Shiprite said. 'What keeps me honest is having a partner to work out with.'

Again that curious look, and Goodnight wondered if he'd heard of all of Shiprite's hobbies.

'You might be interested in coming out here in the daylight sometime, and I'll show you my gym.'

Right, Goodnight thought. And the golden rivet and the bosun's whistle, as well. He made meaningless agreeable noises, then said, 'Actually, Mr. Shiprite, what I've been wondering is when you plan to start running the letters between the unfortunate Miss Adrianopole and Premier Ladier.'

'Unfortunate my ass,' Shiprite said. 'She murdered one of the best journalists in the Dampier System!'

'I apologize for misspeaking,' Goodnight said.

'I . . . or rather the *Pacifist* . . . will begin running excerpts from those letters sometime during the trial,' Shiprite said. 'I haven't decided on the timing as yet.'

'Ah,' Goodnight said. 'You said excerpts?'

'Of course,' Shiprite said. 'We'll only run bits of concern to my readers.'

'Something else that has interested me,' Goodnight said, 'is this Sufyerd case. I understand there are some things in the letters that pertain to that man's crime.'

'Perhaps,' Shiprite said. 'I confess I haven't read every word of them. But if there are mentions of the traitor, I see no reason to upset things by running anything about Sufyerd that might bring into question a verdict that's already been justly decided.'

Goodnight smiled politely, and was glad someone else came up to Shiprite and began asking him an involved question about old lifters.

That was that for Shiprite's ass.

Goodnight drifted on.

Half an hour later, a bit after midnight, he found himself upstairs, in a deserted hallway that led, he'd been told, to Shiprite's private quarters and home office. Goodnight tried one of the doors, found it to be unlocked and a closet. He slid his bomb out of his waistband, spun the timer to fifteen minutes, activated it, put the bomb in the closet, and went back downstairs.

He treated himself to his first alcoholic drink of the evening, waited.

A dull thud came from upstairs as the bomb went off, and someone screamed. Someone else shouted fire.

Goodnight was watching Shiprite carefully. The man

looked about wildly, darted upstairs, and Goodnight went after him, down a corridor, and into a room at the end. His office. That was predictable.

About then, the smoke bomb went out.

Smoke boiled through the house, then, as the manufacturer promised, combined with the air and dissipated. The case itself was supposed to be consumed in providing material for the smoke, and the bomb was guaranteed not to leave scorch marks. Goodnight didn't care – there were so many closets in the house it'd take a lifetime before anyone opened that particular one.

Goodnight wasn't paying attention anyway. He was crouched, looking under the smoke into the office, watching Shiprite move a rather grotesque painting of a lifter at speed out of the way, and start fiddling with the dial of a safe.

That was enough for Chas.

It was, in fact, very very good. Goodnight had learned, years ago, that when a fire starts, people will either panic and grab a fishbowl and run out, leaving their children to fry, or instinctively go for their most precious.

Goodnight had figured those letters between Ladier and Adrianopole might qualify as precious, and now he knew Shiprite's hiding place. He went back and joined the party, which, recovering from the momentary shock, started getting louder, in giddy relief.

Things started breaking up about three. Goodnight had found a small storage room near the back of the ballroom, slipped inside, and found stacks of towels. They made a comfortable seat, and he shoved a wedge under the door to lock it, and waited.

He smiled reminiscently. This was feeling more and more like the old days, when it was just him against the universe. The legit universe, he corrected.

It took another hour for silence to set in and for the lights to go out.

Goodnight put on skintight ultra-thin gloves, pulled the wedge free, went silently out into the ballroom, across it, to the stairs. He saw a couple of snoring drunks sprawled here and there, and grinned.

That would provide his alibi.

Goodnight went upstairs into the office area and down the hall to Shiprite's office door. It was locked. Two minutes with old-fashioned picks, and it was unlocked.

Goodnight closed the door behind him, used the wedge to block the door shut, and took out a small light, which he set on a stand next to the painting of the lifter. He took the painting down, examined the safe, and sneered. Nothing better than a twenty-year-old Willig model Twelve.

One reason – besides the fact that that was where the jewels were – that Goodnight had started robbing the rich was his discovery that they put their faith in showy guards, and robots, and guard animals, and then put their riches behind tinfoil.

He attached an ear to the safe next to the locking sensor, put a listening bud in his ear, and an ultra-sensitive pickup on the other side.

Then he started touching buttons on the sensor.

He heard nothing, no clicks, no muffled thuds, which was what he'd expected from a Willig, which was old and simple, but relatively efficient. But the pickup twitched on a certain number.

Goodnight went through the same ritual again, got a second number, then a third and a fourth. That was all the settings a Willig allowed.

He hit the keys in sequence.

The safe stayed locked.

He tried again, then a third and fourth time, varying the number sequence each time. There weren't that many possibilities.

On the fifth attempt, there was an almost inaudible click.

Now he had all the time in the world – fifteen seconds – to lift the latch and open the door.

Goodnight brought up the light, looked in the safe.

Inside were papers. He sorted through them quickly, but they gave him nothing. There was also a small box with some very interesting unset jewels, probably theones, he guessed. These he pocketed. They'd go to the fence whose name he'd gotten from the 'King of Thieves' for walking-about money. There was no particular need to tell Star Risk about them.

Besides, the missing gems would provide a bit of cover for his other theft, which was a tiny storage device, the only thing in the safe that could contain the letters. That went into a tiny pocket hidden in the tail of his coat.

Also in the safe were Shiprite's passport, a pocket dex with com numbers on it, and a small-caliber, elaborately engraved pistol. The dex, which might provide some sort of info for Grok or King, and the gun, which Chas rather fancied, also went into his pocket.

Goodnight closed and locked the safe and went back out, cleaning up all traces of his visit. On the landing before he reached the main floor, he stopped.

Now was the time to take care of the details of his getaway, distasteful though they were. Goodnight stuck a finger down his throat and threw up all over himself quite silently. The odor was disgusting.

He went toward the main door, stumbling artistically. There were two guards just inside.

'Home . . .' Goodnight mumbled. 'Go . . . home . . . go my place . . . sick . . .' He started to retch again.

'You have a lifter, sir?' one of the guards said, trying to hide his repugnance.

'Got lim,' Goodnight managed. 'Stay . . . told to stay . . . fire the bastard if . . . got to go home. Home.'

The guards helped him out to his lim, which was sitting with ten others, their pilots patiently waiting for their drunken employers to wake up.

Goodnight kept the drunk act going until the lim driver dropped him off, three blocks away from the mansion.

The streets were deserted, except for a pair of streetsweepers. Goodnight crouched behind a parked lifter until they went past, then trotted on toward home.

In spite of the stink, he was feeling good. Very good, with the mission accomplished, no discovery, no casualties, and what had to be those scandalous love letters secure in his hidden pouch.

This sort of clean solo operation was what Goodnight lived for. He was feeling so very good, he thought he might even cut Star Risk in on the profits from the sales of the theones.

Chas Goodnight caught himself. He wasn't sure he felt *that* good.

FORTY

'I have a mention of Sufyerd,' Jasmine King announced, looking up from her computer.

She was searching the fiche of the letters between Hyla Adrianopole and Premier Ladier that Goodnight had stolen from Shiprite's safe. The others hovered over their own screens in the mansion's operating center.

'A mention?' Goodnight said. 'That's all?'

'A mention,' King said. 'I've searched half a dozen times, using every variant I can find of Sufyerd's name.'

'And what do we have?' von Baldur asked.

'I quote,' King said. '"On a minor note, darling, I was curious about this traitor Sufyerd's guilt, since there are a few fools questioning the military court's verdict. I was assured by the good L'Pellerin as to his absolute, unquestionable guilt, so that's something, at least, I don't have to worry about, compared to this abysmal mineral lease scandal, about . . ." end quote, and that's all there is.'

'Shit!' Goodnight said. 'For this I risked my life . . . or anyway my good reputation, and ruined a perfectly good, brand-new formal?'

'It appears so,' King said.

'Well, what about the dirty parts?' Goodnight said. 'Since this twink went and shot somebody to keep from getting her good name despoiled, at least there should be some hot and heavy.'

'Here's something,' Jasmine said. 'Patching it over to you.' She touched sensors.

Goodnight read his screen.

'*That's* hot and heavy? I did better than that when I was fifteen!'

'Including with the snake?' Riss asked.

'Snake? What snake?' Goodnight sputtered. 'I didn't see anything about any snake.'

Then he realized M'chel was laughing.

'Goddamnit, Riss,' he started.

'I also,' Jasmine went on, 'found something very interesting, since I was wondering whether this Hyla Adrianopole is a bubble-brain, or if there's maybe another game being run.'

'Why,' Grok asked, 'do you think possibly Adrianopole is of less than adequate intelligence?'

'Well, we actually know she's close to that,' Jasmine said. 'Shooting down Editor Fall wasn't that bright, especially since she didn't then have her hands on the letters, or even proof that Fall hadn't made copies.'

'Jasmine,' von Baldur said patiently, 'you're veering. You said you had something interesting.'

'I do, and doing a search suggests there's many things in that category. Unfortunately, they don't pertain to our assignment to free Sufyerd.

'But they are *very* interesting. I'll give you one quote, which is pretty well borne out by other references. I quote, "after two hours with the ambassador from T., I feel vastly relieved that they intend no harm to the Belfort Worlds, and that all this sword-waving is but an excuse for the T. navy to completely rearm," end quote.

'Here's one even more interesting, and I quote, "After very private talks, it seems that a viable alternative to the present conflict between T. and ourselves would be to suggest a conference, and . . . this was the ambassador's suggestion . . . that a pacifistic solution to the B. problem would be some sort of powersharing," end quote.'

There was stunned silence.

'Son of a bitch,' Goodnight said. 'I didn't waste my time.'

'T like in Torguth,' Riss said. 'Yow!'

'I do not understand,' Grok said.

'It is simple,' von Baldur said. 'Ladier and his party have been maintaining a peaceful stand, saying that the Belfort Worlds will remain under Dampier control, and that the Torguth have no intentions of fighting a third war.

'Now, just from these two quotes, we have mixed signals. One is that the Torguth navy has big eyes for war, and the Torguth ambassador is dissembling to Ladier, and secondly that Ladier has no objection at all to giving up the Belfort Worlds to Torguth.

'Anyone who proposes sharing power means to have all of it in time, and anyone who accepts such a proposition is preparing themselves for surrender.

'While this does not pertain directly to us, it surely will be of interest to Mr. Reynard.

'This is the sort of thing that makes governments fall. Now I see why Adrianopole was so eager to shoot Fall, and risk everything to get her hands on those letters.

'Jasmine, you were right. There is at least one fool in this whole mess. But it is not the woman, but rather Premier Ladier, for being stupid enough to reveal secrets like this to anyone in writing, let alone to a mistress.

'Yes,' von Baldur continued thoughtfully. 'I think Mr. Reynard will complain a great deal less about our expenses when he hears of this matter. I shall make an appointment with him, and provide him with pertinent extracts from these letters, if you would be so good as to prepare such for me, Jasmine.'

'Well,' Riss said, 'while you're being a political animal, I'm going to hunt down that mailboy Chas's ever-so-passionate friend told us about. I think it's time for a little direct action.'

FORTY-ONE

It took only three days for M'chel Riss to find Strategic Intelligence's mailboy, Runo Kismayu. Since IIa and L'Pellerin's Dampier Information Bureau were hardly cooperating with Star Risk, it took a day longer than it should have, but still was fairly simple. Riss, after running into security holds checking the conventional ways of tracing IDs, finally had one of Reynard's minions check Kismayu's basic security clearance form, and that was that.

She wanted to do a bit of burglary before she confronted Kismayu, and so enlisted the light-fingered Goodnight.

She put in a com for Kismayu at IIa. If he was at work, the coast should be clear for some sedate B&Eing. The somewhat chatty com operator said Kismayu hadn't been in for three days, and they supposed he was sick.

Riss got off the com and said, in low voice, 'By the prickling of my thumbs . . .' and let her voice trail off.

'What?' Goodnight asked.

'Never mind. You don't know anything about wicked. Let's go a-visiting. Are you heeled?'

'Lady,' Goodnight said, 'I don't use the bathroom without having a gun close at hand. Particularly around here.'

They parked their lifter two blocks away from Kismayu's address just after noon, when most of Montrois's citizens would be thinking about or consuming their customarily heavy lunch, and went unobtrusively to the mailboy's address.

The area had tree-lined, very quiet streets with older, impeccably kept town houses and small apartment buildings on either side.

'A bit posh around here,' Riss said, looking about.

'Maybe our boy lives with his parents,' Goodnight said. 'Or maybe he's like his frigging boss, and able to maintain a lavish life without effort . . . and without anybody asking about it.'

'Don't be bitter, Chas. Sooner or later you'll figure out how Caranis can fly so high without an engine,' Riss said. 'Here it is. I'll go knocking.'

She went up the steps, found the sensor with 3 – KISMAYU on it, and rang. She waited, and there was no response.

'Here,' Goodnight said loudly. 'Let me try.'

He came up the steps, and a pair of picks flashed into the door slot.

'Hey, Kissie,' Goodnight said into the speaker, as if someone had answered the ring. 'It's us. Buzz us right on in.' The lock came open. Goodnight pocketed his lock picks, bowed Riss in.

There was a small landing with an atrocious bronze of some hero on it. They went up steps to Apartment 3.

Riss had her hand inside her rather smart jacket, on her gun butt. Goodnight had a small, ornate pistol

M'chel hadn't seen before concealed in his hand.

Automatically, they stood on either side of the door. Riss knocked.

No response.

There were three very modern locks on the door.

Goodnight considered, took out an autopick, turned it on, and fed the tendrils into the first lock. After a moment, it clicked open. He went to work on the second.

Riss sniffed, wrinkled her nose, touched it and the door. Goodnight made a face, nodded. He'd smelled the same thing. The second lock came open, and Goodnight took only a second to break the third.

They went in fast, crouching, guns ready.

Nothing.

Riss had a good idea what the smell was, pointed to a slippered foot sticking out from the dining area.

They got up and swept the apartment, ready to shoot. It was empty, except for them and the corpse sprawled in the dining area. The body'd begun to swell and turn black.

Riss had smelled a lot of corpses, gotten to the point where she could operate around them, but still felt her stomach knot. The stink didn't seem to bother Goodnight.

The corpse lay facedown, wearing a very old-fashioned, but very expensive dressing gown. There was a glass lying near the body, dried wine splattered out from it across the highly polished floor.

Goodnight used a foot to turn the body over. The face was distorted, but distinguishable as a young man with complexion problems and overly styled hair, who was far too young to wear that dressing gown.

'Kismayu,' Goodnight said, pointing to holos here and there in the apartment of its late tenant with a succession of cheap, clearly available young women in various stages of undress.

There was the remains of a meal on the table. Riss went into the kitchen, found more food in delivery cases on the stove, more than enough for one person.

She opened cabinets, found wineglasses. Using a napkin, she lifted the front one. It stuck for a moment to the wood. None of the others did.

She checked the stored plates. Again, the top one stuck for an instant.

Riss nodded, went back into the dining area, knelt, and, carefully using the napkin, picked up the wineglass and sniffed at it.

She made a face, held it out to Goodnight. He, too, sniffed, shrugged.

'Poison,' Riss whispered. 'I'm pretty sure nobody'd ever drink wine that smells that crappy.'

On the table was a near-empty bottle.

Goodnight pointed around, at the expensive holo set, a home theater complex, furniture upholstered in what looked like real leather. They went into the bedroom, which was furnished as a young man's nest of lust. There was a money clip on the dresser, fat with bills.

Goodnight looked at the pictures in the bedroom. Again, provocatively posing women.

Riss pointed to the door. They slid out, relocked the locks, went down the stairs and away. They kept their guns at hand, just in case.

Half a block away, Riss thought it was safe to talk. 'There was another person there,' she said. 'To be sexist, a man.'

'I'm not arguing, but why?' Goodnight asked.

'Whoever was there . . . maybe brought the take-out . . . ate with Kismayu. When Runo'd had enough wine so he wouldn't smell anything, the visitor put poison in his glass.

'Exit one mailboy, who also was the nice, invisible Torguth spy on the inside of IIa, the one who stole the plans that Sufyerd was accused of taking. Nobody ever thinks about mailboys or custodians.'

'Hang on to that thought,' Goodnight said. 'I say again my last. Why a man?'

'The killer thought he was clever, and after Kismayu fell over dead he took his glass and plate to the kitchen, rinsed them, and put them away.'

'Again, why did it have to be a man?'

'Not for certain,' Riss said. 'But a woman probably would've dried them, rather than putting them away wet, so when they dried they'd stick to the shelf.'

'You are a very clever woman,' Goodnight said, and there was honest admiration in his voice.

'It gave me something to think about instead of puking,' Riss said.

'All right,' Goodnight agreed. 'No pictures of family anywhere, which suggests he wasn't particularly tight with anyone who might've been sending him regular checks. But he had a wad of bills that'd choke Grok. If Kismayu came from money, he'd never be so vulgar as to carry that much cash. Real richies have an account.'

'So he was on the take from someone,' Riss agreed. 'Someone who was furnishing him with a nice, lavish lifestyle.'

'And who got worried,' Goodnight went on. 'Maybe

about the time we started digging, and decided to clean up the traces of their boy.'

'Who sure as hell wouldn't have been smart – or educated – enough to have known what the defense plans would've looked like or meant without some serious guidance,' Riss said.

'All we got is the dead little man. His control . . . whoever's really the traitor . . . is still out there. Running ahead of us.'

'True,' Goodnight said cheerily. 'But not that much farther. When they start cleaning up with murder – and I'm not dumb enough to think that our target would've been stupid enough to do the murder himself . . . or herself – they're generally getting worried about the hounds on their ass. Which means us. We're closing in.'

'I hope you're right,' Riss said.

'Have I ever been wrong?'

Both of them broke into laughter.

'Now, let's get out of this oofrawfraw neighborhood, and find ourselves a nice strong drink,' Goodnight said. 'Something that'll let my stomach forget what it saw.'

'You got bothered, too?'

'Don't I look human?' Goodnight said in an injured tone.

FORTY-TWO

Star Risk had assumed that Reynard would take the information that Premier Ladier, and conceivably the entire Universalist party, were in league with Torguth to the media.

'And that is why,' Reynard had said, 'you are soldiers, and I am a politician. Besides, don't you think there's something interesting in the fact that Fall, and his publisher, Shiprite, had these letters for some time, yet never quite got around to going public with them?

'Perhaps Shiprite is trying to cut a deal with the Universalists to get back in favor if he doesn't run the letters. Or perhaps not. I'm not trying to second-guess him.

'I have a lasting distrust of the media. Their reporters may be relatively honest, and relatively incorruptible. But their bosses, the publishers, are as crooked as a sea snake in a whirlpool. No. I have my own plans for this information.'

When Riss found out exactly how Reynard wanted to play his cards, she agreed that she and the others had no talent at all for political schemes.

Reynard made a point of encountering a man named

Faraon. He was a ranking leader of the Universalists, and, more importantly, the man who wanted to be Universalist party leader and then premier, but had lost to Ladier in a vicious bit of in-party fighting that included party brawling and rumored blackmail.

It took almost a week to arrange a meeting, since neither Reynard nor Faraon trusted the other.

It was finally agreed upon to take a small dining room at Tournelle's. Remembering the bugs that Star Risk had found, Reynard proposed they sweep the room before the meet. Faraon grudgingly agreed, and specified that a team of specialists from his own party team up with Star Risk.

Reynard worried about this, until von Baldur reassured him there would be no problems with a Universalist bug. 'Nor,' he added, 'will you have to worry about not having a record of the meet later.'

The Universalists were awestruck by Grok, and very impressed with King's expertise, especially when she pointed out the two windows in the dining room, and then explicated.

'Now,' she said, 'I'm sure you're aware a window has certain resonances when sound impacts it, and a proper parabolic microphone can pick up and translate those almost as well as if the mike were in the room.'

'We are,' the leader of the Universalists sniffed. 'A very ancient device. We Dampierians may be on the fringes of civilization, but we're not isolated.'

'My apologies,' Jasmine said hastily. 'I didn't mean to offend. Here's my countermeasure.'

Both windows were covered with a thin, clear film.

'This gives us dead air between the room and the window glass, so whatever's said in the room stays there.'

She and Grok then made sure they were completely open about searching the room with the Universalists. They found two bugs.

One was very ancient, that might have been planted a century earlier. The other was fairly modern, hidden in a wall cavity behind a screwed-down portrait of the restaurant's founder, who had an expression like someone who'd just learned his refrigerators had seized.

'Yours?' King asked.

The others shook their heads.

She took out that bug's power supply, then said, 'Perhaps one of L'Pellerin's.'

Grok took it, crushed it underfoot.

From then until the meet, a Universalist and a Star Risk guard stayed in the room. There was a last-minute attempt by one of the waiters to put a vase of flowers in the room. It, of course, had a microphone.

Rather than destroy it, King took it back to the mansion. After Reynard and Faraon arrived at Tournelle's, she fed that microphone a series of speeches by the two men made on the floor of Parliament.

Both politicians arrived with armed guards and were searched for body wires. Neither wore one, and pretended mild offense at the search.

The transcript of Ladier's letters and a copy of the fiche were removed from Reynard's briefcase, the briefcase was taken away in case it had a built-in mike, and the two men went into the room.

Grok waited a few moments for the amenities to be exchanged and any further sweeps made.

Then he put power on to the window films King had installed, just enough to activate them as a pair of large, high-resolution vibration-sensitive microphones. The microphones fed into a transmitter hidden in the frame of that portrait of Tournelle's first patron. The bug that King had 'found' in the wall behind it had, of course, been a quite successful mask that Jasmine had planted earlier.

Then Grok turned on the recorder, and started making notes of what was going on in the nearby room.

REYNARD: And so, my friend, to work. This may be thirsty business. There's an excellent forty-five Hico, already opened and breathing on the sideboard, if you'd care to try it. Or there's vintage cognac, which I prefer. If you wish something else, I'll send for a barman.

FARAON: I do not consider you a friend, Mr. Reynard. And I'll not drink until whatever mysterious business is complete, not wanting fuddled wits.

REYNARD: Your option.

Sound of the clink of a glass against a bottle, the splash of cognac, and then the rustle of papers.

REYNARD: My business is simple. I want to give you, without strings, a transcript of the letters between Hyla Adrianopole and Premier Ladier. These are the ones Adrianopole shot Editor Fall for. I understand she's claiming innocence, and the right for a woman to defend her reputation. These transcripts say her motives might well be otherwise.

FARAON: How were they obtained?

REYNARD: I have not inquired into that, nor should you. You'll note these letters have yet to be introduced in the trial of Miss Adrianopole. I think you will see the reasons as you read. The letters contain confessional material from Premier Ladier that I think you – and all Dampier – should know about what I am afraid comes perilously close to treason.

FARAON: I think, as usual, Reynard, you are making grandiose statements that the truth seldom bears out.

REYNARD (*clearly enjoying himself*): Read for yourself. And I assume that if you still doubt the veracity of these transcripts you can manage to get a copy of what the court is holding that I personally doubt will ever appear in open court.

Now the rustle of paper, and a very long silence, broken twice by Faraon's inaudible mutter, then a whispered 'Dear God.'

REYNARD: Interesting, aren't they?

FARAON (*in a broken voice*): I know . . . Ladier has said privately that he wants . . . wants to keep all channels of communication open with Torguth, to ensure peace. But . . .

Another long silence.

FARAON: I'll have a glass of the cognac, if you please.

REYNARD: Of course.

The clink of glasses and a bottle.

FARAON: Assuming this information is genuine . . . I hardly know what to say.

REYNARD: You don't need to say anything. I have faith enough in your probity that I know you . . . and the other uncorrupted members of your party . . . will do the right thing.

FARAON (*weakly*): If these letters are genuine . . .

REYNARD: They are. You may apply whatever tests you want, and seek whatever verification you need.

FARAON: What is your price for this?

REYNARD: The price is very expensive. You may have the papers for free, since I want my beloved Dampier, and those citizens of the Belfort Worlds, to live in peace, and I want a government, whether it is mine, yours or someone else's, that is aware of the constant threat Torguth poses; a government that will stand firm, bold, and confident against them, and take whatever measures may prove necessary to maintain not just the peace, but the current relationship we have with Torguth.

FARAON: Yes . . . yes. I must think about this . . . consult my colleagues. If you'll forgive me . . . I really must leave.

REYNARD: Take good care. My friend.

Again the rustling of papers, and the door opening and closing. Then Reynard's low chuckle as he pours himself another drink.

REYNARD: Not bad. Not bad at all.

It took two weeks, and then an emergency plenary session of Parliament was called by the Honorable Faraon. All five members of Star Risk attended, even though Goodnight grumbled about how badly politics bored him.

Premier Ladier, a chubby, normally cheery man, now looking sadly perplexed, opened the session, and Faraon asked for the floor.

His speech was very succinct, as aides went down the aisles, giving copies of the transcript to all members, not only the Universalists.

'If the honorable members will take a moment to peruse the documents I've had handed out,' Faraon said, 'you shall see the reason I now call, even though my own party heads the current government, for a vote of "no confidence."'

Ladier sputtered.

'And I further call for elections to be set as quickly as

possible, so the ship of state will not continue its rud-
derless course onto the rocks.'

The vote, held about an hour later, was 358–16, the
sixteen being either diehards or slow readers, Riss
thought.

Ladier looked as if he'd been sandbagged.

There was a riotous party at Tournelle's that night, with
very, very tight security provided by Star Risk operatives.

Star Risk held a private party in an upstairs dining
room, while the Independents rioted happily in the
public rooms below. Reynard joined them for a few
minutes.

'I do love it,' Reynard chortled. 'Ladier's famous for
backstabbing . . . that's how he took out Faraon three
years ago. Now it's become his turn. It's a new dawn for
me . . . for us.'

'So what comes next?' Grok asked.

'The Universalists will no doubt caucus,' Reynard
said, 'and Premier Ladier will have his wilderness years
begin. The election for party head will go, without any
doubt, to Faraon. I can beat him like a drum.

'So in the general election, my Independents will be
returned to power. The other, minor parties owe me full
well.

'This means Maen Sufyerd will be returned to
Montrois, and I will force a measure through
Parliament giving him a civilian retrial. Within a year,
he'll be a free man.

'You've done wondrous well, ladies and gentlemen of
Star Risk. May I toast your abilities.'

Von Baldur got to his feet. 'You might wish to hold

that toast for a minute. I have a question. You said Sufyerd could be free in a year. The election is three months distant.

'What is to prevent Ladier – and the certain person we are seeking, the Torguth high-level agent who remains on the loose – from arranging for Sufyerd's immediate execution?'

Reynard's face fell. 'Nothing,' he said softly. 'Except public opprobrium.'

'And that won't mean a damned thing to a corpse,' Goodnight said.

'Nor to his family,' Riss added.

'No,' Reynard agreed, his joy a bit vanished.

'Jasmine, did you arrange for certain supplies, as I requested this afternoon?'

'I did,' King said. 'They were immediately available, and are on the way. They should arrive in a day, two at the most.'

The Star Risk operatives looked at each other.

'Fine,' Riss said, 'let's go get Maen.'

FORTY-THREE

An excerpt from a holo, distributed by the Torguth Ministry of Truth:

VIDEO: A long shot of a formation of warships passing close by an orbital station.
Fade through to:
Close, a stern-looking man in a bemedaled uniform, sitting in an office. There are official-looking books, two flag stands, holo cases, and starship models on the shelves behind him.

AUDIO OVER: We welcome Fleet Admiral Garad.
GARAD: It is my pleasure to be able to show the men and women of Torguth some of their Imperial Navy's might, and prove that Torguth has nothing to fear from its enemies, or potential enemies.

Your Navy stands firm on the frontiers, not only protecting the Torguth Worlds, but our immigrants to other systems, such as the Belfort Worlds, who have been woefully discriminated against by the illegitimate Dampierian occupiers.

Mobs of degenerate Dampierians have continually attacked our immigrants, and the Dampierian authorities refuse to take action.

Be warned, Dampier!

In the event of continued foreign persecution of these immigrants, we of the Navy shall be the first to fight, to defend our women and children. No matter what has happened in the past, the future is ours.

Some of our secret weapons I cannot show you, for fear of informing the enemy of our strengths. But you will see enough to make your hearts pound more heartily, and for you to lose any fears you might have of the past's repetition.

First we shall examine our fleet escorts, those small but strong-thewed craft that patrol our frontiers, and would be the first to encounter any surprise attacks . . .

FORTY-FOUR

Two days before the rescue attempt of Sufyerd was to be mounted, Fra Diavolo and a rather severe-faced woman arrived at the mansion.

M'chel greeted them, and Diavolo told her that she was unquestionably the most beautiful thing around and he'd love to dally with her, but he, or rather his companion, had business with von Baldur.

'You owe me money,' the woman said without preamble when Friedrich entered the operations room.

'I do?' von Baldur said, having no idea who the woman was, then it suddenly came back to him.

She was the second agent on Torguth whom he'd contacted, asking for the Torguth maneuver specifics in the scheduled war games off Belfort.

'Oh yes.'

'I was in the Café of Dawn Delights as scheduled,' she said. 'You were not. I had . . . and have . . . the information you wanted.'

'I unfortunately became entangled in difficulties, and had to precipitately leave the planet. But I agree, I owe you money,' von Baldur said, still not sure what he was going to do with the details on the war games.

'My friend here,' Diavolo explained, 'had an application in to visit to the Alliance Worlds her parents came from that was finally approved, for some unknown reason.'

'Hardly unknown,' the woman sniffed. 'After some unknown Dampierian agent murdered someone, and eluded the hue and cry, things became somewhat warm in the bureau I worked in. I think I might have fallen under suspicion, since I was the only one in it who wasn't fourth or more generation Torguth.

'So someone in Torguth Counter Intelligence decided to give me some running room to see where I'd go. Naturally, I was to be closely followed, and if it turned out I was working for someone other than the Mother Worlds, action would be taken.

'I broke contact with my ever-so-clever followers, jumped passage three times before I . . . but you aren't concerned with that,' the woman broke off. She took out a small fiche.

'I plan to settle here on Montrois, which I understand is expensive. I also plan to be utterly invisible, which I know is also expensive.'

Von Baldur took the fiche. 'You shall find me more than generous.'

'And you will find me more than grateful.'

FORTY-FIVE

The guards at Fortress Pignole had gotten so used to Jasmine's visits to Maen Sufyerd they no longer made her use the secure visitor's room, since she always had reams of paper to pass across for Sufyerd to sign, although they still thoroughly searched her person and possessions.

Sufyerd, being the meticulous sort he was, insisted on reading each and every document, and frequently complained to King that they were meaningless, as far as he could tell.

They were just that, intended merely to give King physical access to Sufyerd, but when Sufyerd would protest, Jasmine put on an icy demeanor, and implied he was collaborating in his own death.

This time, King had only one sheaf of forms, these clearly pertinent, since they authorized Star Risk to try to locate his vanished wife and children and help in their support. Two visits earlier, King had managed to kite a note to Sufyerd saying that his family was safe, and for him not to worry.

These new forms he signed cheerfully. King reached for them, and accidentally scratched him with a sharp-edged cufflink on her blouse, enough to draw a speck of blood. Sufyerd winced, and King apologized profusely.

'You know,' he told her, as she was packing her briefcase, 'sometimes I almost think I'm going to live through this . . . maybe even have another trial that'll prove my innocence.'

'Of course,' King said. 'Isn't that what we've been telling you all along?'

'I just wish the law . . .' Sufyerd's voice trailed off.

'You wish the law what?'

'I'm being absurd,' he said. 'I wish the law wasn't so damned . . . I'm sorry for the language . . . arbitrary.'

'Better,' King said, 'the arbitrariness of law than of the whims of people.'

Sufyerd managed a smile. 'You're right. I didn't mean to sound like I was losing faith.'

As soon as she reached the patrol ship and reported to the other four Star Risk heads aboard, she cycled those contaminated cufflinks she'd been wearing into space.

The patrol ship, obviously not heading back to Montrois, jumped into N-space, unobtrusively leaving a tiny link satellite.

Six hours later, the fortress contacted Montrois with an emergency. Prisoner Maen Sufyerd had fallen ill. Terribly ill, and neither of the station doctors could diagnose his sickness other than high fever, nausea, and intermittent vomiting.

The station's code, bounced into N-space by the planted satellite, was decoded and read by Star Risk.

'I should damned well hope they cannot identify it,' von Baldur said. 'Denebian rabbits do not even show up in zoos on this side of the universe, let alone their expensive damned venom.'

'Time for us to suit up,' Riss said. 'And then wait some more.'

Montrois replied. They were sending a medical ship up to the station, to bring Sufyerd back to the planet for specialist treatment.

'Of course,' Goodnight said bitterly, 'the sons of bitches would never dream of letting somebody in a death cell just die a natural death. Shit!'

'The word,' Grok said calmly, 'is hypocrisy, and everyone, even my own people, practice it most lovingly.'

Star Risk's tiny snitch reported when the med ship, clearly marked, arrived an hour later, and linked to the orbital satellite.

The ship, Sufyerd aboard, disconnected from the fortress's lock and set an orbit back for Montrois.

'Now?' the pilot of Star Risk's patrol ship asked.

'Wait a bit,' von Baldur ordered. 'Let us make sure we shall not need our backup.'

'I think maybe you're being too paranoiac,' Goodnight said. 'Not to mention maybe spending too much of Reynard's credits that we could have stolen and spent on necessities like liquor and sex.'

Von Baldur didn't bother answering, but made a fast commo check to another station.

The medical ship was bare minutes out from the fortress when another starship dropped out of hyperspace.

'Medship Y423, Medship Y423,' it 'cast on the standard emergency frequency. 'Stand by to be boarded.'

There was a gabble of protest from the medical ship. The other ship repeated its message, adding, 'Go into a stationary orbit or be blasted.'

The medship bleated to the fortress-prison, and the prison broadcast alarms to Montrois and empty threats to the other starship.

'Looks to be, from *Jane's*,' one of Star Risk's pilots reported, 'a pretty standard close convoy escort. If it's armed –'

'It is,' von Baldur said with certainty.

'Well then, it's a little heavy-duty for us to take on.'

Von Baldur smiled, a trace smugly, and reached for a mike on another, preset hyperspace frequency. 'Friedrich One, Two, this is Friedrich Control. Come on in.'

'Friedrich One,' a voice came back. 'Breaking out.'

Riss and the others knew the voice – it was the mercenary pilot Redon Spada, sometimes rated the hottest starship operator available on the open market. Star Risk had used his talents before, and Goodnight thought it most funny that Spada seemed to have a perpetual, almost adolescent infatuation with M'chel Riss. So far, Riss hadn't en- or dis-couraged him.

Very suddenly the space just off Montrois got a little crowded, as two destroyers came out of N-space. They were a shade on the obsolescent side, but far better armed than the escort ship.

Von Baldur ordered his pilot to do the same.

'Friedrich Control, I assume you want us to booger the gunship,' Spada cast.

'This is Control,' von Baldur said. 'You assume right.'

'Stupid bastard doesn't even see us,' Spada 'cast.

'Target acquired. Two, launch on my command. Four . . . three . . . two . . . *fire*!'

Two heavy missiles spat from each destroyer and intersected in the space occupied by the escort ship. In concentric balls of flame, fiery bubble theory, that ship ceased to exist. The orbital prison yammered even more loudly.

'I love a good double drygulching,' Goodnight said dreamily.

'This is One,' Spada 'cast. 'What next?'

'Go on home and cash the paychecks,' von Baldur said into the mike.

'This is Two. Easiest pile of credits I ever made.'

'This is Control. Now you see why everyone likes working for us,' von Baldur said.

'This is One. Kiss M'chel for me, and we'll catch you on the uptick.'

The two destroyers vanished, back to whatever base they'd come from before von Baldur chartered them.

'Now can we go get Maen?' Riss said.

'Certainly.'

The crew of the medic ship sputtered as armed people in suits with darkened faceplates stormed through the lock, but none of them made any effort to resist, including the two guards who accompanied the unconscious Maen.

Grok, being too easily recognized, had been left aboard ship.

Goodnight wanted to crack wise before Star Risk left the medship, but knew better than to chance later voice recognition.

They hurried Sufyerd, on his stretcher, through the

lock into the patrol ship, disconnected from the med-ship and, seconds later, went into hyperspace, even as Riss was administering the antidote for the poison.

'You know, technically, we could deliver Sufyerd, as soon as he comes to, on Reynard's doorstep, collect our money and just go home,' Goodnight observed.

'And of course, you think he would cheerfully authorize the bonus check from the escrow account,' von Baldur said.

'Um,' Goodnight said. 'Probably not.'

'Certainly not,' Grok corrected. 'We might as well resign ourselves to proving Maen innocent before we see all those credits. Besides, we still haven't found the real Torguth agent, and that is still piquing my curiosity.'

'Speaking of morality,' Riss said, 'which I wasn't, how much would you like to bet that young Sufyerd here, as soon as he comes to, starts bitching at me for not letting justice take its course, and that now his rep-utation is forever clouded. Even odds? Six to five? Two to one? Ten to one,' Riss tried in desperation.

Even at that, nobody was willing to bet against her.

Two hours later, Sufyerd, fully recovered, indignantly confronted von Baldur about now being a fugitive, and that he would never be able to hold his head up in front of his fellow officers.

'Aw, shaddup,' Goodnight said rudely. 'At least you're going to *have* a frigging head.'

That quieted Sufyerd. But only for an hour or two. He didn't stop sulking until the patrol ship had landed at one of Montrois's more secluded airfields, one of Fra Diavolo's pilots had picked him up and taken him to a certain location even Star Risk didn't know about, and reunited him with Cahamla and his children.

FORTY-SIX

Riss idly stirred the bowl of unset precious stones called theones that Goodnight had, somewhat grumpily, given to 'the cause.' He didn't bother to explain that the 'King of Thieves' had given him a bum steer when it came to recommending a fence. The address turned out to be a vacant lot, and Guayacurus had disappeared from his usual haunts.

Goodnight, knowing how closely they were watched, couldn't figure out another, absolutely safe way to get rid of the gems, and so decided to go for the good will.

As she stirred, Riss considered the screamer headlines floating in front of her.

The headline read: TRAITOR ESCAPES. The deck continued: TORGUTH FREES DEATH ROW AGENT.

The com buzzed, and since Riss was watch officer, she fielded it. 'Star Risk,' she said cheerily.

L'Pellerin of the DIB filled the screen. His face was cold, hard. 'I wish to speak to von Baldur,' he said.

'A moment, sir,' Riss said, muted the call, and buzzed von Baldur, who was investigating the kitchen for the possibilities of a feast.

'Freddie, it's the secret cop.'

Von Baldur took the call.

'I assume,' L'Pellerin said without preamble, 'that you have an alibi for yesterday.'

'I beg your pardon?'

'You were nowhere near the orbital fortress Maen Sufyerd was confined in, correct?'

'Good god, man,' von Baldur said in utter astonishment, 'of course I was not. Nor were any of my people, after Miss King's visit earlier in the day.'

'Of course you weren't,' L'Pellerin said. 'You, and the rest of your hierarchy, are directed to turn yourselves in to my Dampier Information Bureau's Central Headquarters, for questioning. Bring your passports, for if no charges are pressed – which I doubt – you and your entire crew will be subject to immediate deportation.'

The five Star Risk heads were met at DIB headquarters by armed guards and ushered through a side entrance into a medium-sized chamber, bare, with stained walls, a single bench along one wall.

There was a high desk, and behind it were two DIB plainclothesmen. Two others, equally goonish, stood on either side of the desk.

'You will surrender your papers,' one said. The five obeyed.

'You are being held for questioning in the disappearance of Legate Maen Sufyerd, a condemned prisoner of this system. Due to you all being offworlders, bail will be denied to you, even after appropriate charges have been filed. I advise all of you to offer full cooperation, to avoid possibly uncomfortable circumstances.'

'What rights do we have?' Goodnight asked.

'Those,' one of the plainclothesmen on the floor said, 'we choose to give you.' He looked at both King and Riss, and smiled a very unpleasant smile.

'Frigging goons are the same all over,' Goodnight said, and his grin was no less dangerous.

'Chas,' von Baldur said mildly, 'there is no need to be hostile. I am sure there is a simple explanation to our problem.'

'There is,' one of the goons agreed. 'Full cooperation.'

'Even when we know nothing?'

'I was told you were unlikely to be cooperative.'

Goodnight looked at Grok, nodded slightly. Both imperceptibly braced for a response. One of the plainclothesmen looked nervously at the towering Grok, reached inside his jacket.

Goodnight was about to put pressure on his right jaw and go bester, when the door they'd just entered came open, and a tall, balding, red-faced man entered. Behind him were ten uniformed policemen, all in riot gear, all with heavy blasters at port arms.

'Good afternoon,' the man said. 'I am Deputy Guy Glenn, of Parliament's Upper Chamber. I am also a lawyer, licensed to practice in front of all Montrois courts, from military to Supreme.'

'I know who you are,' one of the men behind the desk grudged. 'A damned Independent and one of Reynard's toadies.'

'Excellent,' Glenn said, unbothered by the insult. 'Then there shall be no problem in your accepting this document, which frees these five beings, nor this one, which, filed in the Tuletian Supreme Court, also restrains you, or any other member of DIB, or any other justice official, from putting these beings into custody again, or in any way restraining their right to practice their chosen profession.'

There was utter silence in the room.

'You can't do this!' one plainclothesman said, his hand continuing toward his gun.

'Ah, but I just did,' Glenn said. 'Further . . .' and he snapped his fingers. The blast rifles came down from port arms, were aimed at the DIB officers. The sound of their blaster safeties clicking off was very loud.

The Star Risk operatives sidled left, out of the line of fire.

'I . . . I must summon L'Pellerin,' one DIB managed.

'Please do,' Glenn said, in a voice as smooth as his smile. 'That will ensure proper understanding of the situation at the highest level, to prevent a repetition of this parody of justice.'

L'Pellerin read the two documents Glenn had brought, twice. He looked up.

Von Baldur slightly admired him, for the only sign of his rage was a slight twitch to the right side of his mouth.

'This is totally illegal.'

'But it is not,' Glenn said. 'Or are you accusing our Supreme Court of criminal practices?'

'In front of witnesses?' L'Pellerin said. 'I'm not a fool.'

'Then we shall be on our way,' Glenn said, turning to the Star Risk operatives. 'If you would accompany me?' The five obeyed.

L'Pellerin waited until they were at the door. 'Tell Reynard he will bitterly regret what he did this day.'

Glenn smiled, nodded his head, and the sixteen left.

Outside, Riss nodded to Glenn. 'Thanks. I really wasn't looking forward to a good rubber-hosing.'

'Or worse,' King said grimly.

'Or worse,' M'chel agreed. 'Freddie, I was wondering who you called before we left the mansion.

'Mr. Glenn, I owe you.'

'No,' Glenn said. 'My brother happened to be a bit of an anarchist, and the DIB picked him up and worked him over very thoroughly. He still walks with a limp, and his mind wanders.

'No,' he said again. 'All this was my pleasure. Now, if I could only live to see L'Pellerin rotting in chains; and this building, and the goons it houses, destroyed; and the land, perhaps, sown with salt.' He caught himself, and became the smooth politician once more.

'If you would hold on for a moment, Chas,' von Baldur said, making sure the operations room door was secure, 'I think it is time for a caucus of our own.'

'I always like to get a little drunk every time somebody springs me from jail,' Goodnight said. 'Especially when it's a secret policeman's jail.' But, obediently, he replaced the decanter on the sideboard.

'I would like everyone's tentative opinions as to who you think the real traitor might be,' von Baldur said. 'Chas?'

'I still don't know where that damned Caranis gets his money from,' Goodnight said. 'Otherwise, just out of general pissoff, I'd vote for that goddamned L'Pellerin, not being a fan of dungeons and such.

'It would've been easy for Ceranis to know about the Belfort defense plans, and to pay that idiot mailboy to swipe them for him. I go for Caranis.'

'But what about Kismayu's murder?' King asked. 'We've agreed he probably isn't the sort to play assassin.'

Goodnight made a face.

'Jasmine's right,' Riss said. 'We know there's at least some DIB men in the Masked Ones . . . or maybe the other way around. And those idiots wouldn't mind a little wet work, even if poison's a little neater than their crowd-control methods.

'I see a hole in our work,' Riss said. 'We don't really know squat about the Masked Ones. Maybe I should do a little investigating on those idiots.'

'Let me remind all of you,' von Baldur went on, 'that starship that tried to hijack Sufyerd obviously knew of his sickness and that he was to be taken groundside, which means someone else who was privy to the basic military code at the very least. This person . . . or group . . . also knew enough about the medical ship to use its call letters.'

'Caranis, maybe,' King said. 'L'Pellerin could also be the one. Or some other high-ranker that we haven't uncovered yet.'

'Good,' von Baldur approved. 'Thank you for keeping the options open. Let me add another spice to our stew that you might have forgotten. L'Pellerin told me at that dinner we had that, once Sufyerd was convicted, all his operatives were removed from the operation.

'Yet there were operators, many of them, dogging both the late Elder Bracken's Jilanis church and the Sufyerd family. When M'chel attempted to extract them, the military was instantly involved in an attempt to stop her, and either recover or kill Sufyerd's family.

'Possibly Caranis could still be our villain, although

I question whether he has the necessary clout to keep that many soldiers on standby.

'Even more to the point, could Caranis, after the operation's failure, be able to completely suppress any reports of what happened, including the names of the casualties, of which there were more than a few?'

'L'Pellerin definitely could do that,' Grok said. 'Or someone very, very high-ranking. I don't think ex-Premier Ladier is our traitor, even though he is proven to be close to the Torguth. Very seldom does a success-ful politician get that close to the action.'

'Yet another interesting piece of information,' von Baldur said. 'This from Ladier's letters. When he won-dered about Sufyerd's guilt, who reassured him but Mr. L'Pellerin. That I find quite interesting by itself. Either the head of DIB is a cocky fool or . . . or something else.'

'I'll vote for L'Pellerin,' Riss said. 'It's real easy for me to get pissed at some asshole who wants to pull my fingernails out.'

'I have a question,' King said. 'Assuming, for the sake of argument, that L'Pellerin is the traitor, why? He's got as much, probably more power, than anybody else in the Dampier Systems, scandals in his files that are enough to keep from getting thrown out, and is behind the scenes enough to be almost assassination-free. Why is he risking everything?'

'There's a story I read once, about a guy who was the head secret cop for some dictator,' Riss said. 'All he wanted was to be made . . . I don't remember what . . . a star marshal or a nobleman or something that would give him a public triumph. The dictator turned him down, shocked as all hell, saying that secret policemen never get made noblemen or have parades in their honor.

'According to the story, that crushed this guy, so much so that he tried to betray his boss the first chance he got. Maybe something like that happened to L'Pellerin.'

King considered. 'Or maybe,' she said finally, 'it's something as simple as people who want power never, ever can get enough. But what could Torguth be offering him?'

Riss shook her head. 'I dunno.'

'Let's continue with our straw vote. I, too, pick L'Pellerin,' von Baldur said. 'Although we should not forget Caranis. Chas, would you devote considerable energies to investigating him?'

'Cheerfully,' Goodnight said. '*Now*, can I have a drink?'

'You may,' von Baldur said.

'The problem,' King said, 'assuming our theorizing is correct, and L'Pellerin is the traitor, is that we will now be proving that the head of the secret police is a double agent. And, by the way, I'm going to reserve my vote for the moment.'

'It shall be a task,' von Baldur admitted. 'Mr. Goodnight, would you pour me a dram? Perhaps alcohol will lubricate my few remaining brain cells.'

FORTY-SEVEN

'Things are going quite well indeed,' Fra Diavolo said. 'First – and I'm sorry, M'chel, to sound unsentimental about poor Sufyerd's continuing problem – is that we have toppled Ladier and the Universalists. Or, more correctly, Ladier committed political suicide. The only people who should save their letters are the innocent. If there is any such animal.

'Then we have a Torguth traitor within IIa exposed and murdered by his own people.

'And, in your eyes most importantly, Maen Sufyerd is freed and with his family. When circumstances are right, we shall arrange for another trial, an honest one this time.

'The only thing I find displeasing are the Torguth mobs on the Belfort Worlds, obviously trying to stir things up, and Torguth itself, which also seems to be flexing its muscles toward a fourth confrontation with Dampier. But there appears little I can do about that at the moment.

'I am having a perfectly lovely time with my pamphleteering, hoping to guarantee that the Universalists don't stand a chance of being returned to office, although, to be honest, I'm not that convinced that Reynard and his Independents are much better — although, at least, they don't appear to be in bed with Torguth.'

'Star Risk may not have been directly responsible for all this, but you surely have acted as a catalyst.'

'I thank you, sir,' Riss said, lifting her wineglass. She still didn't entirely trust Diavolo, but had at least downgraded him from roué to old, gentlemanly roué. 'You . . . and your people . . . have been of great help.'

'And I would suspect,' Diavolo said, smiling slightly, 'that you've come out to my estate for more than a dinner.'

'Correct.'

'Let me ask what you need, before we start contemplating the meal. Tonight we are having a seafood salad, sweetbreads, and a torte, with cheeses and the appropriate wines. I would rather not be worrying about whether I'm going to be able to provide what you need, and think about my digestive system.'

'I need a former Masked One,' Riss said. 'One who'll talk . . . or one I can make talk. By preference, someone who's blown out of the organization in a decent state of pissoff.'

'Oh my,' Diavolo said mournfully. 'You don't ask for the easy things, do you?'

'If I wanted something easy,' Riss said, 'I wouldn't need to come to you.'

'Flatterer.'

Chas Goodnight eased into the mansion, looking most pleased with himself.

'Did you finally find someone who'll listen to your wily ways?' Jasmine King asked.

'Nope,' Goodnight said. 'I've been doing good deeds.'

'Such as?'

'Visiting our next-door neighbor, who's a wonderful little old lady. I spent the afternoon listening to her talk about the old days, when there weren't all these horrid politicians and good homemade bread was a tenth of a credit a loaf.

'Naturally, I didn't believe her for a minute. She never bought a loaf of bread in her life, but sent the servants round.'

'But you stayed with her,' Grok said, peering around a corner. 'Because you found out she doesn't have a will.'

'You've been around too many cynics too long,' Goodnight said. 'Actually, I was apologizing to her for the loud bangs we've had go off around here, even though they're hardly our fault.

'She didn't mind them at all. Said it made life a little more interesting, which is all you can ask for when you're her age.'

'That was the only reason you went to talk to her?' King asked suspiciously.

'Of course,' Goodnight said carelessly. 'There might have been two or three other items we touched on, but hardly anything of importance.'

Grok and King exchanged utterly unbelieving looks.

It took almost two weeks to find an appropriate Masked One, which didn't surprise Riss. Someone who'd left or been thrown out of the Masked Ones would most likely be lying very low, afraid of retribution not only from the citizenry, but from his former fellows.

The one Diavolo's scurrying minions located ran a small store on one of Montrois's islands, and reluctantly agreed to talk to the person Diavolo sent. Riss took Grok along for backup.

The weather was cold, misty, and the buildings on the island were gray, forbidding, and wet.

The storekeeper was small, but wiry-muscled. He said his name was Givoi, and turned a CLOSED sign on the deserted store's entrance. Then he ushered them into a back room, frequently giving Grok's immensity a frightened look.

M'chel didn't know what had convinced the man to talk to her, but from his behavior, suspected it was blackmail rather than a bribe or a desire to unburden his conscience. Riss hadn't seen many people in the Dampier System who seemed overly troubled by conscience.

'I really won't be able to tell you much,' Givoi said. 'I was just a lowly member . . . what they called a believer.'

'Sit down,' M'chel said, in a friendly voice, indicating one of the two chairs in the room. Givoi obeyed.

'Why did you become a member of the Masked Ones?' Grok asked, truly curious.

Givoi was silent for a time, then reluctantly said, 'I've always been a patriot, believing in my system, but that men are weak, and should be ruled by a stronger man.'

'Who, for the Masked Ones, would be . . . ?' Riss asked.

He shook his head. 'I wasn't told that sort of thing. None of us on my level were. Orders came from the Council, and we never saw any of them or heard from them directly, either. Orders came to our cell leaders.'

'Could the Council have been one man . . . or woman?'

'No,' Givoi said. He stopped himself, thought. 'Well, I can't say for certain, but I can't believe that.'

'But you don't know,' Riss said. 'So you joined the Masked Ones just out of your ideals?'

She stared straight into Givoi's eyes. He started to answer, then stopped.

'No,' he said, looking down. 'Or, rather, that was just one of my reasons.'

Riss waited.

'When you're a nobody . . . like I was . . . I guess, like I am, you want to have some kind of power. I wasn't anything but a clerk in a big grocery, and so, when a friend of mine started talking about the Masked Ones, well, that was something that called out to me.

'To have a secret, to know that you, and your friends, can be out there, on the streets, actually trying to change things, trying to make a better society . . . that was like nothing else I'd felt.'

'You weren't married, or with a partner?' Grok asked.

Givoi shook his head. 'I've never had the time for women.'

'Tell me about the structure of the Masked Ones.'

Givoi needed frequent prodding, but talked. The Masked Ones were organized into operating cells. Some of these cells had a common headquarters, but the members of one cell wouldn't know someone from another cell except by face.

'They said it was good for our morale to get together, just before an operation, so we wouldn't feel alone. They were right.'

Members would get instructions about the next operation at these meetings, or directly by com in the event of a sudden crisis. They would be told what to do, and the extent of violence they were permitted.

'After a year,' Givoi said proudly, 'they trusted me with a gun. Although,' and his voice showed disappointment, 'I was never ordered to use it. But I carried it on half a dozen of our operations, in the event of an emergency.'

'You always backed the Universalists,' Riss said.

'Almost always.'

'You said you were patriotic. But why would you support the Universalists, since Premier Ladier always talked about peace, and now he's been proven to be in league with Torguth.'

'That's a lie! The media made all that up!'

'Calm down,' M'chel said. 'What goals did you Masked Ones have? You couldn't think that your whole lives would be spent beating people up.'

'Of course not,' Givoi said. 'Eventually, we were told, we'd have a chance to reach real power. We weren't told exactly how that'd happen. I thought maybe we'd bore from within, take over the Universalists, and then seize the government. But . . .'

'But what?' Riss asked.

'It just seemed to go on, always the same, for the five years I was a member. I got arrested twice, and that cost me my job, and I lived on the dole, plus what my cell leader would give me to help with my expenses.

'Then an aunt of mine died, and left me this store, and an apartment down the street, and I thought maybe it was time for me to leave Tuletia anyway. Really, I can't tell you what you seem to be looking for.'

'What about the names of your cell leader, anybody else who might know more than you do?' Riss asked.

'I couldn't betray them! That'd be . . .' Givoi broke off, staring at Grok. 'What are you doing?'

The alien had taken a kit from his pouch, and took out a airspray syringe, an ampoule, a rubber tie-off, and a sterile towel in a package. He spread the towel out and clicked the ampoule into the syringe.

'This,' Grok said, 'is something that'll help you talk to us.'

'No,' Givoi said, shaking his head from side to side. 'No. I can't stand injections.'

'You aren't going to be consulted.'

'You can't make me take truth serum!'

'Actually,' Riss said, feeling a little unclean, 'this isn't truth serum. I'm not sure there is anything like that. You might call this babble juice. You'll just talk about the closest secrets you've got. If one of them happens to be that you used to sleep with your mother . . . well, that'll come out. Then I'll be prodding you to talk about certain things. Eventually, we'll find out what we need to know.'

'You don't happen to have a weak heart, do you?' Grok asked. 'Or a tendency to nervousness that might lead to a breakdown?'

Givoi looked about wildly for an exit, but there was none.

'Now,' Riss said, in her most soothing voice, 'if you'll just roll up your sleeve . . .'

'No! No! I can't!' Givoi's voice was rising in pitch. 'I remember someone. Someone big. Someone important.'

'Ah?'

'His name is Juda Abiezer, and he started as a believer, just like me. But he was good, always ready for a brawl, and he was made a cell leader, and then an overleader.'

'How do you know all this?' Riss asked. 'I thought you didn't know anything about your leaders.'

'I don't . . . I didn't,' Givoi said. 'But Abiezer was always ready to talk to us believers, and even buy us a glass of wine every now and then, and never behaved like he was better than us. He was a real leader, some-body who was in the trenches, but you always knew he was in charge, and we'd follow him anywhere.

'He was . . . is . . . the bravest of us all. A big man with a scarred face that some damned anarchist gave him. But it never slowed him down. He's big. He knows the leaders. He could help you with what you want to know, things I don't.'

'Why are you willing to betray him to us?'

'Because . . . because he's just barely a Masked One now. He got as tired as some of the rest of us of just beating up people carrying signs, or firebombing some store for some reason we never got told about, and wanted us to start moving on Parliament, to start either getting deputies on our side, or else neutralizing them.

'The Council, I heard, reprimanded him two or three times, but he wouldn't shut up. I think they were afraid of him. And so one day he vanished. We were told that he was sent on a special mission, to where his talents would be turned loose.

'He was sent to the Belfort System, to break up the damned Torguth supporters, traitors and secret agents. He now heads a more or less aboveground organization he's calling the Patriot League. I've seen things on the holos about the Patriot League, and seen him. That's where he is now.'

FORTY-EIGHT

'I assume,' Grok said, 'that we should be considering a visit to the Belfort Worlds, to interview this Abiezer.'

'I don't think we'll get much from interplanetary com,' Riss said. 'Not to mention I'd bet that anything going to the Belfort Worlds has an automatic bug on it, setting off alarms when it comes to hearing things like "Masked Ones," "Torguth," "Council," and things like that.'

'I, for one,' Friedrich said, 'would welcome a chance to visit the Belfort Worlds, especially since nothing in particular appears to be happening here on Montrois.'

'I, also,' King said. 'It would give us a chance to determine whose propaganda is the most dishonest – Torguth saying its poor immigrants are being massacred, or Dampier's saying the other way around.'

'So we're going to jaunt on out to the Belfort Worlds, find thisyere Juda Abiezer, who'll be more than willing to sing about the Masked Ones, when M'chel blinks her beautiful greens at him,' Chas Goodnight said. 'Right.'

'It does sound a bit unlikely,' Jasmine King said.

'So let us consider the options,' Grok said. 'We can kidnap and beat what we want out of him.'

'The beating is not a problem,' von Baldur said 'The kidnapping of someone running a paramilitary order sticks in my craw a bit. It might prove a little difficult.'

'Or, dare I say the words, frigging impossible?' Goodnight said.

'We could go to him, and ask him to help us.'

'Even more damned unlikely,' Goodnight said. 'First, he's some sort of muckety with the Masked Ones. Assuming L'Pellerin is their head, and assuming that he's the double agent who's trying to sell Dampier – or the Belfort Worlds, at the very least – down the river, that won't sit well, by which I mean believably, with Abiezer. Dreams tend to die hard, particularly for a fanatic.'

'Friendly persuasion doesn't sound like it would work,' von Baldur agreed.

Riss had been listening, shaking her head sadly. 'And I thought I worked with a pack of scoundrels,' she said. 'You four ought to start teaching church school.'

'Obviously, you have an idea,' von Baldur said.

'Obviously, I do,' Riss said. 'I remember reading an old book once, talking about the problems early medicine had, and one of the worst was treating a patient with what they were sick with in the first place. For instance, if you banged your head up, and had internal bleeding, they'd bleed you more. Or they might give you a vaccine that, in theory, was a minor version of whatever disease was killing you.'

'Quite barbaric,' Grok agreed.

'That's me,' Riss said. 'A true barbarian. Jasmine, how fast do you think a couple of cargo containers could be schlepped here from your friend Asamya?'

'Depends on what you need,' Jasmine said. 'If it's

nothing out of the ordinary, and we pay for a rush, maybe an E-week, on the outside.'

M'chel explained her plan. King looked at her in a bit of shock, Grok nodding in agreement and von Baldur stroking his chin, thinking.

'I shall be damned,' Goodnight said. 'I didn't think you were capable of that kind of scumbucketry.'

'Hey,' Riss said. 'When you go to do a job, you do a job.'

FORTY-NINE

'Has the jury reached a verdict?'

'We have, Your Grace.'

'Hyla Adrianopole, please stand.'

'How do you find the defendant, Hyla Adrianopole, of the first charge, of premeditated murder?'

'Not guilty, Your Grace.'

The other not-guilties weren't heard as the court-room went into pandemonium.

'I don't like this at all,' Reynard grumbled.

'Why not?' von Baldur asked. 'I did not think you cared much about this Adrianopole one way or another.'

'I don't,' Reynard said. 'But now, with her free, the *Pacifist* won't be running the letters between her and Ladier, which I was counting on to give me the edge in the election.

'Now, nothing. Poof. I had an aide check. Bernt Shiprite has evidently used the letters as blackmail to get back in the good graces of the Universalists. There are currently no plans for them to appear anywhere. Damnation!'

Von Baldur smiled sympathetically, made his

excuses, and blanked the com. He immediately dialed another number. 'Fra Diavolo, please.'

The secretary recognized him.

'One moment.'

Diavolo's face appeared onscreen.

'Yes, Mr. von Baldur?'

'How would you like some interesting material for your pamphlets?'

'What is this Unwritten Law that the media says is the real reason Adrianopole was acquitted?' Grok asked.

'Generally,' M'chel Riss said, 'it's the right of a husband or lover to murder his partner if he catches her in bed with somebody else. Males only need apply. It seems to be different here on Montrois.'

'How barbaric. There should never be laws beyond the law,' Grok said. He reached across the dinner table, speared another soya steak, and inhaled it. Goodnight, chewing on his second, very bloody chunk of real meat, winced.

'I don't know,' Riss said. 'It's nice to find a place *somewhere* where women get a few extra licks.'

Grok rumbled. 'That settles it,' he said. 'I have not been certain of my intents on your proposed visitation of the Belfort Worlds, due to my extreme recognizability, if there is such a word.'

'There is now,' King said.

'I shall now leave Jasmine here to man the fort. I shall go to Belfort with you other three, and remain low, as I think the saying is. In the event of any excitement, I shall be delighted to participate.

'I feel confused, and there is nothing like a bit of bloodshed to clear the air.'

FIFTY

It was easy to see why the Belfort Worlds were so high on the Interplanetary Lust List: there were four inhabitable planets. One was perfect for mining light minerals; two others, for heavy.

The second planet from the sun was the closest to E-normal, and the most heavily settled, with a population of about forty million. There were only a handful of cities, the biggest, the space-seaport of Lavre, with a population of about a million. The rest of the people were in scattered hamlets, farming in the old-fashioned style of people living in villages and going out to their holdings to work.

The four Star Risk operatives had taken their own yacht to Belfort II, Goodnight having suggested they might need to get out of town fast, and wouldn't want to be dependent on passenger manifests and such time-consuming nonsense.

Von Baldur watched the screens as the pilots brought the ship in on an old-fashioned braking orbit, which gave them a chance to look at this world.

'Nice,' he said. 'It looks most peaceful.'

'Very agrarian,' Grok agreed.

'I would go insane here within a week,' von Baldur said.

'Now, Friedrich,' Riss said. 'You're putting down the virtues of long walks in the dusk, quiet fishing on a stream, perhaps a game of ball on the village green.'

'I would rot,' von Baldur said flatly. 'Or kill myself just to find something interesting.'

'Enough piff-paff,' Goodnight said. 'We should be discussing how we're going to find Juda Abiezer.'

'Something tells me,' Riss said, 'he won't be difficult to find if he's masquerading under the name of the Patriot League.'

He wasn't.

They had their ship parked on the far side of the field, next to the cargo ship from Asamya, and told the crew to take some time off but listen for their recall beeper.

Von Baldur, Grok, and Goodnight waited while Riss hired a lifter and flew out into Lavre.

Goodnight wanted to come along, for security, but M'chel withered him with a glare and suggested there was never a time when a Marine needed back cover from a goddamned soldier, no matter how modified. She grudgingly agreed to keep an open com link between the ship and the lifter.

A river ran through the city, which had been laid out in a comfortable sprawl, with broad avenues like Tuletia. Business districts were built in cells, with residential areas between them.

'What a charming, bucolic little burg,' Goodnight said over the com. 'Hey. There's a cop. Go ask him.'

That officer claimed not to know anything. Riss went on.

'I should've known better,' Goodnight said. 'Of course he wouldn't know. Did you note the slight drool from one side of his mouth?'

'Shut up, Chas,' M'chel said. 'I'm trying to fly . . . ah-hah. I'll try this pair of coppers.'

She waved their lifter down, went over, and came back a few moments later, grinning. 'Pay dirt,' she said. 'The driver is a member, and told me I ought to join, to keep Belfort Dampierian if I valued my life and those of my children.' She grimaced. 'What is it about these thugs? Every woman is assumed to be a baby factory.'

Juda Abiezer's nose had been broken and reconstructed so many times that the surgeons on the last break evidently decided to leave his face matching the city's sprawl. One eyebrow drooped a little, and a scar ran straight up the middle of his veined forehead to disappear in his shaggy hairline. The man looked in his late forties, going on sixty. He was heavily built, and moved carefully and walked with a limp. Evidently Givoi hadn't been exaggerating when he said Abiezer was always ready for a brawl.

Riss hid a grin, remembering what one of her hand-to-hand combat instructors had told her years ago, when she admired somebody else on the committee who looked equally broken up.

'Wrong, young lieutenant. The guy you ought to respect is the one who *gave* him those scars.'

The Patriot League might not have had any signs, but it had been easy to pick out – a low brick building painted with Dampier's national colors that had paired sentries walking around it. There was open land on three sides of the building, which made it easy to defend. The parked lifters were all commercial, fitted with seats, except one, which was a lim about fifteen years old.

The male secretary was less interested in Riss's false ID and her equally false explanation of why she was here, claiming to be a political writer from another system, than in her neckline.

She was searched, ineffectually. The secretary and a summoned matron-looking woman didn't find any of Riss's small arsenal, nor the two microphones she had hidden.

Juda Abiezer fawned over her, saying that he was delighted that his cause had attracted attention on other worlds, and so on and so forth.

At least his office was huge, big enough for Riss to get completely airborne and kick Abiezer's testicles up around his earlobes if he got cute. But while Abiezer leered, he stayed on the other side of his immense steel desk, big enough to land a starship on.

'It's hard,' he said mournfully, 'being so far away from the Alliance, and trying to keep up the good fight for the freedom of Belfort. It's a long struggle, and Torguth's infiltrators are on the increase. Perhaps what I share with you will bring in some donations, which we can always use.'

'Actually,' M'chel said, 'what I told your receptionist was, to put it politely, a crock.'

Abiezer reacted, one hand sliding toward a desk drawer.

'No,' M'chel said hastily. 'I mean no harm. What I want to do is trade for information.'

Abiezer relaxed, and put the leer back on. 'What would you be interested in trading?'

'Four standard cargo packs of current-issue Alliance small arms, plus ammunition,' Riss said briskly. 'You might be able to use those in your long struggle.'

Abiezer blinked, recovered, blinked again. 'We, uh . . . I should make you aware that I'm recording this conversation, and if you propose anything unlawful, I'll be duty-bound to report you to the proper authorities.'

'Yeah. Right. What I'm proposing is to give you guns for words. I have no idea what the gun laws are here on Belfort, and don't give a damn. And I don't think you do, either.'

'That's as may be,' he said carefully. 'Something like what you propose would suggest you want some very valuable words from me.'

'I do,' Riss said. 'I want to know a few things about the Masked Ones.'

Abiezer's lips thinned. 'I have no idea what you're talking about.'

'Bullshit,' Riss said bluntly. 'You were one of the Masked Ones' hierarchy, and supposedly your constant demand for taking action against the current government got you sent out here in exile.'

There was a long silence.

'No,' Abiezer said. 'Not exile. But a place where a man of action is appreciated.'

'Call it what you want,' M'chel said.

'What do you want the information for?'

'I'm not asking you what you want the guns for.'

Abiezer grinned, showing the overly white of rebuilt teeth. 'No. You're not. So who trusts whom the least? I mean, who goes first?'

'I'll tell you what,' Riss said. 'I have a ship . . . and

the cargo . . . at the spaceport. My ship has more than adequate security. You can send, say, three or four people to make sure the guns are there, and there's no surprises in store. When your people come back to you, then you and I start talking. When I'm satisfied, you can bring in your stevedores.'

Abiezer thought, then nodded. 'I'll be right back.'

'All right,' von Baldur's voice came through Riss's ear bud. 'They've got four men here, and Grok is going to escort them over to the cargo ship. We're on standby.'

'Big rog on that one,' Riss said, and turned her attention to Juda Abiezer, who lounged in his chair behind the desk.

'I'm miking all this, and bouncing it back to my ship,' she said. 'Not for any kind of legal use, but just so I don't miss anything.'

'Good,' Abiezer said. 'Nothing like common trust.'

'Let's start with now, and work backward,' Riss said. 'What's the real situation like here on Belfort?'

'You mean with Torguth? They've got agents all over the place, been sliding them in for at least ten years. Some are honest-to-Wotan immigrants, but most of them are either agents in place, infiltrators, or, lately, just plain hooligans.'

'Strength estimate?'

'Probably four or five thousand,' Abiezer said. 'And they're well-trained, so that makes their numbers more than enough to paralyze society here. That's what the Patriot League is for – we break up every demonstration, every meeting, every riot they try to put on.'

'What do the police do about that?'

'Nothing,' Abiezer said. 'Some of them don't want to create trouble, others back Torguth, and others are on our side. I think we've got more cops with the League than they do. I think,' he repeated with emphasis.

'Which is one reason I'm very damned glad to get the guns. They'll be just a bit more of my edge, since the League's somewhat outnumbered.'

'What are your numbers?' Riss asked.

'Sorry,' Abiezer said. 'I don't tell that to anybody.'

'I suppose that doesn't matter,' Riss said. 'Now assume that your society is able to stop this disruption, and that Torguth itself is turned back. What are you going to get from this?'

'Saving a system that's important to Dampier, keeping its citizens here free, and standing up to tyranny,' Abiezer said.

He spoke just a little too quickly. Riss hoped it was because he'd been asked that question many times already, and not that the response was nothing more than a convenient lie.

'Now,' she said, 'let's talk about the Masked Ones.' She gave him a succinct version of what Givoi had told her.

'You've got somebody on the inside,' Abiezer said.

'I don't tell *that* to anybody,' Riss said, and got a grin from Abiezer.

'So what do you want from me?'

'You were in the hierarchy,' Riss said.

'I was. Fat lot of good it did me.'

'How many people are in the Council?'

Abiezer shook his head. 'I don't know . . . and I'm being honest. I had contact with only one man.'

'Could it be possible that there is no Council? That there's just one man running the Masked Ones?'

'Of course not!' Abiezer said vehemently, then stopped, frowning. 'You know,' he said after a bit, 'I've got to pull that one back. I don't know. I guess . . . I guess there's no reason there couldn't be.'

Riss nodded, took out a slip of paper, wrote something on it, and turned the paper over. 'In a second, I'll let you see who I think that man is.'

'I don't know if I can confirm that.'

'Fine,' Riss said. 'All you have to do when you read it is tell me I'm wrong. But I've got something first. Mostly, it appeared to me that the Masked Ones' demonstrations and head-beatings were in support of the Universalists, correct?'

'Yeah,' Abiezer said. 'Those damned Independents are too damned leftish for me, or for anybody else who wore a mask. And, since we want to take power eventually, the Universalists were the best stepping-stone to the counterrevolution.'

'You're aware of the recent murder trial of Premier Ladier's mistress.'

'Of course. Damned glad she got off. I'd hate to live in a society where a woman's name can get dragged through the mire by any hack who can get access to a printing press.'

'One thing that didn't come out in the trial is that Ladier is . . . was . . . increasingly cozy with representatives of Torguth.'

'What?' Abiezer was truly shocked.

Riss waited.

'Why hasn't that come out?' Abiezer demanded.

'It is, right now,' M'chel said. 'You can have anyone

you know back on Montrois check around for the latest pamphlets Fra Diavolo . . . I assume you know who he is . . . is circulating.'

'That lying son of a bitch is worse than any holo asshole,' Abiezer growled.

'Maybe,' Riss said. 'But for your information, I can attest that he's not lying this time.'

'And why should I believe you? I never heard of you before today.'

'Think guns,' Riss said. 'Why would I be giving you guns if I was blowing smoke?'

Abiezer puzzled.

'I don't know. Things like this get beyond me.'

'You can turn over that piece of paper now,' Riss said.

Abiezer obeyed. His eyes went wide . . . a little too wide, Riss decided.

She waited.

'I won't shake my head no,' Abiezer said. 'But it'd be my life to say yes.'

M'chel got to her feet. 'Thank you for your time, Juda. You can have your men take the cargo.'

Abiezer stared at her, then nodded slowly and reached for the com, then caught himself. 'Just to make sure there's no slips,' he said, 'why don't you stay here with me until the unloading's finished?'

Riss didn't like it, but couldn't think of a way out. 'Why not?' she asked. 'We're both creatures of our word, aren't we?'

Three hours passed. Riss got increasingly nervous. This was taking too long.

Abiezer had asked her to excuse him, and left her in the cavernous office.

At least she'd managed to make a call on her secondary com device, a throat mike, so she didn't have to vocalize, assuming the office had a bug.

Abiezer came back in, then. 'The last case just came off the transport,' he said. 'So you kept your end of the bargain.' He went to his desk. 'Unfortunately, circumstances prevent me from keeping mine.' He slid open a drawer.

Before his hand went in, Riss slid an obsidian throwing knife from her inside arm, and flipped it, underhand, at Abiezer's neck.

The blade spun sideways, Riss not being any more of a knife artist than anyone else outside a sideshow, and hit him, very hard, in the bridge of his nose.

Abiezer screeched, stepped back.

The second knife didn't miss, burying itself in the base of his throat. Abiezer gagged unpleasantly, staggered, and fell on his face.

Riss took a small blaster from the inside of her thigh, went to the window, kicked its security grate free, and was halfway out when the secretary came in. He had a gun in his hand.

She triggered one of the small blast grenades that'd been hidden behind her belt buckle, threw it at him. It went off, and he jumped in shock. Before he could recover, she shot him twice in the heart, and was out the window.

'I'm on the run,' she managed into the mike, spun as two of the sentries came around the side of the building. She crouched, braced against a small tree, and shot them down.

'And we're here, as summoned, your royal marineness,' came back the thin voice in her normal mike.

There was a roar overhead, and the yacht slashed in, went forty-five degrees from vertical on full braking, lowered on antigrav down into the open land behind the building.

Riss heard a grating behind her, looked back. The roof of the Patriot League was opening, and a multi-barreled chaingun appeared. Three men were behind it, feeding belted rounds into the breeches.

There was a ripping sound, then a crash, like that made by a missile launcher, and M'chel went flat and rolled. The missile from the yacht smashed into the League building, and it exploded in fire, the cannon and crew spinning away in the mushrooming cloud.

The yacht was down, and its airlock was open. Riss pelted to it and in. The lock slid closed behind her, and the ship went vertical, although with ship gravity on, it felt perfectly normal to her. She recovered her wind, then went through the inner lock into the main crew space.

Goodnight wore a missile launcher helmet, and was concentrating on a pull-down screen. Von Baldur was at the controls of the yacht's small autocannon. Grok sat glowering in the only chair that would accommodate him.

'If we scoot like we should,' von Baldur said, 'we should be out-atmosphere before the local yokels even realize we have been and done.'

'Good,' Riss managed. She went to the sideboard, poured herself a very long brandy, and drained it. 'Booze always tastes better,' she said to no one in particular, 'just after you've almost lost being able to drink it.'

Goodnight took his helmet off. 'We're in-space,

and . . .' The world spun a trifle, and strange colors flashed at the only open port. Goodnight irised it shut. '. . . and,' he said unnecessarily, 'on our first jump. Home free, and all that.'

He looked at M'chel. 'You owe me, you know. If I hadn't been there, sharp as a thimble, that cannon would've produced shredded M'chel. You owe me.'

'I owe you,' she grudged.

'Repeat after me . . . sometimes even a bootneck is full of shit and needs all the help she can get.'

Riss gave him a deadly stare, but obeyed.

Goodnight grinned. 'And, to finish the payoff, pour me one of those.'

He noticed Grok's expression. 'If I read your face right, and I'm still not sure I do, what do you have the ass about?'

'I came out here with you,' the great being said, 'when I should have been doing paperwork, in the hope I would find a few necks worth wringing. Instead, I just sit here, the action having gone on about me, but without me. I am not pleased.'

'Tough,' Riss said. 'If you need something to think about, what the hell happened with Abiezer? I thought we were getting along just ducky, and he went and turned his coat on me.'

'No thought required at all,' Grok said. 'You shocked him when you told him the Universalists were hand in hand with Torguth.

'So he checked with his master.'

'L'Pellerin,' Riss said. 'Shit. For what we got . . . basically no more than confirmation of our theories, we . . . I . . . might well have stirred up a shitstorm.

'I guess I got a little too cute for my own good. Once

he had the guns, there was no reason to keep the deal going with me. I should've come up with something better. Creeping up behind the bastard with a sock full of sand and then letting Chas pull his toenails out until he sang in C sharp comes to mind.'

Grok nodded agreement, then said, 'That L'Pellerin is the traitor, as well as the head of the Masked Ones, is very very clear now. Abiezer confronted him, and, no doubt, was offered a deal for you . . . and the rest of us . . . to become dead.'

'What sort of deal?' von Baldur asked.

'Oh, I could theorize,' Grok said. 'Let us assume that Torguth made L'Pellerin an arrangement some time ago. Something such as he would become the puppet ruler of the Dampier System. That could well be the equivalent of the marshal's baton Riss talked about earlier that another spymaster was denied.

'Since Abiezer was working for L'Pellerin, and had no doubt been offered some sort of satrapy to accept exile on Belfort, it would have been very easy for L'Pellerin to reassure Abiezer that his deal was still intact. Just the supreme bosses would be changing slightly.

'All Abiezer had to do was remove the four of us, and the situation continues as before, except that, no doubt, the street-fighting between the Torguth thugs and Abiezer's Patriot League suddenly stops.

'Torguth takes Belfort, and names Abiezer quisling. The deal with L'Pellerin remains in place, and when Torguth inevitably takes Dampier, either from without by invasion, or from within by subversion and anarchy, L'Pellerin now sits the throne.

'One, two, three . . . and I think we should get back to Montrois as rapidly as possible. L'Pellerin has heard of Abiezer's death by now, and, I must assume, is moving on us.

'Without slighting her qualifications in the slightest, our Jasmine is very much alone except for the hired help.'

FIFTY-ONE

The big surprise at the mansion was that there weren't any surprises waiting. All was very quiet.

Star Risk thought about throwing a Very Minor Success party, but didn't think hangovers would improve matters if surprises did develop.

Surprises did just that, a bit after dawn the next morning. Evidently L'Pellerin had decided to wait until he had all of Star Risk penned in the same coop before striking.

The attack started with a heavy commercial lifter, crashing at as much speed as it was able to reach holding close to the ground and having to make a hard turn off the boulevard, through the heavy iron gates. It was enough to smash down the gates, then, bursting into flames, it killed the two sentries.

The Masked Ones didn't attack from above, assuming that Star Risk probably had some sort of antiaircraft provision. It did – small autotracking AA missiles hidden in three of the mansion's front bedrooms.

But rather than catching everyone asleep, the new shift of guards was already awake, and finishing breakfast in the dining room. Half an hour earlier, and the

Masked Ones might've been able to successfully follow up the first shock attack on the sleeping mansion.

Instead, the two lifters that came in next, modified with armor plating in front of the driver's compartment and filled with heavily armed gunmen, were immediately engaged by the guard shift commander and his fellows when the intruders lifted over the burning crash, exposing their soft bellies. One lifter spun sideways, crashing beside the initial attacker. The second tried to retreat. The driver was killed by a heavy blaster bolt, and the lifter slid sideways and smashed down in the driveway.

'Go, go, go,' Star Risk's hired guns were chanting, as they deployed out into the mansion's yard, finding cover behind parked lifters, trees, and statuary, and finding targets. 'We got 'em now, we got 'em now.' No one could complain about the guards' morale.

By then, the five Star Risk principals were awake, half dressed, and had their combat harnesses on.

There was a brief, brisk firefight that killed another Star Risk guard and half a dozen Masked Ones. They fell back, and found cover.

'We have got fire superiority,' von Baldur shouted.

'No,' Riss called back. 'The bastards are waiting for something.'

'Well, let's not let them get bored,' Goodnight said, and burnt a burst from a crew-served blaster through the rising smoke.

'Did you notice something interesting?' King asked, and Riss was impressed with her calmness. 'No sirens.'

'So we're to work out our fate by ourselves,' Grok said. 'L'Pellerin is making sure his thugs aren't interrupted. I don't mind that, since I am of a mind to wreak total havoc.'

Goodnight's loader made a small, frightened noise.

Riss heard it before she saw it, then a huge self-propelled gun on tracks ground toward the mansion. Its firing spade cranked down, and it reversed, and the spade dug in to ground the weapon securely. The cannon tube lifted, pointed at the mansion.

'Eat dirt!' Goodnight said, and obeyed his own command, chewing carpet, as the gun's crew aimed and fired. The shell shattered the mansion's enormous front door, smashed through the foyer. It was an armor-piercing round and tore on, not exploding until somewhere in the rear storerooms.

The gun moved forward and smashed into the wrecked lifter. It pulled back, smashed into it again, trying to push it out of the way.

Von Baldur had a throwaway anti-track launcher popped open. He came up in a shattered window, fired. The rocket shot out, hit the SP gun on its heavily armored mantle. It ricocheted upward, not penetrating, and exploded harmlessly.

'Out the back!' von Baldur shouted. 'We shall bust it from the side.'

He motioned to a guard, and each of them grabbed two launchers. They doubled through the house, and went through the tunnel into the garage. Von Baldur started to pry the door open, and blaster fire chattered around him.

'Damnation! They appear to have discovered our secret,' he said, and the two went back the way they came.

The SP gun was still battering at the lifter, slowly moving it aside. The gun fired again, this time high, and took off a good percentage of the mansion's roof.

'Urban renewal,' Goodnight managed, trying to see if he could go bester and get out the front for a flanking shot.

A grenade arced through a window, hit, and bounced. Riss watched it roll in slow motion, then it exploded. The blast caught King, sent her rolling back, and shrapnel ripped into Goodnight's leg. He screamed, went down. Jasmine King lay motionless, then she moved slightly without getting up.

Riss was on her knees, and she spotted the two Masked Ones who'd gotten close enough to throw the grenade. One of them was about to throw a second grenade. Her burst took both men down, and the grenade fell out of the man's hand, blew up.

'Thanks,' Goodnight gritted, trying to sit up. 'Get some of those launchers . . . third floor, side bedroom. There's a plating to go across into the place next door.'

'So that's why –'

'You didn't think I was cultivating that old bat for her sex appeal,' Goodnight said. 'Now go, goddamnit! Be sure and tell her I sent my love, and that we'll pay for damages.'

He slid back behind the crew-served blaster. His loader lay moaning beside it. Goodnight let the rest of a drum blast out into the yard, spattering bolts across the SP gun, which was slowly bulldozing the lifter aside.

Riss saw ten guards scattered around the front rooms, shooting at the Masked Ones, who seemed content to let the gun do all the preliminary work, as she went upstairs, a launcher in each hand. Behind her came Grok, effortlessly carrying a crew-served on its tripod in his arms, a pair of drums under one arm.

M'chel made the third floor landing, ran down the hall, and kicked the unused bedroom door open. It was empty except for a long, heavy steel strip with a dropper harness lashed to either end. The bedroom had double windows, and Riss booted them open.

Less than four meters away was a jutting turret of the next door mansion. Riss turned on the dropper anti-gravs, and she and Grok slid the strip across, crashing through the other house's turret windows.

The Masked Ones' artillery piece fired again, and the mansion rocked.

Riss slung the two launchers, ran across the gang-plank, and jumped through the broken window. She fell down into a nursery filled with dusty, old-fashioned dolls. Behind her came Grok, delicately balancing as he walked across, the strip bending under the bulk of him and his weapon.

M'chel pulled him into the turret, and they found stairs, went down them. A frightened face peered out of a door, the door slammed closed before Riss could give Chas's greeting.

Part of Riss's mind noted the house's musty smell, dust and unwashed body, and then she was at the front door and had it open.

The front garden was overgrown, bushes and trees reaching high – perfect cover. The two went down the walk to the locked gate. Riss shot it off its hinges with her heavy blaster, the noise buried in the battle-din next door, and they were in the street.

Two Masked Ones, crouched behind a lifter, turned startled faces before Riss killed them.

Grok braced his crew-served gun on the rear lid of the lifter. About thirty meters distant was the entrance to their mansion, the self-propelled cannon slamming at the lifter like a crazed robot. The crew in the open gun tub was concentrating on the gate.

Riss took the safeties off a launcher, aimed carefully. The crew of the gun was loading a shell into the cannon's breech.

Things became very slow.

Riss noted, as she depressed the firing key, a crew member turning, seeing her, lifting an arm, mouth opening to shout a warning. The rocket crawled out of the tube, crossed the space to the SP gun, struck the cannon just inside of its shield, and exploded.

There was a double blast as the shell also exploded, tearing the tube off the gun mount and sending it spinning away. The crew in the tub vanished in the blast, and then the gun's engine caught fire.

The Masked Ones along the avenue gaped in shock for an instant, then Grok opened up with his blaster. That broke them, and, as they'd done before, they pelted away, up the avenue.

M'chel Riss aimed carefully and fired her second rocket.

It took the woman she'd aimed at in the middle of the back, tore her in half, then struck a parked lifter and exploded.

Grok sent the rest of his drum, then another, after their attackers.

Bodies and burning lifters strewed the street, but there was little sound but moans, the crackle of flames, and the occasional pop of a round going off in a fire.

Only then did the 'rescuing' sirens start.

*

The toll was heavy.

Of the twenty guards, six had been killed, eight were wounded badly enough to warrant their contracts being paid off, and wound bonuses paid. The mansion's staff, to a person, insisted this was far too risky a job, regardless of pay, and demanded they be given the return ticket to their home worlds and released.

Jasmine King lay on a couch, Riss and one of the two doctors von Baldur had brought to the mansion next to her. Without opening her eyes, she said in a little girl's voice, 'I don't like these people.'

Riss lifted an eyebrow.

'Concussion,' the doctor said. 'She'll be wobbly for up to a week. I'll be coming by daily to check on her.'

Chas Goodnight sat on another couch, watching the second doctor finish splinting his broken leg. He looked around the room.

The mansion was somewhat of a shambles, missing a good percentage of its roof, all the windows on the front and side, plus suffering extensive interior damage from blaster bolts and the cannon shells. Plaster dust hung thick in the air.

'I think,' he observed, 'our insurance rates are about to go up.'

He winced. 'I'll have another of those pain pills, if you please,' he said.

'In a moment,' the doctor said. 'I just want to make sure I don't get any of you in the splint before I seal it.'

Jasmine opened her eyes, struggled up. 'Everything is going roundy-round,' she said, still in the little voice, then: 'I think we're going to have to do something about this Mr. L'Pellerin.'

FIFTY-TWO

But doing something wasn't exactly that easy.

L'Pellerin's DIB building was reconned, and regarded as invulnerable except for a full-out attack by a space fleet or a burrowing nuke. The headquarters was also protected by guard posts hidden in the surrounding buildings. Very alert snipers, relieved every hour, were stationed on the rooftops around it.

When L'Pellerin went out, he was buried in bodyguards, and traveled in lims that were armored personnel lifters with civilian paint jobs.

'Besides,' Grok said, 'killing him will solve nothing, except that Torguth will not have their easy in to the secrets of Dampier. In fact, simply assassinating him, assuming that we're prepared to accept this as an option, will more likely make him a martyr to the sanctity of Dampier . . . a man who gave his all . . . and so forth. The matter needs considerable thinking.' There wasn't that much else to do.

King recovered fully, although for two months after the grenade blast she would still have periodic headaches. Goodnight was also recuperating. The shrapnel wounds were healing nicely, his doctor said, and his leg was knitting. Goodnight didn't help the process any, furiously stomping around the shattered mansion, growling about not, goddamnit, being able to do his job.

Riss said, sweetly, that there was no problem. She could take on the load, since, 'After all, a soldier's task is light compared to a Marine's.' She patted his cheek. 'I know you've been having problems with Caranis, either tying him in with the spy ring or proving him innocent. Ooo don't have to worry yer little knickers about it. Riss has the situation well in hand.' That didn't improve Goodnight's mood at all.

The damage to the mansion was quite considerable, and the owning agency was just as unhappy as Goodnight had predicted. But workmen, each watched by a Star Risk employee, swarmed over the structure. Goodnight insisted on putting up a banner across the driveway: NICE TRY, with a Masked One's face mask at either side of the banner.

The casualty count for the Masked Ones was dreadful – the police who belatedly arrived dragged away some eighty-three bodies in various stages of disrepair. The self-propelled gun had been stolen, so von Baldur was told by the authorities, from an arms depot by Masked Ones who'd had military training. Von Baldur didn't embarrass them by scoffing except in private.

There was one piece of good news: Cerberus Systems, evidently feeling well out of things, quietly withdrew from the Dampier System, with never any indication of what their assignment had been.

'Beat without even a face-to-face,' Goodnight chortled.

'Let us hope,' Grok said, 'all our enemies fade away like boojums.'

'Huh?'

'Never mind. It's poetry. Ancient poetry.'

'Yaak. Damned right I'll never mind. Probably the kind of shit that doesn't rhyme, either.'

The campaign was going hot and heavy.

The Universalists were running on a platform of continuing prosperity, keeping the peace, and business as usual, with, as Reynard had predicted, Faraon leading the campaign. They were ignoring the incident on Belfort, saying that it was unfortunate that the Patriot League building had gotten blown up in some sort of industrial accident, but, after all, that was what happened to thugs who were willing to go beyond the law.

Reynard's Independents took quite a different tack. What happened on Belfort was clearly an attack by Torguth commandos on the League, which, even though it espoused methods beyond the law, had some good, solid patriotic points.

The switch by both parties must have puzzled the thugs with masks, and von Baldur chortled at the convolutions L'Pellerin must be going through to keep his dunces with truncheons happy.

Reynard promised if the Independents were returned to power, 'Dampier would have to face the price of its freedom and independence.'

Universalists hissed that Reynard's adventurism would bring war, and that the first thing he and his fellow crazies would do, after taking office, was to order mobilization, and who knew what Torguth would respond with?

Reynard, interestingly enough, didn't deny that the current 'classes' – men and women of a certain age – might well be called into the service.

The Masked Ones, so far, had played little part in the campaign, only attacking a few Independent rallies, and those were quickly broken up by the Independent's own security.

The theory around the mansion was a bit different – that the Masked Ones and the DIB operatives under-cover with them had taken such a beating they were still stumbling around in shock, licking their wounds.

The holo ads seemed about equally split. Normally the Universalists, since they were the party of the rich, could blanket the frequencies. But with Reynard call-ing for increased military presence, a number of defense contractors changed sides, knowing on which side their weapons systems would be buttered.

Also, Fra Diavolo's propaganda machinery was in full swing, and his followers were requested to give a bit to the Independents.

Naturally, Montrois's police kept a carefully neutral stance, or so they claimed.

'Wittgenstein with a bubble pipe,' Grok said. 'I'm glad we run our government differently. There seems to be no logic on either side, no talk of peace talks with Torguth. It's either ignore them or start shooting.'

'How do your people run a government?' Riss asked.

'We discuss things thoroughly, make sure everyone is in agreement, and then whoever seems to want a posi-tion is free to take it.'

Riss shuddered. 'That sounds too much like a dicta-torship. It wouldn't work for humans, since we don't seem to be able to agree about anything for longer than a week or so without somebody bringing out the rubber clubs for persuasion.'

'I have heard it said,' von Baldur put in, 'that democracy is the worst form of government, and its only virtue is it is better than all the others that have been devised.'

Grok snorted.

The voice asked for M'chel Riss. There was no picture. Riss took the call.

The voice, clearly feeding through an alteration device, said: 'I heard you are interested in the doings of Division Leader Caranis, of Strategic Intelligence.'

'We are.'

'Twelve kilometers beyond Tuletia, on the S'kaski Road is the Montpelier Inn. Tonight, at eight. Be early.'

The com cleared.

'And who was that?' King asked curiously.

'Either a trap,' Riss said. 'Or one of Diavolo's little footsoldiers doing what his master asked him.'

'Who'll you take for backup?'

Riss shook her head. 'Don't know. I'll have one of the patrol ships in a high orbit, for certain. On the ground . . . if Caranis is going to be there . . . he's seen Grok and von Baldur, and I don't want to think about what would happen if our Chas went bester with a busted leg. Maybe one of our rent-a-goons?'

'I'll go,' King said.

Riss considered for half a second. 'Surely. Why not. We could both do with an evening in the country.'

The Montpelier had been somebody's elaborate country manse, tastefully converted into a restaurant clearly intended for the wealthy, judging from the expensive lims and lifters parked in its tree-thick grounds. There was no sign of Caranis's Sikorski-Bentley.

Riss landed their lifter, pointing it out for a clear, fast takeoff. It was just 7:30.

'Good place for an ambush,' Riss said, as they sauntered up the steps.

Both women were dressed formally, if a little on the sensual side. It was Riss's theory that the more she could get men reacting through their gonads, the better chance she'd have. Riss wore a black skirt with a cream blouse, and a black jacket. King had formal pajamas on, in green and white. Both women wore flats, for ease in running if they had to, and carried a pair of guns hidden in various places.

'Ours or theirs?' King asked.

'Either one,' Riss said.

'I think,' Jasmine said, 'maybe you've been around the military too long.'

Riss thought about it. 'There's no maybe to that,' she sighed. 'Wouldn't it be nice to come here, and not be thinking "boy, that tree could put up a couple of snipers, and I'd emplace my mortars over there," and so on and so forth. And we can't even go and get drunk.'

King patted her shoulder. 'Later there's time for almost everything.'

They were greeted at the door, escorted to the bar, since they deliberately didn't have reservations, where they asked for a window seat.

Riss ordered a very light liqueur with sparkling water, King a glass of wine. Both nursed their drinks, made idle chit-chat. Five minutes before eight, a long, black lim grounded.

The driver and one man got out. The driver looked about warily, while the other man came into the inn, looked around, and evidently saw nothing to worry about. He went back to the lim, and a third man got out. He was older, very tall, with a shock of white hair. The man came into the inn, looked in at the bar.

Riss and King gave him friendly smiles. He raised his eyebrows in interest, smiled back broadly, went into the dining room.

Two minutes later, a Sikorski-Bentley landed. Again, two men got out, cased the inn, went back to the lifter.

King had to suppress a case of the giggles. 'These people really trust each other,' she whispered.

Division Leader Caranis got out. He was dressed casually, but expensively. He came into the inn, didn't look in the bar, went into the restaurant and sat down with the older man.

One bodyguard covered the back of the restaurant, one just inside, the third the front entrance.

King and Riss decided it was time for dinner. The dining room, in mid-week, was only about half-full. The women were seated, by preference, across the room from Caranis and the older man.

Both men had three drinks apiece before ordering dinner. The two women finished theirs, and ordered. The men ordered sparkling wine, and the older man poured lavishly.

'Don't we wish,' King said through motionless lips, an invaluable trick, 'we had a bug on that table?' Riss nodded and laughed as if her friend had told a very funny joke. She was thinking hard about what to do next.

Halfway through the meal the older man burped politely, and got up to use the restroom.

Riss had it. She waited a minute, excused herself to Jasmine, and went for the other restroom herself. She went in and waited, listening.

She downrated the bodyguard at the door. He should've been dogging his client, waiting outside the restroom. But maybe the older man didn't think he was in any particular danger.

She heard the fresher flush, came out, as if in a hurry, and bumped hard into the older man. She stumbled, went to her knees, and the man was bending over her.

'Are you all right?'

'Yes . . . yes . . .' M'chel said. 'I just feel clumsy.'

He helped her to her feet, and she smiled at the man, a warm, inviting smile.

'I should buy you a drink,' she said, 'for banging into you.'

'No, no,' the man said. 'I think I should buy you . . . and your friend . . . one. Do you come here often?'

'Every now and then,' Riss purred. 'When there's the promise of good company. Sometimes with my friend, sometimes alone.'

'Ah,' the man said. 'I'd certainly like to join you in the bar for an after-dinner drink, but I'm here on business.'

'Perhaps we could make it another time,' Riss said. She dug in her tiny cocktail purse, careful not to expose her small gun, took out a business card.

It read:

MANDY DAVES, RECREATIONAL THERAPIST.

Under that was one of the com lines into the mansion that was answered only with 'Hello.'

The man looked at Riss, licked his lips without realizing it, reached inside his suit, gave her a card: LESNOWTH ALMAHARA, CHIEF EXECUTIVE OFFICER, CHETWYND INDUSTRIES.

'We should think about giving each other a call,' M'chel said. 'I do prefer older men . . . they have so much more to talk about.'

Almahara smiled back, a bit hungrily, and the two returned to their meals.

'Got him,' King said. 'Chetwynd Industries is a major defense builder . . . one of the bidders on the Belfort Orbital Defense System.'

'You satisfied?' Riss asked Goodnight.

'A nice quiet little dinner,' Goodnight said dreamily. 'And, no doubt, a discreet envelope passed to the head of Strategic Intelligence over the dessert, to make sure he stays happy.

'Now that's somebody to have on the pad,' he continued. 'The head of IIa would know anything and everything proposed for defense spending, and, no doubt, the bid ceiling, and who else will be bidding. Including, maybe, that orbital system for the Belfort Worlds.

'Our Caranis,' he said, and now a bit of disappointment came, 'is no better than a common crook, not a big time spy. Hardly worth worrying about. And I was wrong. It's L'Pellerin all the way.'

'Umm-hmm,' Riss said.

'So why aren't you gloating more about not only being right, but getting the bastard cold?'

'Because,' M'chel Riss said, 'I'm looking over Jasmine's shoulder, staring at the good Almahara's itinerary, and an announcement of a Traditional Event, according to the *Pacifist*, and suddenly I think I've got a good way to nail L'Pellerin.

'Good and final, putting him dead at the crossroads with a stake in his heart. Not to mention publicly exposed. Assuming, of course, I'm still as sneaky as I used to be.'

FIFTY-THREE

From an advertisement, discreetly placed in several of Torguth's business holos:

Interested Investors

Get in at the beginnings of a mammoth profitmaker. Major investments are now sought for work in a new solar system, soon to be open for full exploitation, for those seriously interested in Torguth's future growth. Areas of potential development include light and heavy mineral works, agricultural, and heavy and light manufacturing. A docile workforce and working conditions designed for the serious entrepreneur are guaranteed, without interference. This opportunity fully approved by Governmental agencies. For more information, contact . . .

FIFTY-FOUR

The trap for L'Pellerin would have to be carefully set and sprung.

It involved a rather strange gathering called the Artists' Ball, which was not a ball, nor were any artists, unless they came from the very rich, ever invited. Perhaps they had been, in the early days of Dampier, but no more. Instead, the Ball was a five-day-long gathering of Dampier's hierarchy. There were no media, no 'outsiders,' certainly no social critics invited.

The Artists' Ball was held on a secluded island of southern Montrois. There were cabins small and large, dining halls, conference rooms big and small, plus all the recreational facilities anyone could want. The staff was specially hired for the five days, and flown in. Certainly the staff was either superbly professional or equally attractive and handsome.

A handful of journalists and populists had tried to infiltrate the Ball over the years, and uniformly had been caught by the island's heavy security and escorted back to the mainland, not infrequently with thick ears.

There had been rumors about the Ball for over a century: This was where the Dampier System's future was planned; This was where the rich divided up their spoils, and agreed not to step on each others' toes; This was where conglomerates were formed and dissolved.

Most of these were true.

There were other stories: No one ever brought his or her legal mate; Anyone leaking to the media about anything that happened was liable to end up without a career or worse; There had been at least two hushed-up murders; Some industrialists had gone bankrupt after rounds of high-stakes gambling; There were orgies every night.

Annually, the Artists' Ball was derided by the leftish holos as a rich degenerates' playground, and every year the suites of the wealthy and powerful were vacant for those five days.

Two days before the Ball, M'chel went to Reynard, meeting him in his party's campaign headquarters, where Reynard had a party-leader-size office, decorated as a successful pol's sanctum should be.

First, she told him their suspicions – near certainty – about L'Pellerin.

The man was honestly shocked. 'He has too much power,' Reynard said, 'and has been known to misuse it. I told you once he was crooked, but I never, ever, thought he was a traitor. No wonder he was so quick to condemn poor Sufyerd. I was right, I was right, but gods, what a price this is going to cost.'

M'chel added that L'Pellerin was also the single head of the Masked Ones. Reynard's hands were trembling. He sat down behind his desk abruptly.

'Can I get you something?' Riss asked.

'Yes . . . yes. A brandy. There's a decanter in that sideboard.'

M'chel held back a grin. Things were going much, much better than she'd planned. She went to the sideboard, fumbled for the decanter, and poured Reynard a snifter. Riss brought it back, and he drained it.

'What are we going to do? What are we going to do? If I accuse him now . . . that'll be a debacle. A disaster. There are stories, reliable stories, that he has private information on most politicians that could destroy them. If he's fighting for his life, I have no doubt that he would make sure that information is disseminated. We do not need, in these parlous times, a disaster of this size.'

Riss declined to ask if L'Pellerin had anything on Reynard himself.

'Don't worry,' Riss said. 'At least, don't worry too much. Star Risk has a way, I'm fairly sure, of defusing the situation. But I need your help.' Riss explained what she needed.

Reynard nodded jerkily. 'That's not much . . . and yes, I'm certain I can ensure L'Pellerin attends the Artists' Ball, even at this short notice, though he's loudly denounced it from time to time.

'And the second thing you need . . . again, that isn't a problem, particularly with the current situation with Torguth.

'But . . . to speak frankly, my dear Riss, I don't think I should attend this Ball. I hate saying that, for it makes me sound most cowardly, but this election will be close run, at least at this point, and I . . . or rather the Independents . . . can't risk any problems.'

M'chel, privately thinking that Reynard did, indeed, come across as a coward, assured him that Star Risk could also make sure he wouldn't be able to attend the Ball, and there would be no questions raised about the convenience of Reynard's absence.

That had already been thought of and taken care of.

Goodnight watched Grok move through a small array of glassware, admiring the alien's deftness.

'I do appreciate the concoctions you devise,' he said.

'Thank you, Chas,' Grok said, holding up a test tube. 'This is a particularly strong version of trithiopental, and should, assuming all goes well, be exactly the wonder drug we need.'

'Better living through chemistry,' Goodnight murmured. 'I wish to hell I could see what happens when it works . . . just like I'd love to see what happens when that hellbrew M'chel put in Reynard's booze kicks in.'

FIFTY-FIVE

No one, at least in the Dampier or Belfort systems, ever knew exactly what happened to the Dampier Patrol Ship *Webb*. It was one of half a dozen aging warships loaned by Dampier to the Belfort Worlds, primarily as an adjunct to their customs service.

The only information was that the *Webb* sent a 'cast, on its standard frequency, to the patrol command on Belfort II, reporting that an unknown ship had emerged from N-space, and they'd been unable to reach it:

Suggest ship is most likely the cargo carrier expected to arrive in-system in one E-day, running early. But will close, and ensure nothing's awry. Stand by on this —

The transmission broke off.

The *Webb*'s command tried to contact the ship, at first routinely, since the old tub's electronics were forever going out, then with increasing urgency.

No reply ever came.

Search ships went out, but were unable to find any traces of the *Webb*.

The mostly Universalist caretaker government waffled suspiciously, then announced the *Webb* had met with an unknown accident, adding that, even in this modern age, starships still did meet with unfortunate calamities. That was bad enough, but the release went on to say 'there is absolutely no evidence of any Torguth involvement in the catastrophe.'

Star Risk theorized it'd found a Torguth spy ship who shot first.

The accident happened the day before the Artists' Ball.

Riss hated to celebrate someone else's death. But this played into Star Risk's court.

Within hours one of Tuletia's street singers, using the tune of an old folk song, had written a ballad called 'The Death of the *Webb*.'

It spread across the planet, and was picked up and recorded by one of Tuletia's best-known singers.

FIFTY-SIX

It wasn't scheduled to be much of a speech. In fact, only a few of the holos bothered to cover ex-Premier Reynard's announcement that, tomorrow, he would be taking a break from the 'cares and pressures of the campaign trail to confer with trusted aides and others.'

Which meant Reynard didn't want to go to the Artists' Ball. Which M'chel Riss had promised to find an out of.

But he couldn't contact her, and he was very worried about what she thought was a Star Risk certainty, and hoped it didn't involve a phony assassination attempt. That played hell on the knees of custom-made suits.

Reynard took a reassuring nip of his brandy before going down in the lift to the press room. His stomach roiled a bit, and he told it to be still. Soon enough he'd be out of the camera's eye, and could relax as much as he ever allowed himself to.

He smiled at the handful of holo reps in the press room and greeted those he knew, which was most of them.

'This is fairly routine, gentlepeople,' he said. 'As my aides have told you, I shall be taking a few days —'

Very suddenly matters became unroutine, as he threw up all over his podium. He staggered sideways, was rackingly ill again, and went to his knees. Riss's potion went into high gear, and Reynard into parabolic vomiting.

Only one of the holos showed footage of the fairly disgusting sight. The others cursed that they were not there for the momentous footage.

There certainly was no question whatever that Reynard would be bedridden for at least a few days, and unable to travel anywhere.

FIFTY-SEVEN

L'Pellerin's chief aide noted the secret policeman's sour expression as the lifter began its landing approach to the nameless island.

'Chief, are you all right?'

'Fine,' L'Pellerin said. 'I do not like this waste of time, especially on a topic such as I was asked to discuss. "The Perilous Situation with Torguth." Pah. What fools these politicians be. You prove to them that there is no concern, and what do they do? They want you to talk some more about how safe they are.'

'Yessir,' the aide said neutrally, looking out the port.

L'Pellerin's lifter, as befitted the head of Dampier's secret service, was escorted by two patrol ships ahead, and two to the rear, plus his armed guards in lifters on either side of his ship. In addition, a pair of destroyers flew high cover.

Below was the island, an amoeba-shaped tropical forest in turquoise seas. On this, the first day of the Ball, lifters swarmed around the landing area.

There were some early arrivals already sporting with watercraft in the water.

'At least,' the aide ventured, 'we'll be able to keep early hours.'

'You, perhaps,' L'Pellerin grumped. 'I have more than enough paperwork, not to mention what the office sends on.'

'Yessir. Sorry, sir. Of course I'll work along with you.'

L'Pellerin nodded. 'I know you will.'

It was a definite statement of fact.

The patrol ship lay on the bottom at thirty meters. It had landed two hours before, some kilometers out to sea, coming in low and landing without a splash. Submerged, it sought the bottom, then 'flew' along it toward the island.

'Sorry to be preoccupied, M'chel,' the first pilot said. 'I don't have a lot of hours playing submarine.'

'That's all right,' Riss said. 'You just keep us from swimming into some giant squid that eats spaceships.' She was feeling more than a little claustrophobic, fought the feeling down.

'We're grounding where you wanted to exit,' the pilot said over his shoulder. 'I guess that's the word for it.'

'I'll beep you for pickup when I'm finished.' She avoided using or thinking the word 'if.'

Riss wore a wet suit and full helmet with breathing apparatus, fins, and a bulky pack. She cycled herself out through the lock into the dark green world, adjusted her fins, and pushed off. She had to stop to adjust the buoyancy to perfect neutral on the pack, then swam on, following the guide her wrist compass gave.

She wasn't much pleased with her progress or her physical shape. There hadn't been much time for working out lately, especially at swimming.

The bottom was rising, and she could look up and

see the silvery sheen of the surface. Her breathing apparatus was built to bleed exhaled air out into the water in tiny bubbles, so there'd be no giveaway on the surface to any watchers.

She held close to the bottom for a few seconds as a boat, maybe pleasure, maybe security, swept overhead at speed, leaving a deep wake behind. The waves gave her cover to move closer to shore.

She came to the surface, popped her head up on the far side of a small wave. She was on the far side of the island, away from the arrivals and the excitement, which was just where she wanted to be. Ahead should be a cove that on the chart had been marked for deep water.

It was.

She went for the depths again, swam into the cove. Small waves three meters above her broke on craggy rocks. She discharged air from the pack, let it sink her to the gravelly bottom.

Her watch finger told her it was two hours until sunset. On the island the last of the guests should be arriving, being assigned their cottages, and getting ready for the first night's banquet.

As it grew dark, Riss reinflated the pack, let it take her to the surface.

This was the most dangerous part.

The sea was calm and warm, and a gentle wind was blowing.

There was no sign of life.

She clambered up onto a ledge and stripped off the diving gear.

From her pack, she took a phototropic coverall and other gear. Riss put her diving gear into the pack, held it underwater, and adjusted the buoyancy to negative.

Naked, she dove to the bottom with the pack, and grunted a small boulder on top of it. If a storm didn't come up and blow her pack to who knows where, it would be waiting when – not if – she returned.

M'chel surfaced, clambered up on the rocks, put on the coveralls, a pair of tight-fitting boots, and, comforting feeling, her combat harness.

The only other item she had was a slender meter-long tube of dark metal, with a pistol grip and a tiny-apertured peep sight. It was a single-shot, high-pressure air gun.

She pulled the coveralls' hood over her head and took a small receiver from a harness pouch. She crawled, very slowly, to the top of the rocks. There was an inviting, romantic beach in front of her. The receiver vibrated in her hand. She saw where the motion detector line was, crawled up to it.

Another bit of electronics came out of her pouch, and she 'buzzed' this detector relay into harmlessness. Then she crawled through the zone, and brush rose about her. Very good. Very, very good.

Now she had all night to get where she was going. She waited awhile, to make sure nobody was stalking her, then went on, never moving faster than a meter a minute.

Twice the telltale said there was an electronic device ahead, twice she momentarily confused it, passed through without setting off any alarms.

A pair of guards came through, but they were talking, and hardly any bother. Now she could move faster. Riss crested the mountain's ridge, and could hear music, happy laughter from below, where the Ball's estate spread.

Enjoy yourselves, ladies and gentlemen, she thought. Drink hearty. So you'll sleep really, really well.

She heard rustling, and went into a bush. In the dim moonlight, she saw two more guards . . . and a dog. She hated dogs – at least when she was at work, and they weren't on her side. Riss heard the dog whine, knew it had scented her.

'What's the matter, boy?' one guard asked.

Riss took a pack from her pouch, tore it open and dumped it on the ground, then crawled backward.

'Let's see what's bothering you.'

The guards and the dog were coming closer, the whines getting more and more eager. Then the dog hit Riss's defense, and started wheezing, then choking, then coughing convulsively as the white pepper did its work.

The guards knelt over the dog as it rolled about. Tough, dog, Riss thought. You'll be all right in an hour.

She crawled around the commotion, and then, ahead of her, was a building. Riss checked it from memory. Just about where she'd wanted to be.

All she had to do was move north a hundred meters or so, where the aerial photo showed some thick brush, and go to ground. The path she wanted, which led to one of the tree-hung outdoor speaking areas, was less than twenty meters from that brush.

Now, if the weather report only held true, and it didn't rain, and everything got moved inside . . .

If that happened, she'd have to chance entering the main cottage area the next night, and who knew how hard that would be.

*

'A beautiful morning, isn't it, Chief?' the aide tried.

L'Pellerin looked about the sun-dappled wilderness around him. 'Somewhat of a waste, I think,' he said. 'In my province, this would've been cut down and turned into productive farmland a century ago.'

The aide thought about arguing, realized it would get him nowhere, kept silent.

L'Pellerin, with a sour expression, looked about the path they were walking down, toward the speaking area somewhat absurdly called Truth Zone III. He was deliberately a little late, giving time for everyone to assemble and for their anticipation to build.

Suddenly he jerked.

'What's the matter, sir?'

'Damned fly, or something, just bit me,' he said. 'You see? Farmland doesn't bite.'

'Nossir.'

He didn't see the tiny, sharp-pointed plas ampoule on the ground, and a second later, it melted. Nor had he heard the soft *paff* of Riss's airgun.

They walked around a bend, and L'Pellerin saw, with satisfaction, the speaking area was packed. Everyone who was at the Ball was there, or so it looked.

The assembled dignitaries came to their feet, applauding, as they saw him. L'Pellerin's aide dropped away, and L'Pellerin walked alone to the low platform.

He waited until the applause had died.

'Good morning,' he said. Most speakers begin with a joke or a pleasantry. L'Pellerin had no time for such fripperies.

'I assume you know me,' he said. 'And I know you, or know of you, very well indeed.'

There was an uncomfortable laugh. L'Pellerin let the reminder of his secret files sink in.

'I was asked to be here, and discuss with you the current situation with Torguth. I don't have any speech, don't think I need one. You may have questions. Feel free to ask them at any time.

'To begin with, you should be aware that I, and my men and women of the Dampier Information Bureau, work night and day to ensure that Dampier, and, yes, Belfort, are secure and free.

'There have been some insecure, or even subversive-minded, citizens who doubt that. There is no cause for alarm, no reason to worry.'

L'Pellerin swallowed, feeling suddenly a bit ill. It must have been that overly rich breakfast he'd had. He should have gone without and just had his normal bread, cheese, and tea.

'Our two systems are as safe, and we are as far from war, as we have been since the first colonists landed on Montrois, centuries ago.' L'Pellerin felt a bit of sweat on his forehead, noted the worried look his aide, sitting in the front row, gave him. A bit too much sun the day before, certainly.

'We have defeated Torguth twice within two hundred years, and that system has learned its lesson. I can assure you that –'

A man whom L'Pellerin recognized as one of the fortunately absent Reynard's toadies, stood and quite rudely asked, 'How many Torguth agents are there on the Belfort Worlds?'

L'Pellerin reached for the obvious answer, but his tongue escaped him. 'At least five thousand. Perhaps more.' He couldn't believe what he'd just said. He tried to retract his words, but the man persisted.

'And how many here on Montrois?'

'Two hundred, at the least.'

There was an uproar. The man persisted. 'How much have you been paid by Torguth?'

Now there were shouted insults at the man.

This one L'Pellerin could answer honestly. 'Nothing.'

'Then what have they promised you?'

Again the world swam about him.

'Power,' L'Pellerin said weakly. 'A share in the . . . in their government. After they seize Montrois and our other worlds.'

Now there was chaos. The man had to shout loudly.

'So that makes you, the head of DIB, a traitor!'

It wasn't a question, but L'Pellerin found himself nodding.

'Yes . . . yes . . .'

His words were lost in the tumult.

They took L'Pellerin, near collapse, back to his cottage.

His aides called for an emergency lifter to take the man to a hospital. Clearly, he'd suffered some sort of breakdown.

The ambulance came in hot, crushing a pair of benches as it landed on the aide's signals. L'Pellerin's guards were surrounding the cottage. The aide ran to the door, knocked on it. There was no answer.

'Sir! Your lifter's here.'

A flat thud came from within.

'What . . .'

'Out of the way,' a bodyguard, who knew what the sound was, growled. He and another man put shoulders against the door and smashed it off its hinges.

L'Pellerin lay sprawled on the floor. There was a small-caliber pistol beside his right hand, and a small blackish hole in his temple.

As the ambulance came off the ground with L'Pellerin's corpse, Riss cycled the lock open, flapped to a seat in the patrol ship, and collapsed.

'I ain't no merwoman,' she said. She managed to kick off her fins and shrug out of her breathing apparatus. 'The swim back was a lot worse than going in.'

'Well?'

'Get us out of here,' she ordered. 'When we're well clear, send Star Risk One a com. On the way home.'

'What happened? Or can you tell us?'

'A cop got bit by the truth bug. Hell if I know what went on from there.'

FIFTY-EIGHT

Riss took the next day off, as did the rest of Star Risk, letting the smoke settle, and not returning Reynard's coms. But they took pity, finally answering one late at night, and suggested Reynard might want to drop by the mansion the next day.

He did, and joined Star Risk at its breakfast table, but ate nothing, still looking somewhat peaked.

'Great Egg,' he said, 'but you people really go for the throat.'

'That is our reputation,' von Baldur agreed comfortably. 'More caff?' He poured.

'What is going to happen about L'Pellerin?' Riss asked. She had already read the confidential report Reynard's assistant had made about the debacle at the Artists' Ball.

'Not much of anything,' Reynard said. 'We don't need to shatter the government. The word is that the poor man suffered some kind of seizure, most likely from working too hard.

'There'll be a funeral, just small enough so it's obvious he died in some sort of disgrace . . . details will get out, if they already aren't . . . and just big enough so the exact truth won't be common knowledge.'

'What about the Dampier Information Bureau?' Grok asked.

'They're in desperate trouble,' Reynard said. 'No matter which side wins the election, there'll be a massive shakeup. I'm thinking, if I become premier again, of dissolving the whole damned thing and starting over. Spies don't seem to learn their lessons that easily.

'Or maybe I'll put a deputy of our party, a man named Guy Glenn whom you might remember, in charge. He would enjoy that.

'Right now, all their agents, overt and covert, are keeping close to cover.'

'Better question,' Goodnight said, buttering toast and putting a very large slice of mustarded ham on it, 'is what about his private files? The ones that supposedly had who was sleeping with who and all that.'

'Immediately after hearing of his death,' Reynard said, looking a bit uncomfortable, 'a special police task force took custody of all of L'Pellerin's papers. Even as we speak, those files are being destroyed.'

'*All* of them?' von Baldur asked.

'Well . . . all but a few . . . and those pertain to planetary security.'

King and Riss exchanged cynical looks. Planetary security no doubt meant having full information on all Universalists' private lives.

'What I'm concerned about is what will happen to the Masked Ones?' Reynard asked. 'They're still an unknown quantity, and I don't know if L'Pellerin had a subordinate qualified to take over.'

'Do not worry about them,' von Baldur said. 'There is no subordinate worth concerning yourself about once his superior has been dealt with harshly. And a leader-less mob dissolves within hours.'

'Then the election should be a certainty for us,' Reynard said. 'And then the house of cards will begin to tumble. Sufyerd can be brought into the open for another, fair trial, and your commission will be fulfilled.'

'Not quite,' von Baldur said. 'I obtained some information some time ago, not sure what I was going to do with it. After due cogitation, and considering that your checks have been delivered promptly, with a minimum of complaint, I have decided to attempt a favor for you, and for Dampier.'

'Which is?' Reynard asked.

'I'm going to prevent war with Torguth.'

Everyone at the table looked incredulous. Reynard noted the expressions.

'All by yourself?'

'Not at all,' von Baldur said, scooping eggs and fruit onto his fork, and downing them. When he finished chewing, he added, 'I will have some help.'

'From where?'

'Now, I do not think I need to be specific,' von Baldur said. 'Especially if my scheme . . . er, plan . . . does not work as smoothly as I hope.'

'I should have learned by now about asking details from you people,' Reynard said, getting up. 'I have things to take care of, with the election only three weeks away.

'Especially after having been under the weather for the last two days.'

'Oh,' M'chel said. 'I forgot. You might want to dump that decanter of brandy in your office out.'

'You? You did that to me?'

'You said you didn't want to go to the Artists' Ball, and wanted an impeccable excuse,' Riss said.

'But did you have to be so damned drastic?' Reynard said. 'My stomach lining is still in knots.'

'As you noted,' M'chel said. 'We go for the throat. Or lower areas.'

FIFTY-NINE

'Gods of above, below, and the hinterlands,' Fra Diavolo said. 'You certainly dream large, von Baldur.'

'It's not a dream at all,' von Baldur said. 'With your resources, a reality. I've only got my yacht and two patrol craft, you know.'

'My people will volunteer . . . although I'm sure there are some that will need to be recompensed for taking time off from work,' Diavolo said. 'And fuel costs will be interesting. Are you sure you aren't trying to bankrupt me?'

'Would you like to see the bills we have been submitting to our main client?'

Diavolo shuddered. 'No. No, I think not.' He thought for a time.

'It would be an accomplishment,' he said thoughtfully. 'I don't know if I'll ever be able to brag about it. But I've certainly never heard of anybody stopping a war in the manner you propose.'

'It should work well,' von Baldur said persuasively. 'Especially remembering that every dictatorship is professionally paranoiac.'

'True,' Diavolo said, and considered some more, then came to his feet.

'Why not? It'll be a tale long in the telling for my nonexistent grandchildren.'

Exactly on schedule, the Torguth fleet blasted off from its various bases in the system. Each ship commander had a copy of the maneuver plan, with his part in it precisely timed.

The entire fleet first rendezvoused in empty space, between systems. Strangely enough, there was a large ship, a rather elderly in-system transport, hanging in a dead orbit nearby.

A pair of destroyers scouted the ship, and reported it was just what it appeared to be, except that its registry was in the Dampier System, which was a bit unsettling. Fleet Admiral Garad gave orders to ignore the ship and begin the war games.

About a quarter of the Torguth ships vanished on cue into hyperspace. They would reappear later, playing the maneuver enemy.

War games can be played in a myriad of ways. The chanciest – at least regarding the military and its leaders' reputations – is to merely posit a situation, and let what happens happen.

Chance is not a favorite of the military, particularly in peace time. Since Torguth was a precisely run system, their grand maneuvers were to be played to a precise scenario.

The Torguth fleet made two jumps, the second emerging from N-space as planned, beyond the Belfort System.

Waiting for them were a pair of ex-Alliance Pyrrhus-class patrol ships, who took no notice of the Torguth, nor of a designated flagship's attempt to communicate with them and ask their intentions, which Friedrich von Baldur listened to most happily.

After a nervous hour, the patrol ships vanished, just before, again, as planned, the Torguth fleet was attacked by the aggressors, playing the part of Dampier warships.

After careful skirmishing, to ensure there were no embarrassments such as a collision, the attackers were driven off, as the script dictated. A space yacht appeared as this was happening, watching and evidently recording.

Fleet Admiral Garad was beginning to get a trifle nervous about unexpected appearances. He commed the problem to his High Command on Torguth, and was advised to take whatever action he felt necessary, neatly dumping the ball, and any catastrophe that might occur, back in his lap.

Garad decided to proceed with the games, and ordered the third fleet jump, this into the heart of the Belfort System.

Yet again, two ships were waiting for them, one a converted minesweeper, the other an ultraluxurious yacht. Both refused attempts to communicate. If this had been a real war, Torguth would have now ordered the attack on the Belfort Worlds.

But it was not, and so the fleet made two jumps to a dead system, four of whose worlds were approximately the same distance from their dying sun as the populated Belfort Worlds.

They would represent the target and, since they were unpopulated, would provide targets for live fire exercises.

Impossibly, since this system was light years from

anything, two more Dampierian ships were there ahead
of him. Confusion on the command decks of Torguth
warships was bubbling.

Garad didn't know what was going on, what scheme
Dampier had mounted, but knew better than to chance
his precious ships. He ordered the games canceled, and
for all ships to return to their bases.

The very worried High Command met to discuss the
matter.

It had already been clear that Dampier had at least
one, probably more, agents on Torguth. One had almost
been apprehended some time ago. It was also evident
that their main agent had to be high in the military
hierarchy, perhaps almost as high as the late L'Pellerin,
for how else could their top-secret war games have all
their details exposed?

The question was, why did Dampier choose to let
Torguth know of this agent, and that their innermost
sanctums had been penetrated? It was here that expla-
nations proliferated, and chaos began to set in, since
none of them made a great deal of sense. Clearly,
though, the planned invasion of the Belfort Worlds
must be set aside for a time.

For quite a time, it was pointed out, since Dampier's
elections were less than a week away, and it appeared
likely that saber-rattling Reynard would be returned to
office.

When he did, there was no doubt in any mind on the
High Command that the aborted Belfort Defense
System would be constructed, which would make invasion far more difficult, and the Dampierian military
would be on far greater alert.

It was also assumed that Dampier's fleet would be heavily reinforced.

In the meantime, Torguth could proceed with a fine pogrom of its various intelligence apparats, until the mole, or moles, were winkled out.

There was major bewilderment at high levels on Torguth, and the military despises perplexity even more than they dislike chance. And so the decision was made to do nothing until the situation clarified itself, in the fullness of time.

'Now,' von Baldur boasted, 'do I deserve the title of Great Peacemaker?'

'You do,' Riss said. 'All you have to do is convince people to believe what happened actually went down.'

Von Baldur slumped a little. 'Oh well. As the good Diavolo said, it shall at least make an extraordinary bar story.'

SIXTY

The election was a total disaster for the Universalists. Reynard may have labored under some sense of fair play in not releasing the details of L'Pellerin's treason – not to mention his railroading of the innocent Sufyerd to protect himself, and forgetting the murder of the vanity-stricken Kismayu – but Fra Diavolo had no such scruples, and sent his broadsheet writers in for the kill.

Ladier, already in disgrace, was brought up again and again as representing true Universalist thought, and the point was hammered that the rich always think more of their bankrolls than their nation.

The election ran 70–22 in favor of Reynard's party, the missing numbers going to various fringe parties.

With that great a mandate, Reynard had to move more quickly than he'd planned.

He announced plans for the Belfort System to be amalgamated into Dampier's central government, and that 'henceforth any hostility toward Belfort will be regarded as an attack on the home worlds, and dealt with immediately and with devastating force.'

He also proclaimed the DIB was to be broken up, although von Baldur was certain its agents wouldn't spend more than a few days unemployed before a new espionage agency was formed.

Maen Sufyerd and his family were brought out of whatever hiding place Diavolo had hidden them in, and, naturally, the holos immediately made him a hero. It was some other press villains that had hounded him as a spy and a traitor.

Star Risk paid off the patrol ships, and most of the contract workers, keeping only enough to guard their backs until they got offworld.

Maen Sufyerd insisted on thanking them in person. Reynard had the media present, although the guards were able to keep them out of the mansion proper.

There were tears and laughter, and Sufyerd's daughter, Abihu, announced that she'd changed her career choice yet again, and was back to wanting to go home to study to be a soldier with M'chel Riss. Riss, a bit nervously, said that would be interesting, when she was old enough, and to be sure and stay in touch.

Sufyerd, with a bit of a smile on his face, the first Riss could remember seeing, took her away from the others.

'It is as I planned from the beginning,' he said in a low voice. 'There shall be no war, even though the path had turnings I could never envision.'

M'chel, puzzled, stammered something.

'I also never allowed for you,' Sufyerd continued, 'or for the others of Star Risk, and we shall always owe you for saving my life.'

'Uh . . . yeah,' Riss said. 'It was, uh, nothing. I guess.'

Sufyerd smiled again, a very saintlike smile, and went back to his wife.

SIXTY-ONE

A month and a half later, M'chel was lounging, naked, on one of Trimalchio IV's golden, empty beaches. Pulled up on the beach was a small waterjet. In it were chilled drinks, a lunch, and the latest edition of *Equations Leading to the Theory of an Alternate Hyperspace Drive* that she'd been looking forward to for six months.

Now it was enough to lie there, think nothing, let the sun turn her into a vegetable.

Well, think about one thing, perhaps.

She considered lazily if the singer with the band at the luxury resort she was staying at was as good-looking as she'd thought last night, and if so, should she invite him up for a drink after tonight's performance?

The com buzzed.

She ignored it.

It buzzed again . . . three . . . two . . . three.

Riss cursed, got up. That was Star Risk's code.

She went to her waterjet, leaned over, and touched a sensor, leaving the picture blank.

'Riss,' she announced.

'This is Jasmine.'

'All right,' Riss said, and opened the camera.

'And my, don't you look relaxed and all,' King said. She was at her desk in Star Risk's offices, evidently having returned early from her vacation.

'I am . . . or, maybe, I was. What's the news?'

'Hang on,' Jasmine said. 'Put something on. I'm patching through everybody else.'

Riss obeyed, pulling on a pareau, returned as the screen split four ways.

Von Baldur was wearing an archaic suit, and was in the tiers at a racetrack with, Jasmine suspected, real Earth horses. Grok was in some library somewhere, surrounded by computers and printouts. Chas Goodnight, impeccable, if a trifle haggard in evening dress, was in an expensive high-rise apartment. Riss saw movement behind him, identified two people, both female.

'We have a slight problem,' Jasmine King said. 'I was checking the mail that came in when the office was closed. I'd submitted the last bill owed to us by Premier Reynard of the Dampier System before going on my trip. Now it's been returned. It's marked ACCOUNT CLOSED.

'Son of a bitch,' Goodnight said. 'The bastard clipped us.'

'Only on one payment,' King said.

'Still,' von Baldur said, 'I agree with Chas.' He smiled wryly. 'Although it may be apropos that there do not appear to be any heroes in the scoundrel worlds.'

'Except, maybe, Fra Diavolo,' Riss put in.

'This is more in the nature of a formal notification,' King said, 'rather than something for your concern. I've been padding Reynard's bill from the first, expecting something like this, so, technically, we've been paid some one hundred forty percent of our contractual amount. And we're ahead on the expenses as well.'

Goodnight grinned.

'Godlets bless you, Jasmine. I was getting that terrible feeling that we were going to have to go back to work. Another time.' He turned off.

'Soon,' King said to the blank screen. 'But not quite yet.'

'And if I make this double,' von Baldur said, 'sooner may well be later.' He smiled, blanked off.

'And I, my faith in you restored, can return to my studies,' Grok said, and his part of the screen closed as well.

King was about to tell M'chel goodbye, when she noticed Riss's expression.

'What's wrong? You can still remain in your lap of luxury.'

'I was just reminded of what Sufyerd said, just before we lifted off Montrois,' Riss said. She repeated Sufyerd's remarks.

'Oh dear,' Jasmine said.

'Just so,' M'chel said. 'I've been brooding off and on about what this could have meant for about a month. Did that mean that he *was* spying for Torguth? That there was more than one agent in IIa, and he was part of the apparat? Or that he had his own channels, and the L'Pellerin-Kismayu conduit was something coincidentally else?

'If any of that's true, that means we spent time and a great deal of substance freeing a guilty man.

'Or was what he said just some Jilanis weirdness?

'You see why I've been going over and over it.'

'I do,' King said gently. 'And I don't. But do you think we'll ever find out?'

'No,' Riss said. 'Not until I learn how to be psychic.'

'Oh dear,' Jasmine said. 'Psychic. You sound like you need a drink . . . and somebody to drink with.'

'That might be a good idea. The only person who might be on the agenda's a damned lounge smoothie.'

Jasmine looked offscreen at a clock. 'Let's see. I can close up here again, catch a fast lim out to where you are, and be there in two hours to get drunk with you.'

'Well, come on, girl!'

'One thing,' Jasmine said. 'Don't worry about Sufyerd or anything anymore.

'After all, at least we got paid.

'And that is surely what life is about.'